DEATH
Southern Style

BEVERLEY BATEMAN

OTHER BOOKS BY BEVERLEY BATEMAN

A Cruise to Remember

A Murder to Forget

Don't Go

By Design

Hunted

Missing

Targeted

The Foundation – Sarah's Story

www.beverleybateman.com

DEATH
Southern Style

This book is dedicated to my friends who helped with the editing, Joyce and Stephanie.

CHAPTER ONE

Perrine Dupré hurried down the street. She needed to get home. Dark New Orleans clouds hovered overhead. Thunder rolled. Large drops of late May rain pelted the streets of the French Quarter. It sounded like hail as the fat globs bounced off the pavement behind Perrine. The ozone mixed with the scent of magnolia and the smell of shrimp and fish cooking in the area.

The older African American woman struggled against the wind. It whipped her umbrella inside out. She clutched it tightly so not to lose it. Rain blurred her vision. Thunder crashes caused her to jump. She stumbled up the three steps to her front door. Her daughter was coming home for a visit. Perrine's pulse increased and a smile sneaked out.

Perrine loved her New Orleans. She hated to travel, but two years ago she'd gone to New York to see Julie Ann and her new business. It was a mass of busy airports and crowded flights, but she'd enjoyed seeing the city and staying in her daughter's apartment. Her daughter had showed off her new interior design business, introduced Perrine to a few of her friends and dragged Perrine to some of the typical tourist activities. Julie Ann had been getting her designing business established then and had a challenge taking time off to leave and come home. Recently she'd taken on a partner. It freed up a little extra time. Tomorrow Julie Ann would be home in New Orleans and Perrine could give her a big hug.

Juggling her parcels, umbrella and the key Perrine jabbed it in the direction of the lock. Finally, the key found the opening and turned.

Thunder rumbled a little louder, sounding like pins crashing in a bowling alley.

Perrine turned the doorknob and froze.

One of her psychic visions flashed in front of her. Her shoulders sagged. A man stood inside. Her visons didn't lie. She wasn't going to see Julie Ann after all. And she'd miss their regular telephone call tonight, too.

She wasn't prepared to die. A single tear shimmered down her cheek. Her heart pounded. She clutched her parcels to her chest. *Why now?*

Lightning flashed. Thunder crashed again.

He waited for her to come inside.

The vision showed her crumpled on the ground in front of the house. She'd run, but obviously she wasn't going to get far. Even if she managed to escape, they would kill her eventually. And after tonight Julie Ann would be home. She would also be in danger.

The family was too rich and powerful. They didn't care about collateral damage or anyone who might get hurt. Had they killed off all the other people involved? Was that why the documentation wasn't important anymore? The birth certificate should have been enough.

There was so much she should have shared with Julie Ann. At least then she would be aware of the threat.

Perrine didn't want to die in the house. It would leave a permanent stain and memory. Julie Ann might never enter the house again if Perrine's body was found inside.

In her mind, Perrine stared into the depths of the house, hands trembled, freezing cold filled her chest. She had to make a decision. He was getting ready to make a move. Perrine dropped her parcels, turned and raced down the steps.

The skies opened wide and lightning flashed across the sky, turning it an electric white. Perrine crumpled to the street. No one heard the shot. An icy shroud of death enveloped over her.

The front door closed. The lock clicked.

She felt no pain, not even when a boot kicked her sharply in the ribs—twice.

The feet moved away.

A gate squeaked.

A car engine roared to life.

The phone rang. No one answered it tonight.

Her spirit prepared to leave.

Perrine regretted that she'd never shared any information about Julie Ann's real mother with her daughter, or how her mother had been murdered. She'd tried to protect her baby.

Julie Ann's birth mother had kept records and passed them to Perrine, to be used for blackmail purposes for everyone's protection.

It hadn't saved Elizabeth, Julie Ann's birth mother. She'd been killed before Julie Ann was a year old. That had been an ominous sign. Perrine had spent years looking over her shoulder, but there had been no issues. No one ever threatened them. Even today, there had been no demands or threats.

To the best of Perrine's knowledge, no one else had been in danger since. Although she had never looked up any of the people involved at the time of Julie Ann's birth. Now, for whatever reason, death had reared its ugly head. The documents hadn't saved her. There'd been no threats, just the shooter.

What had changed? Why now?

She wished she'd at least told Julie Ann about the documents. It might help save life.

Perrine's mind dimmed. She prayed to her god to help her keep Julie Ann alive. Her spirit gradually left her body and floated away. Using her fading power, Perrine pulled on the power of the Priestess to allow her to remain on earth, in any form.

Julie Ann would be at risk. Perrine might still be able to protect her. She needed to be there, at least in spirit, for her daughter.

Sheriff Tozer hefted his overweight body out of the police car, shoved his hat on his head and stepped through the crime scene tape being careful not to put his foot in what was left of the dark circle of blood from under the body, or touch the area markers. Most of the blood had been washed away in the rain.

He hadn't planned on coming out to the scene until he realized there was a relative. No one had contacted him yet, but they might and if they started asking questions, he needed to make it look like the death had been properly investigated.

"Find anything?" He approached the forensics officer snapping pictures of the street, area markers and the gate.

"No sir, not much so far. Apparently, she was running from the house when the perpetrator shot her in the back. He must have been inside, when she opened the door, saw him, turned and ran. If it was a break-in and robbery, why would he shoot her in the back?" The officer shook his head.

"Probably high on something. You know how pot-heads can be."

"I don't know, sir, it doesn't seem to fit. The shots came from over by the doorway. No shell casings. He must have stopped and picked them up. A pro does that. It looks like he exited by the front door and locked it behind him. That doesn't sound like someone high on drugs, too organized."

Tozer shrugged. "If he was outside the door the casings could have rolled down the steps and been washed away."

"That's a possibility. I'll see what Frank wants done. In the meantime we'll check the street and surrounding area, maybe see where the sewer drains are located."

"The casings could have gone down the sewer drain and got carried a mile away in that rain. There's little chance you'll find them."

"Maybe… There's not a lot of evidence. No one heard anything. The thunderstorm would have masked the gunshot. The neighbor across the street called it in when she came over to borrow some red beans about eight o'clock last night and found the body on the street."

"I wouldn't waste too much time on what's obviously an interrupted robbery. Write it up and stick it on my desk." Tozer lumbered up the steps and into the house. "Frank, are your forensics guys almost finished?"

The tall, thin man with a goatee and clipped moustache glanced across the room. "We've taken pictures and done a cursory check of the main floor so far. We haven't checked the courtyard or the upstairs yet."

"That sounds good enough to me. It happened outside. I wouldn't worry about the rest of the house." Tozer replied. "Is the body in autopsy?"

"I understand Cormier took it last night."

"Okay, wrap it up. You guys finish and head off to your next case. Get me the report when you have time." Tozer shuffled back toward the door.

Frank frowned. "Are you sure you don't want us to do a thorough forensics work up on this one? I'm not sure it was a simple robbery. Lots of little things don't fit."

Tozer paused. "I'm sure. There doesn't appear to be any other motive. It looks like an interrupted robbery to me. We've got other more pressing cases. I'll leave the tape up for a day or so, in case you need to return, but I don't expect you will."

Frank shook his head. His forehead wrinkled, his eyebrows knit together, and his lips tightened into a straight line.

Tozer could see him struggle. The man had always been a perfectionist. He hated not making a full investigation so he'd be able to answer any question that might come up, especially if he had to testify in court.

"Trust me, Frank. If anyone asks, you can say it's my decision. It's not good utilization of staff on something this open and shut. It's not cost effective. Wrap it up. Do a quick report and move on to one of the other cases you've got backed up. I'm going back to the office. Lock up when you guys leave." Tozer waddled back to his car.

Leaving the tape up would make it look like they were still investigating the old lady's death. It should keep the neighbors happy and keep everyone out of the house. He didn't want people nosing around inside. Not that they'd find anything.

Tozer drove off.

As the vehicle pulled away the curtains at the upstairs window inside the house parted slightly, then closed.

Back at the police station Tozer headed down to autopsy.

The room was cold and sterile. The scent of bleach mixed with the copper smell of blood reached his nostrils when he opened the door.

The only sound was a saw cutting through bone.

"Hey Doc, you got that woman from the French Quarter?" Tozer asked from the door, out of sight of the body.

"From the Esplanade Ridge district, yeah, John, my assistant, picked her up last night." Dr. Alan Cormier, the coroner, pulled down his mask, stepped away from the body on the table and took a sheet of paper from a nearby desk.

"John put his gloves on before he touched the body. He found her lying face down at the bottom of her stairs, just inside the gate. She'd been shot in the back."

Cormier paused.

"She was running from the shooter. Interesting that he would shoot her in the back if it was a random break-in."

"That seems to be the general observation. I still think it was probably some hophead on drugs. Who knows?" Tozer shrugged, still standing by the door.

"A very organized hophead. I don't recall seeing one like that. She'd been out in the rain for a while when John got there. He methodically examined the body and checked the extremities before he bagged her hands."

"She was shot outside the house. There won't be anything on her hands."

"It's part of the routine process, Tozer. Maybe she scratched him before she ran." Cormier proceeded to read from the report. "John continued his examination. Three shots hit her in the back. From John's report it looks like one bullet hit her heart. His opinion is this guy was a crack shot. It doesn't look like he used any Saturday night special gun either. I'd say it was a professional job."

"Do you have any proof?" Tozer paced back and forth not looking at the body.

"Not yet. I haven't started the autopsy on her. I'll pull the slugs and send them to the lab. Maybe they can match them to a specific gun, or one used in another case."

Tozer nodded. "No rush. It's a robbery gone bad and a victim in the wrong place at the wrong time. Twenty minutes later, he would have been gone and there would have been a different ending. The report doesn't have to be that detailed."

He made a mental note that the gun might be traced. He couldn't tell Frank or Cormier to deliberately ignore evidence.

"According to John, he rolled the body over so he could examine the exit wounds. When he finished his exam, he placed the body in the body bag and then put it on the stretcher and brought it to the autopsy room where he signed her in."

"It sounds like he wrote a thorough report. Send me a copy."

"I'll get it to you when I finish the autopsy and have a completed report."

"Good." Tozer turned and headed toward the door.

It looked like forensics, or the coroner, both had concerns about whether it was a robbery gone bad. Damn it. This wasn't going the way it was supposed to go.

He pulled the Dupré folder from the top of a pile on the corner of the desk and flipped it open. At this point it only contained the sheet with the initial report from the policeman who had found the body.

The coroner had been called and removed the body. He'd told forensics they could do their routine inspection in the morning and had the police officer locked the crime scene and put up crime scene tape last night. It might not be actual protocol, but it would work for this case. First thing this morning he'd sent forensics out to check the scene but told them not to waste a lot of time on it; do a quick and dirty to confirm it had been a robbery gone bad.

Frank Reynolds, the head of the team, had given him a questioning look, but hadn't challenged the direction. Forensics always ran short of staff and had enough cases to work on, so they wouldn't be upset about not spending hours on this one. The only problem being, Frank always did a thorough job, but Frank also followed orders so it shouldn't be an issue.

Once Tozer got their report, he'd be able to write off the case. There was no other obvious motive except robbery. No one had a description of the shooter and if Reynolds didn't turn up any forensics, the old lady's death would be added to the long list of unsolved murders. Everything should work smoothly unless the relative showed up and started asking questions. That might cause problems, but what more could he do?

CHAPTER TWO

Julie Ann Dupré sat in the JFK airport lounge waiting for her flight to board. Pulling the crumpled piece of paper out of her pocket, she smoothed it and read the number. The police officer who had come to her apartment last night to notify her of her mother's death had written down a contact number for her in New Orleans.

She hadn't called before because she'd spent most of the night crying. And then she'd needed to get ready to fly to New Orleans. The flight had already been booked. She had planned a visit with her mother. A sob caught in her throat.

This wasn't the best time or place to call the New Orleans police, but she should let them know she would arrive today. Hopefully she could hold herself together for the length of the call.

Julie Ann pulled out her cellphone and slowly punched in the number.

"New Orleans Police Department, how may I direct your call?"

"Sheriff Tozer, please?"

"Thank you. Please hold."

She clutched the phone. Heaviness filled her body. Exhaustion and emptiness from crying filled her body.

How could this have happened?

"Sheriff Tozer."

Julie Ann swallowed twice before speaking.

"Sheriff Tozer, may I help you?"

"I hope so. My name is Julie Ann Dupré, I was given your number."

"Yes, ma'am?"

"Perrine Dupré, she was killed yesterday."

"Oh, right, the old lady shot by a burglar when she returned home after shopping."

"By a burglar? Are you sure?"

"Yes, ma'am. That was the motive."

"What was taken?"

"We're not sure. It's possible she startled him before he took anything. He ran off right after he killed her."

Julie Ann closed her eyes.

"Ms. Dupré? Ms. Dupré? Are you still there?"

"We have started the boarding for Flight 5868 to New Orleans."

"Yes, I'm here."

"Will you be coming down to New Orleans?"

"What? Yes, I'll be there this afternoon." Julie Ann dropped her phone into her purse, stood up and proceeded to the boarding gate.

Her mother was really gone. But shot by a burglar? Everyone in the area knew her mother and she had nothing worth stealing. It didn't make sense. There had to be another reason. *Why would anyone kill Perrine?*

The heat and humidity of a New Orleans day after a rainstorm blasted Julie Ann when she stepped through the Louis Armstrong New Orleans International airport doors to the taxi area. She'd forgotten how that combination could make it difficult to catch your breath in the south. It was a different humidity than New York.

A redcap flagged a cab for her and put her luggage in the trunk. She tipped him before she slid into the back seat. She gave her home address and sank into the cushions. She avoided any eye contact that could lead to conversation with the driver. She was too tired for trivial chitchat and she needed to prepare herself for the return to an empty house and the loss of her mother.

That sounded so dramatic but what it really was, was sad. The tears gathered and spilled over. She dug out a Kleenex and dabbed at them trickling down her cheeks. She tried to muffle the sobs.

The taxi weaved through moderate traffic. It was about a thirty-minute drive without construction and heavy traffic. Julie Ann stared out the window.

Crepe myrtle trees dotted the landscape. She'd forgotten the beautiful pink and white blossoms. The taxi passed Metairie Cemetery off to the left. It reminded her she would need to find a cemetery for her mother. Her mother's body—it sounded do strange to think that. Had her soul left her body? Was it still in the area? Would Julie Ann be able to sense it?

Shot? A robbery? Why? Whom? It was a good neighborhood. There would be a funeral to arrange. Hopefully some of the neighbors would help. They were all good people. A random act of violence? It happened. Were Savannah and Charlie still there? Of course, they were, and they'd be there to support her. Savannah and Perrine had been close. She'd always known them as Savannah and Charlie, or Sweetness. What were their last names?

The thought of how her mother had died kept recurring over and over. Her parents had lived in the same house for thirty years. Perrine had been raised in that house on that street and so had Julie Ann. Everyone in the neighborhood knew Perrine. They also knew she had nothing to steal.

If anyone wanted anything she had, she probably would have given it to them. Maybe the person was looking for cash, but they would have been disappointed. Maybe that's why they shot her, because she didn't have anything.

Did her mother have a burial vault already? Hopefully she'd left some instructions somewhere. Mom had a lawyer when Julie Ann last visited. Who was it? She couldn't remember, but she'd need to talk to him or her. So many things to do.

Allison, her new partner, had said she'd take over Julie Ann's clients, but they might have to wait a little longer for service. She'd met Allison in Chicago. They'd hit it off and complemented each other's designs. Now if clients had to wait Julie Ann didn't worry about it. Allison would do her best. And if Julie Ann had to, she'd built the business once, she could do it again. Looking back, if she only hadn't worked so hard at building it, she might have come home more often so she and her mother could have spent more time together. Regrets overwhelmed her. That was time she'd never get back.

She would stay in New Orleans as long as it took to handle all her mother's affairs. And to find out what had really happened.

The taxi took the Vieux Carre exit off ramp and turned into the downtown area. It drove past old buildings locked and boarded.

Thirty minutes later he stopped in front of her home. Julie Ann didn't move.

The yellow crime scene tape across the front door of the pale blue house screamed that her mother wouldn't be opening the door. Someone had tacked a black wreath over top of the yellow tape.

"Ma'am, excuse me? Is this the correct address?" The driver turned his head toward her.

Julie Ann nodded. She reached over to open the door. Her feet felt like cement. She slid across the seat and out the door. She kept her eyes focused on the tape, unable to look away.

Julie Ann paid him and stood on the sidewalk, her luggage beside her where the driver had dropped them. She continued to stare at the house when the taxi pulled away.

She waited for her mother to throw open the door and run down the stairs to envelop her in an enormous hug. That's how it should have been. It wouldn't happen now. In her head, Julie Ann knew that, but she still waited.

Gradually she forced herself to face reality. She couldn't enter the house with all that yellow tape. And there was more tape across the gate and a few markers on the ground between in front of the house. Was that where her mother had been shot? If it was, she wasn't even in the house. Why would a burglar shoot her? It made less sense than the robbery as a motive.

She stared at the yellow tape. Now what?

That sheriff hadn't said anything about not being able to go into her house.

While she stood there, she could feel someone watching her.

She glanced around, but the street appeared empty. Was someone inside her house? It wasn't a threatening feeling. It felt more like someone was watching, like her mother, waiting for her to come inside.

She took a step toward the house. She'd told the police she would arrive today. *How long were they going to keep that damn tape up?*

And where was she going to sleep tonight?

Anger replaced lethargy. Julie Ann grabbed her cell phone and punched in the number for the operator.

"How may I help y'all?"

"Could you please connect me to the French Quarter police station? Thank you." Julie Ann tapped the toe of her four-inch stiletto heel as she waited. She kept glancing around the neighborhood.

"Police station, how may I direct your call?"

"Sheriff Tozer, please."

"I'm sorry, ma'am, he's not in the office at the moment."

"Then please connect me to whoever is in charge of the Dupré case?"

"Sorry, which case?"

"The Dupré case—the woman who was murdered in her house yesterday."

"Oh yeah, the robbery vic. Hold on. Deputy Sheriff O'Reilly's on call. I don't know if he's in."

"If he's not, find me someone who *is* in. I want to get in the damn house." Julie Ann snapped.

"Ma'am?"

"That robbery victim was my mother. It's my house and I want the damn tape removed so I can get into my own home. I'm standing out front in this damn heat right now. You find someone and get them over here ASAP to get that goddamn tape off my door or I'll take it down myself." Julie Ann clicked the phone off and dropped it in her purse.

She opened the gate that led to the front stairs. Theirs was the only house with a gate even though the house was built close to the street.

The hinge was broken so she lifted it carefully. The gate squeaked. A ghost of a smile flickered across Julie Ann's lips. After all these year's her mother had never fixed that hinge. Julie Ann remembered the day it broke. She had climbed on it to swing back and forth against her mother's wishes. One hinge had broken. Her mother didn't fix it. She said no one could sneak in without being heard.

Julie Ann wanted to march the ten feet to the front stoop but stopped because of the markers and tape. She bent down to observe the dark brown stain. This was where her mother had died. The distance from the stain to the door didn't make sense. She placed her hand over the stain and held it there.

Nothing.

Her mother's spirit wasn't in this area.

She gingerly edged back toward the narrow street.

Across the street a young mother pushed a stroller occupied by a toddler with a mass of red curls and waving a bright green sucker. It took a few minutes until the mother reached the corner and disappeared.

She must be new to the area. Julie Ann noticed a few of the older homes had been replaced by newer ones or renovated. There hadn't been a lot of young families when Julie Ann had left for Chicago. It looked like they were trying to renew the area and build more modern homes on the small lots. *Would that have been why her mother was shot?*

She glanced at her watch. *Where the hell were the police?*

The street remained empty. Not even a single car was parked there. Julie Ann couldn't see anyone, but the feeling of being watched stayed with her. It was quiet this time of day. If people were home, they were inside with air conditioning and the TV on, or out in their courtyard sipping ice cold lemonade.

She debated going across to Savannah's, but if Savannah was home and they went inside, Julie Ann might miss the police. After the police removed the tape and she was allowed inside the house, she'd go across and see her.

She swiped at her forehead with her hand and wiped away the rivulets of perspiration. Ice cold lemonade sounded good right about now.

The street remained a mixture of smaller bungalows and small houses, some with a second floor. Unlike New York, where everything was muted colors and similar to your neighbors, here they were painted in a mixture of colors, peach, cream, or bright turquoise like Savannah's house across the street. Her mother always talked about her friend who still lived there.

God it was hot. She'd forgotten how hot a May day in New Orleans could be. She'd have to get a fan. You couldn't exist in New Orleans without a fan. It was the humidity.

Julie Ann dug her airline ticket out from her purse and waved it in front of her face. The slight breeze helped dry a few drops of her perspiration.

If someone didn't get here soon maybe she'd go over to that damn police station and raise a little hell. She could do it, too.

At that moment a dark sedan slowed to a stop in front of the house.

Why did they always drive a dark sedan and think they were inconspicuous? It had cop written all over it.

The door opened. A man in his early thirties unwrapped himself from behind the steering wheel and emerged from the car. He stood over six feet; a rumpled tan suit stretched across shoulders as wide as the car door. He had a strong chin.

She continued to observe the man as he strode toward her. His ragged dark brown hair needed a haircut and a brown, patterned tie loosened at the neck hung slightly off center.

Self-consciously he reached up to straighten his tie. His shamrock green eyes met hers.

An electric arc cross the space between them. Julie Ann held his gaze. Her breathing spiked. Her heart rate took off around the NASCAR circuit.

It's because I'm so exhausted. Nothing more.

"O'Reilly, Deputy Sheriff Conner O'Reilly. You phoned the police station?" He stopped a few feet in front of her.

"Julie Ann Dupré. Perrine Dupré was my mother. She raised me. Yes, I phoned because I want to get into my home." Her eyes focused on his thick, sensuous lips. She gave her head a slight shake.

"I'm sorry for your loss, Miss Dupré." He shoved his hand forward.

Julie Ann slid her hand into his. It disappeared in a warm cocoon when he closed his hand over hers. Somehow it made her feel safe. She relaxed slightly.

"I phoned and said I would be in today. I didn't expect to find crime scene tape still up."

"I see. I can understand why you're upset."

"Can you? I'm told my mother has been murdered. I didn't sleep last night. I've flown in from New York, via a stop in Washington. I'm hot and tired. I want to get inside, have a bath and change into something cooler. This is my home. Please, take that damn tape down."

Connor stared at her and scratched his chin. "We haven't quite finished with the crime scene. The guys were a little busy and we didn't know anyone would be staying here. The team needs to come back one more time."

She found herself staring into those mesmerizing green eyes.

"Sorry?" Julie Ann realized that while she stared into his eyes he'd been talking.

He flashed a killer smile down at her. Deputy Sheriff O'Reilly put a hand on her arm. "You must be exhausted, what with the news of Ms. Dupré's death and then that long trip…"

"Look, I just want to go inside." Julie Ann interrupted him.

"I understand. Unfortunately, that's not going to happen today. I'm sorry. Let me take you to a hotel, on the police department, for the night. You can get a good night's sleep. I'll get forensics back here to finish off the scene tonight. I'll supervise everything myself. Tomorrow I'll pick you up in the morning and move you back into the house. It will be ready for occupancy. You won't be as tired and maybe you'll be able to cope a little better."

Julie Ann looked up at him. Her shoulders slumped. The anger seeped away. Exhaustion replaced it. Her whole body felt on the verge of collapse. Between the lack of sleep and this damn heat she didn't have the energy to fight him. The events of the last day had taken their toll, emotionally and physically. All she wanted was to get into her own house, soak in a hot bath and fall into bed.

With a shake of her head, she had to admit he was being

logical. "All right, one night, deputy, but tomorrow I want to be in my own home."

"Deal," his smile reached his eyes. His thick lips parted to reveal straight, white teeth. A cleft in his square cut jaw caught her attention.

If the effort hadn't felt so exhausting Julie Ann might have considered running her finger over that cleft, before touching those damn, kiss me lips. Instead, she let him pick up a suitcase in one hand and wrap his arm around her waist with the other, guiding her away from the house.

"Let's get you into the car and then I'll get the rest of your luggage."

Julie Ann nodded and allowed herself to be led to the car and inserted in the front seat.

"Deputy, I was told it was a robbery and murder. Are you sure it was robbery? My mother didn't have anything of monetary value. What was missing?" She looked up at him.

"Connor, please. We're not sure what was taken. You'll be able to help with that tomorrow. But there doesn't appear to be any other motive than robbery. That's why we want to do a thorough investigation before you go inside. We don't want to miss anything. If it wasn't a robbery gone bad, then we need to find another motive." He continued to hold her hand until he released it when he handed her the seatbelt. Seconds later he'd grabbed the rest of her luggage and put it in the trunk. He slammed the lid, strode around the car, opened the driver's door and slid in beside her.

"I see." Julie Ann stared out the car window toward the house where she'd been raised.

"Everybody seemed to like her, no known enemies, no reason to kill her. It's one of those senseless crimes."

Julie Ann nodded. He was right. It didn't make sense, but something didn't feel right. As she stared toward the house the curtains moved.

"Is anyone inside right now?"

"No, no one's inside. The crime tape is up and only the police can cross it."

Julie Ann looked back at the window. The curtains were closed. Nothing moved. Her mind must be playing tricks on her. Stress and exhaustion must be catching up with her. Unless…

She stared back at the house.

"You have my sympathy. It must be very hard to lose your mother and then to come home and not even be able to get into your own house to grieve. I do apologize for that. Like I said, we didn't know anyone would be coming."

"I did tell Sheriff…, whoever I phoned, that I would be coming down. I… I…"

Deputy Sheriff O'Reilly turned the key and started the car. "That would be Sheriff Tozer. He didn't mention anything. Sorry about that."

Julie Ann slumped into the passenger's seat. She wiped at the perspiration on her forehead.

Connor turned up the air conditioning.

"I hate to mention this, but we'll need you to identify your mother. It doesn't need to be today, but probably sometime tomorrow."

Cold air blasted Julie Ann. She stared out the window. "Of course, I expected I'd have to do that. I want to see her anyway. I need to say goodbye."

"You can view her through a camera. You don't have to actual see her."

Julie Ann turned her head to look at him. "I want to see her. I need to see her. I want to be able to touch her."

Connor pulled away from the curb. "Sure, not a problem, I'll arrange it."

"Thank you." Julie Ann turned back to the window. Nothing moved.

It only took minutes to traverse the roads from the Esplanade Ridge area to the hotel on Conti Street.

"We're here. You're only a few blocks from your house so you probably know this area."

Julie Ann nodded. "It's changed a little, but not that much."

"I'll check you in and make sure you're comfortable. Then I'll be back in the morning to pick you up. Come on, let's get your luggage. You want to be checked in as Ms. Julie Ann Dupré?"

"Ms. Dupré, yes, thanks." Julie Ann opened the door and stepped out into the oppressive heat. Her head pounded and her body ached. She needed an aspirin; maybe even something stronger, and a good night sleep.

Deputy Sheriff O'Reilly put her suitcase on the sidewalk. "Are you all right? Do you want me to help you inside? You don't look well."

"No, I'll be fine, thank you." Julie Ann shook her head. "I think I'm still in shock and this heat; I'm not used to it."

"Haven't been home in a while?"

"Not this time of year. Last time was Christmas."

No, she hadn't been home in a while. Maybe if she had this wouldn't have happened. She'd been selfish, staying away. Her and her damn drive to become a successful interior designer. She was on her way up, but it had cost her her mother. It wasn't worth it.

"When was the last time you ate?"

"What?" She stumbled on the low step into the lobby. A strong hand shot out, grasped her arm and elbow. The other hand dropped the bags and slid around her waist.

"When did you eat last?"

"Um," she tried to remember. "Maybe lunch yesterday."

"That's what I thought. I think I will carry you, whether you feel you need it or not. And I'll order some food sent up to the room. Eat it."

Julie Ann found herself swung up in a pair of strong muscular arms, her head rested on his powerful shoulder as he strode into the lobby.

"Sit here. I'll check you in and be right back."

He deposited her gently onto a love seat in the reception area.

The bell boy brought her luggage over to her seat. "Checking in?"

"The lady is. I'll go and get a room." Connor responded.

Minutes later Connor returned to the love seat. He gave the bellman the room number and swooped her up in his arms again. He carried her up in the elevator and down the hall to where the bellboy stood beside an open door.

"Deputy, I… I mean I'm sure I can walk on my own," although she really wasn't sure at that moment.

"It's Connor, remember, and don't argue. I don't want a lady fainting in my presence, bad for my reputation."

He passed through the doorway and across the room where he lowered her gently down on the king-sized bed.

Julie Ann reluctantly removed her arms from around his neck. She had felt safe for a few moments.

She lay quietly on the bed and watched as Connor tipped the bellboy, closed the curtains and brought her a glass of water.

"Food's on the way up. Eat, then go to bed and get a good night's sleep. Have breakfast in the morning. I'll pick you up about ten and take you to the coroner's office before we go back to your place. You can move in at that time."

"Thank you. You've been very kind."

"It's the least the department can do." He flashed another killer smile that made her stomach do a slow somersault.

Connor moved his large, muscular frame toward the door, ducked his head and disappeared. The door closed behind him.

He was sexy and kind, but she had no intention of getting involved with anyone. One reason she seldom dated, let alone developed a relationship was she focused on her business. She didn't want anything to prevent her business from being successful. That would be several years away.

Now she'd lost her mother and missed all that time they could have had together, because of the damn business. The business wasn't worth that. Maybe she needed to re-evaluate her priorities, especially right now.

Julie Ann closed her eyes and lay quietly on the bed. She hadn't fully taken in the events of the last two days. She wanted to hug her mother and spend the night catching up on what they had been doing, but that would never happen again.

She'd chosen to stay in New York and get a good start on her career and a new life. Her mother had understood. Julie Ann wondered if she herself did. New Orleans was her home. Her mother had overcome her fear of travel and flown to New York to visit once, a couple of years ago. She'd said how proud she was of what Julie Ann had accomplished, but New Orleans was Perrine's home. Julie Ann had managed to find time to get home, but only for a few short visits. Phone calls had substituted for personal contact.

New York had got into Julie Ann's blood. The shopping, the bistros, the shows, and croissants at three in the morning had been exciting. Interior design was addictive. Dealing with people's homes and their quirks and idiosyncrasies was fun and a challenge. When a project finished, her clients were usually excited and happy with the results. Pride in her accomplishment added to her addiction to New York.

Julie Ann didn't want to leave New York and Perrine couldn't give up New Orleans.

She phoned her mother regularly. They talked for an hour or more every weekend. Julie Ann had convinced herself she'd outgrown New Orleans. There was nothing here for her anymore—except for her mom, and her neighbors, and beignets and the aura and mystery of the French Quarter. Okay, maybe there were a few things she loved about New Orleans.

Room service delivered a tray of soup, sandwich and a plate of fruit and cheese. Her stomach grumbled. It was definitely time she ate something. She had them place the tray on the old oak desk. When the waiter left, she pulled up a straight back chair.

The room was furnished in early nineteen hundred style with dark wood and wainscoting. It was a simple but elegant. She sat down and took a couple of spoonfuls of spicy tomato soup. It tasted good. It slid down nice and warm with that hint of creole spice.

Okay, that was another thing she missed, creole cooking and music. New York jazz didn't compare with New Orleans jazz. There were a lot of things she missed in New Orleans that she had forgotten. She finished the soup and half the sandwich. She started to feel human again and a little drowsy. She pulled down the sheets on the bed.

Allison texted she'd phoned Julie Ann's clients and explained to them she'd be covering during Julie Ann's absence. Her business would definitely take a hit from the absence. Hopefully Allison could hold it together, but somehow it wasn't a priority right now. She had no idea how long she would be away. Her priorities had changed.

She'd stay as long as it took to take care of everything in a manner her mother would approve. She also wanted to find out what really happened. That robbery story didn't make sense.

She checked the lock on the door before she slid into the bed. She was almost asleep before her head hit the pillows. She put her hand on a warm spot in the middle of the bed. Odd. Then someone or something squeezed her hand. She jumped.

"Mom? Are you here?"

She didn't expect an answer but snuggled closer to the warm spot. It felt comforting and she drifted off to sleep.

Who had really killed Perrine? And why? It didn't make sense. The only secret Julie Ann was aware of was the truth about her birth mother. *Had it anything to do with her birth mother and if it did, why now?*

CHAPTER THREE

Connor O'Reilly strode back to his car. He couldn't get Julie Ann Dupré out of his mind. She was the most beautiful woman he'd ever seen—not just physically, although that was pretty good, too. Her body had felt soft, yet firm, when he'd carried her to her room. She'd slipped her hands around his neck and pulled herself closer to him.

Her floral and spicy scent still clung to his jacket. The scent had been unique, maybe a mixture of spice and lilies. Her soul seemed to shimmer through those huge dark brown eyes. She looked like she was about to fall apart, but still wanted to know how and why her mother dies. And she planned to find out, even as she collapsed from lack of food and exhaustion. He wanted to lie down on that bed beside her, pull her close, and hold her until she fell asleep. He wanted to take care of her.

Connor scratched his chin and wondered what had gotten into him. First, he'd never reacted to a woman like that before. Second, he was not into relationships. Being a cop, marriage and family didn't work. Look at the divorce rate. Or look at what a wife went through if she lost her husband to the job. He'd watched that first-hand.

The police never paid to put people in a hotel unless it

was a witness. It had popped out of his mouth after one look at her. Connor knew she needed someone to look after her. How the hell was he going to convince the department to pay for one night for Julie Ann Dupré to stay at a hotel? It would be a challenge and one he most likely would lose. The budget didn't cover items like this. Worst case scenario one night wouldn't take that big a chunk out of his paycheck if he had to pay for it himself. It didn't matter, he had to do it.

What the hell was Tozer doing? He hadn't even mentioned the Dupre house before he took off from the office, without telling anyone where he was going. Either he should have told Julie Ann she wouldn't be able to get into her house or he should have finished with forensics and taken the tape down.

Why had the tape been left up around the house? He didn't understand. He understood from Frank that forensics had finished. Tozer had said to do a quick investigation. Why had it been left up?

No one appeared to know much about what had happened and apparently the word had come down not to spend any time investigating the death. Something didn't feel right to Connor.

On the drive back to the station he decided to pull the file and review the details of the case. If it looked like it might be needed, he'd get Frank and the forensic crew to go back out. He'd even go with them to make sure nothing got missed. Julie Ann Dupré deserved that much at least.

He had to admit that the robbery sounded like a pretty lame excuse for the woman's death, but what else could it be? He would run backgrounds on both the murdered woman and Julie Ann Dupré to see if anything popped there.

He couldn't resist a smile when he thought of how light Julie Ann Dupré had felt in his arms. She'd snuggled in like she belonged there. Of course, it had only been because she was so exhausted. Still... Her head had fitted perfectly against his shoulder. Her hair under his chin had felt soft.

The curls invited his fingers to twist and play with them. He'd felt an attraction when their eyes had first met and he'd gazed into those rich, sable colored eyes.

He drove around the police station, searching for a parking spot. He found one close to the station and backed into it. Connor ran up the stairs to the station two steps at a time.

Tozer's office was empty. Connor slipped behind Tozer's desk and scanned the folders piled up in one corner. The top one was the Dupré folder. Connor grabbed the folder and flipped it open. He scanned the single page.

Dammit. There was nothing in the folder. Not one damn thing. A few paragraphs stating the date, time and victim. No one heard anything. The forensic report was short and inconclusive. The death was the result of a home invasion. That was it. There was little information and a bunch of big holes.

How the hell could they have just written it off so quickly?

He slapped the folder back onto the desk. At his own desk he grabbed the phone, hit speed dial and waited.

He'd make sure they got an accurate account of what happened.

"Frank, I'm having problems with the death of the woman in that break-in yesterday. The crime scene tape is still up. Could you or your guys go back and do a thorough forensics exam of the place?"

"This afternoon or tonight?"

"Either, do it tonight, or have your team do it early tomorrow morning, if you can manage it. The woman's daughter is here from New York and wants to know what happened. She also wants to get back into the house."

"Tozer said to make it quick."

"Yeah, well, I'd like to make it thorough, not quick. I'll take the heat for any fallout."

"No problem. Personally, I hated to leave an investigation half-finished. I had some big questions about motive.

We'll be done and tape down tomorrow morning."

"Thanks, Frank. And put the report on my desk will ya?"

"You got it."

He didn't trust Tozer, hadn't since his father was killed. Tozer had said 'don't spend much time'. Why would he give a direction like that? Was he covering something up or didn't care because it was some poor black woman? Was he covering for someone? Maybe he just wanted to get his statistics up for the month, but still, a murder…

Connor strode back to the car. He jerked it into gear, screeched away from the curb and drove back to the crime scene.

Before he talked to Tozer, he wanted to see for himself exactly what had happened and unless he visited the crime scene, he couldn't do that. He'd also review the forensics report in the morning after Frank finished redoing it. The report would mean more if Connor had actually walked the scene.

He' would also read the coroner's report.

He careened to a stop in front of the tape-wrapped house. He checked to see if any of the neighbors were watching. The street remained deserted. Not a curtain waved behind the small windows on the row of houses. The unusual heat probably had everyone hiding inside with their air conditioning blasting. It wouldn't start to cool down until it was dark.

Connor leapt out of the car and hurried to the gate. He lifted the latch and the gate squeaked. The body had been found at the bottom of the stairs, probably before she got through the gate. She'd opened the gate, seen someone, turned and ran. The shooter had followed her out and shot her.

A robbery gone bad didn't make sense. If she was running away why would someone shoot her? He hadn't been going through the house to steal something. He'd been waiting for her to come through the door. That was the only thing that made sense. It wasn't a robbery. A robber would have heard the gate squeak when she came home. He had time to get away.

Conner squatted down by the markers and used his hand to figure out the general direction the shot came from. He'd get forensics to do a technical check, but it looked like it came from outside the front door and to one side. Connor ran his tongue over the inside of his cheek.

If it had been a robbery, why did it appear that the person stood right there by the door, waiting for her to open it? He should have been searching the house for something he could steal. *Had the killer been waiting for her? Had she even opened the door? Had she known someone was inside? And if she had, how?*

Conner ducked under the ribbon. From his pocket he pulled out the key he'd picked up before he originally came out to check on the angry woman from New York. He shoved it into the old brass lock.

Before he turned the key, he bent down to observe the fresh scratches around the keyhole. Connor took out his notebook and made a notation about the scratches. It looked like someone had picked the lock. Forensics would have picked it up, or they'd pick it up when they returned. He pulled out his camera and took several shots. He wanted to make sure nothing got missed.

Had forensics also photographed the scratches? He'd check with Frank.

He pulled gloves out of his pocket and snapped them on before he turned the key and pushed open the heavy, blue painted wood door. He stood quietly in the doorway. His eyes scanned the room. With the curtains pulled shut, the inside was dark and cool.

Connor closed his eyes in an attempt to get a feel of the robbery and the murder.

Nothing came to him except this niggling feeling that it wasn't a robbery. If that was the case it was a deliberate murder. It made more sense, but what was the motive?

How the hell could he convince anyone, especially Tozer, that he had a 'feeling' it wasn't a robbery? The death needed to be investigated as a murder. Maybe forensics could give him something.

He'd overheard two officers talking about the case after one of the officers returned to the police station. The officer had done a quick canvas of the street. Apparently, everyone liked Perrine Dupré. The few people he'd talked to, spoke about her as a friend, someone always ready to offer help. She and her family had lived here for a long time. And there was nothing in her house for anyone to steal—no drugs, no alcohol, no fancy computer stuff, big screen TV, nothing. Everyone in the area knew that. She didn't keep cash either. She had a small tin by the front door where she put a few dollars each month for the kids who came collecting for a sports team or school event.

He moved into the room, looked and saw the tin by the door. It still held a few dollars and change. The thief, if it had been one, hadn't bothered to take it. Someone high on drugs would have grabbed it.

Perrine must have inherited the house after her parents died. Her bio said she was fifty-five and a single mom. He hadn't noticed anything about her ever being married. He pulled out his notebook again and the short, stubby pencil with the eraser chewed off. He jotted a few words in the notebook. A habit he'd picked up from his father.

Connor wandered carefully through the house, making sure not to disturb anything. He opened closets and cupboards and peered at the neatly organized contents. Nothing in the drawers appeared to be out of place.

If it had been an interrupted robbery in progress, he'd been a very neat burglar. No sign of searching, no mess. In fact, if he had been a burglar, he must have known exactly what to look for and where to find it.

He'd lay bets that the daughter wouldn't find anything missing.

Connor climbed the stairs to the second floor. The first room was a bedroom. It looked undisturbed. The next room could have been an office or library. Papers and books were strewn all over the floor. It appeared someone had been looking for documentation of some kind. Obviously, the person had been searching for something, but it didn't appear to be a thief looking for money or to steal anything valuable from an old lady. It wasn't the usual robbery but appeared the thief had been looking for something specific, documents, legal papers…. Had he found it? Was he supposed to find some documentation, and kill her?

There wasn't anything of value in the room except an old computer. Odd, very odd, Conner thought as he looked around the room. Forensics needed to be checking the second floor, despite Tozer's order that it wasn't necessary. The thief had obviously spent some time here.

Did Ms. Dupré have secrets? Was that what got her killed?

Whoever shot Perrine Dupré had moved carefully through the house and searched for something specific. When they hadn't found anything, they had waited until she returned and killed her. That theory made sense, more sense than the robbery angle.

A third bedroom upstairs was also undisturbed.

Back downstairs Connor checked the back door. It was locked from the inside. He'd have to check the notes from the attending officer to make sure no one had locked it.

If Connor had the scene right, the killer had entered by the front door, searched the house, left by the front door and took the time to lock it behind him. Somewhere in that time period Ms. Dupré came home and ran away. He'd shot her in the back. Then he'd coolly walked past the dead woman after he shot her.

From what he'd heard, the police who had canvassed the neighborhood hadn't turned up anyone who had heard the shot or seen anything unusual. It had been during a thunderstorm so that could have camouflaged the shots.

Then again, the officers had said they were given orders to only check out a few neighbors, enough to make it look like they were actually investigating.

Apparently, Tozer wanted the case closed quickly.

Why?

Nothing about the case made any sense so far. Had the killer used a silencer? Burglars didn't usually carry silencers. But there had been a thunderstorm. Why kill an older woman, living alone on the edge of the French Quarter?

He'd revisit the neighbors and see if he could learn anything more. He'd also talk to Tozer about continuing the investigation. This time focusing on a motive for murder. It would be the least he could do for Julie Ann Dupré.

Connor needed to put a file together and do those background checks. Frank and his team would get back here and finish the job. Connor could cover the neighborhood while Frank worked.

Connor closed and locked the door behind him. He ducked back under the tape.

A curtain flickered in the front window of the turquoise house across the street. Connor noticed it and strode quickly across the street and up to the door. He knocked and waited.

No answer.

He knocked again. Out of the corner of his eye he saw the curtain move. Someone peeked out through a sliver between the curtains, obviously trying to decide whether to open the door. A few minutes later a bolt slid back. The door opened a crack.

"Yes?"

"Deputy Sheriff O'Reilly, ma'am. Could I ask you a few questions about your neighbor?"

"I already talked to the police. I didn't see nothin'." A woman's voice snapped from behind the door.

Connor took a shot. "Her daughter's back. I've put her in a hotel for the night, but she'll be home in the morning."

"Julie Ann? She's here? That's right. Perrine expected her today. Poor child, she must be out of her mind with grief. They were so close." The door opened a little wider. "What you want?"

A short, heavy African American woman, probably in her late sixties or early seventies, sharp brown eyes behind round glasses, stared up at him.

"Julie Ann is very upset, understandably. I'm trying to get more information to try and make it easier for her to understand what happened. Sorry, I didn't get your name."

The woman nodded and wiped away a tear that trickled down her wrinkled brown cheek. "It's Savannah Cheval. That poor baby, Julie Ann hasn't been back home a lot, but she called every Sunday evening like clockwork. She and Perrine had long talks. Six o'clock every Sunday we all knew Perrine would be home talkin' to Julie Ann."

Connor nodded and pulled out his notebook. "So, it was common knowledge about her Sunday schedule?"

Savannah's head bobbed up and down. Her chins bounced against her chest. "Why did this happen to Perrine? I jest don't understand. I mean if it was a robbery, like that policeman said, why Perrine would jest have likely given him whatever he wanted. Why would he go and kill her?"

"Good question. I don't know. I'm going to try and find out. Did she have any enemies? Was there anyone who didn't like her?"

"Perrine? No sir, everybody loved that woman."

"If everyone loved her and she had nothing to steal, who would have shot her?"

"That's your job, ain't it?"

Connor smiled. "Yes, it is, and I am trying to do it. Will you be here in the morning?"

"I might. Why?" She raised her chins. Her eyes narrowed.

"I'm bringing Julie Ann home, maybe around eleven. It would be nice to have someone here to welcome her."

"I'll be here. I'd do anythin' for that child. Poor little thing, you should have let her stay here the night. It would have been better than some old hotel. I could have taken care of her."

"I didn't know you were here. She came to the house direct from the airport earlier, but because of the tape couldn't get in. I guess she didn't think of coming across the street to see if you were home."

"She was probably distraught. I didn't see her arrive or I would have come out. I was probably in the back trying to keep cool. After the murder we're all being pretty careful around here."

"That's a good thing. Keep it up. With the stress and the heat Julie Ann was exhausted, close to collapsing. That was why I took her to a hotel."

"Poor baby, is there anythin' I can do?"

"Not tonight. I'm guessing she's already asleep, but if you could be here for support in the morning, I'm sure she'd appreciate that."

"I be here. I watch for her."

"Good, here's my card. If you think of anything you didn't already tell the police, or if you have any concerns, call me. I want to help you and Julie Ann get to the bottom of this."

"Sure," thick lips compressed into a tight line, "like the cops are really going to do anything to solve the murder of a poor, lady down here. They've already written it off. I know how you all work."

"Not everyone works like that. I'm really going to try and find out what happened." Connor pushed the door open a little farther. "You said murder, not robbery. Do you know something I don't?"

"I know what I know. It wasn't no robbery. Perrine was murdered and if you look hard enough, you'll see that, too.

The rest of those corrupt cops went through the motions. They weren't there long enough to figure out nothing." Savannah stared up at him her eyes glittered with suspicion before she shoved the door shut.

Connor heard the lock snap and then a chain being slid into place. Savannah obviously knew more than she said, but what? Nothing added up. One thing he was sure of, it wasn't a robbery gone bad.

The forensic guys would come back and go over the house and grounds with a fine-toothed comb. They'd look for anything that might provide a lead.

He'd interview the neighbors after everyone got home from work. In the morning he'd interview Julie Ann and see if she had any information that might explain a motive for murder or what the killer might have been searching for in that little office.

He needed to talk to the coroner and then Frank. After that he'd work on background checks, including one on Savannah Cheval, before he picked up Julie Ann from the hotel.

This case was more than just robbery. A murder had occurred, and he wouldn't let the case become another of the unsolved murders, despite what Tozer and anyone else might want. There was a murderer out there. Until they found a motive, Julie Ann might be next on his list. Connor wanted to catch him and make sure that didn't happen. He needed a motive and a suspect.

Could he find anything to give him a clue as to where to start?

A shard of light seeped through a crack in the curtains and slid across Julie Ann's face. She absently brushed her hand over her cheek, to get rid of the sensation. It didn't work. She struggled to open her eyes. The ceiling was ornate, with a chandelier. What room am I in? Where am I? How did I get here? Nothing looks familiar.

The sounds of garbage cans smashed against trucks and pavement. Water sloshed against curbs. The sounds permeating the room brought back familiar memories. The water was to clean the streets after last night's revelry. She was back in New Orleans, in the French Quarter. She didn't know of anyplace else where they cleaned the streets every morning.

Reality crushed around her. Her mother was dead. She'd been shot.

The garbage truck moved ahead, and more cans banged.

Her mother had occasionally got up early and took Julie Ann for a walk through the streets to get fresh beignets from Café Du Monde. They'd strolled past those street cleaners and jumped over water to avoid getting wet from the hoses spraying the gutters.

Her mother had gripped Julie Ann's hand tightly and made up stories about what might have happened the night before. The stories included voodoo queens and ghosts who might have walked through the streets.

The memory caused a severe ache in Julie Ann's chest. She reached for that warm spot she'd found last night. This morning it was cold. She wrapped her arms around herself, holding in the heartache. She'd forgotten about those times. Love for her mother flooded over her. Mom and the French Quarter had provided her with so many wonderful memories.

She'd buried them when she'd left New Orleans. She'd got caught up in the rush and development of a successful business in the city of New York. She should have come home before this. She'd forgotten how much she'd loved New Orleans, but it was coming back.

The events of the last two days flooded over her like a tsunami; Mom's death, the flight to New Orleans, the yellow tape and Deputy Sheriff O'Reilly—Connor.

She closed her eyes and pulled the covers over her head to block out the bad memories, but the heaviness sitting on her chest didn't go away. An overwhelming sadness filled her whole body, but she didn't cry. She'd dried up.

The person she loved most in her life was gone and she couldn't even cry for her anymore. Her throat squeezed shut and blocked the tears that pushed against the barricade like water against a damn. The pain was excruciating; even swallowing didn't relieve the pain. She moved her hand across the sheet again, but no one squeezed back this morning.

Julie Ann threw the covers back and pushed her feet to the floor. She had to get showered and ready for Deputy… Connor. A ghost of a smile flashed across her lips as she thought about the linebacker-sized policeman with kind, amazing Irish green eyes, who'd carried her to her room and ordered food because she hadn't eaten. He'd said he'd pick her up at ten. He looked like the punctual type.

She started toward the bathroom and stopped. Her smile dissipated. Her stomach clenched.

In the corner of one of the chairs sat a small voodoo doll, with blonde hair and a small hole with a drop of red surrounding the heart area.

How had it got there? How had anyone got into the room? Why did someone leave it for her?

She hurried to the door. It was locked. So was the window. She reached for the hotel phone and lifted the receiver. She replaced it. Deputy Sheriff Conner would be here soon, probably already on his way. Besides, if someone got into her room, the hotel staff might be involved.

She hadn't been hurt—yet. Was the doll a warning? It was obviously meant for her. Did they expect her to run back to New York?

Anger flared. She grabbed the damn doll and slammed it against the wall. A vision flashed before her when she touched the doll. It was a group, not one person. They were blurry. She didn't recognize anyone.

She stared down at the doll. She recalled her mother taking her to a small shop. The woman had them join hands. She'd lit a flame, passed their hands over it and recited some kind of spell. Perrine had said something about a vision or passing on a vision. The memory was foggy, and Julie Ann had no idea what her mother meant.

Was this it? She'd had flashes occasionally but brushed them away. They were usually about her or someone she knew. Often when she touched something. If she ever mentioned them in New York people raised their eyebrows and made some comment about seeing a psychiatrist. So she'd tried to bury the visions, or at least not mention them. Her mother had encouraged her to work with those visions and strengthen them.

Julie Ann picked up the doll and held it. She closed her eyes. Again there was a flash of a man and behind him several people. They were so blurred it was hard to make out any features, even if they were male or female. The one in front was definitely male. She'd never seen him before.

The images faded. She only felt emptiness.

In the shower the cold water pelted down on her soft skin like tiny knives. Julie Ann stood under the water trying to bring some feeling back into her body. It didn't help. Like an armor of chain mail the numbness covered her body, making her sag under the weight.

She'd never planned on coming home to bury her mother. After several years of building her career she'd made plans for this visit so she could hug her mother. She had planned to stay a few weeks so they could spend lots of time together. She knew it hurt Mom that she had chosen to remain in New York for so long, but she had tried to understand.

Julie Ann decided to order a healthy breakfast. The police were picking up the tab and she wanted to prevent fainting in front of the cute deputy. After ordering room service, she got dressed. She couldn't do anything about the voodoo doll for right now. She needed to get ready to move back into her home.

What would it be like to go back into the house?

Julie Ann knew the ghosts of her past would be there to greet her.

Would there be traces of her mother's death. Would she feel anything?

She knew it wasn't a robbery gone badly. The police probably wanted to sweep the death under the carpet and write it off quickly. They didn't care about an old lady. Besides Perrine wasn't old.

It had to be murder, but why? Did it have something to do with Julie Ann's background? Julie Ann had asked her mother for years about her birth parents. Starting when she approached her teens, she'd had questions. It had been normal teenage curiosity. She'd loved her mother.

Mom had always said not to worry about it. The details weren't relevant. When asked how she had adopted Julie Ann, Perrine had smiled and said the gods had been kind and put Julie Ann into her life.

Julie Ann knew mom hadn't told her the truth. She'd asked every year or maybe more often until she'd gone to university in Chicago. Even after she'd moved to New York she'd asked about her background occasionally. Mom had steadfastly refused to say anything. She had once said that it would be safer if Julie Ann never knew the truth.

But, if the murder had to do with Julie Ann or Perrine's background, why now, after all these years? It was time Julie Ann found out about her own background and if it was a motive for the murder.

Julie Ann pulled a powder blue, cotton t-shirt over her curls. Her mother said her blonde hair came from her birth mother, but she wouldn't say anything more. The curls apparently also came from her mother or had she inherited those from someone else in the family. Perhaps her father? No one ever admitted knowing anything about him. Could he be part of the reason for the murder? So many questions. So few answers.

Maybe it was time to start a serious search for information about her parents. She had a birth date. She could start with hospital birth records. Maybe she could find a motive that would convince the police her mother's death had been a murder. Maybe then they'd look for the killer.

She finished dressing and ran a comb through her curls.

In her teens she'd been too young to investigate on her own and Perrine would have been upset. In New York her excuse for not trying to find out any information had been the distance from New Orleans. Although with computers it hadn't been a valid excuse, but she'd been busy career building. Now that she had come back, maybe it was time to research her own history and find out about her birth mother and father. How hard could it be in this technological world?

She picked up the voodoo doll from the floor and wondered if Mom's death might be voodoo related. That might be another possibility, except if it had been voodoo related, they would have left a sign where her mother died. No one had mentioned anything so far. She'd check that with Connor.

Perrine had been a practicing voodoo priestess for years. She also attended the Catholic Church. She had taught Julie Ann that the two religions worked well together.

Voodoo taught that you only do good. Any of their spells were always for good. If you used voodoo for evil you received it back three times worse. Perhaps someone didn't understand that. It could be they thought they were getting rid of an evil voodoo priestess. Maybe she should go see Priestess Ava. She might be able to help.

Julie Ann paced across the room and back. She tried to calm her mind and focus on a plan. She needed to make a list of all the things to do in the next few days and put them in priority.

There was a knock at the door. She peeked through the keyhole. It was room service. She opened the door and motioned to the coffee table.

She gobbled down the bacon and eggs. She hadn't realized how hungry she was. And she'd eaten dinner last night. She poured coffee, added three creams and sat down at the antique desk. She opened the center drawer and found a writing pad. Using the hotel pen she began her list.

She had a lot of work in front of her, starting with her visit to identify and say goodbye to her mother. Then she'd talk to Priestess Ava. She'd call Laura to see if she could help. She and Laura had been best friends in school. It had been a few years since they had talked. She'd cut off so many people.

At the sharp knock on the door, she glanced at the clock. A smile played with the corners of her mouth. Ten o'clock—exactly.

She took one more sip of coffee, pushed the chair back and did a quick check in the mirror before she opened the door. Her stomach did a curlicue as the sexy, centerfold policeman smiled down at her.

"Ready?"

"Not quite. There's an added involvement. Someone was in my room last night."

"What are you talking about?" Connor pushed past her. "Didn't you lock the door?"

"of course I did." Julie Ann picked up the voodoo doll.

"This was sitting in that chair when I got up this morning." She indicated where the doll had been.

Connor grabbed the doll. "It's a voodoo doll."

"Very good, deputy. Yes, it's a voodoo doll that simulates me."

"Are you sure it's you?"

"You don't think the blonde hair is a giveaway? It's not my mother. I believe it's meant to scare me so I will return to New York."

"Maybe you should consider it."

"I was tired, hungry and stressed last night. I don't usually behave like a wimpy woman. I'm usually strong, independent and hopefully a little like my mother, I don't scare easily. Today I've decided I'll stay in New Orleans as long as necessary. I'm going to find out exactly what happened to my mother. I want answers."

Connor checked the doll around out. "You're sure your door was locked?"

"Yes, I checked it before I went to bed last night and I checked it again this morning."

He opened the door and checked the lock. "It doesn't look like it's been tampered with. Someone must have had a key."

"That was my thought, maybe one of the staff."

"I'll check it out and do security checks on all the staff and see if anything pops. I thought you'd be safe here. Looks like I was wrong."

"Whoever it was didn't hurt me, at least not this time. Someone being in the room while I was asleep does creep me out."

"It should. I'll see if I can find some answers."

"Thank you. I'd like that, because I have a whole lot of questions. Shall we go?"

"Yes. The crime tape on your door should be coming down."

"Good. The first things on my list are to visit my mother in the coroner's autopsy and then to return to my home."

"You're sure?"

"Yes. I think I can handle it." Julie Ann took the voodoo doll back.

"If it's any help, I'll be there for you." Connor took her hand and squeezed it before he picked up her luggage.

"Thank you." She pushed past him and headed for the lobby.

She glanced at the doll. Great start to the day. What did the rest of the day hold for her?

CHAPTER FOUR

Connor let his gaze slide down her body. He took in the shapely breasts under a short t-shirt that revealed a waist he could span with both hands, a firm, well-shaped butt and a pair of long, slender legs. He wondered how it would feel to have those legs wrapped around his naked body.

Immediately he gave himself a mental slap and tightened his grip on her large suitcase. He followed her out the door reminding himself, one, she was family of a victim. And two, he only did no string relationships. She had strings written all over her. *Back off O'Reilly.*

"You're looking better. Sleep well?"

Julie Ann nodded. "I went out like a light. Thanks."

"Did you eat breakfast?"

Julie Ann nodded. "I'm usually not much of a breakfast person, but with a busy day in front of me I ordered room service and pigged out on bacon and eggs. No grits."

"No grits?"

"I know I'm in New Orleans, but breakfast is bad enough, let alone with grits on the plate."

"At least you got your protein for energy. My mother says breakfast is the most important meal of the day. I'll take the doll to forensics."

"I want to keep the doll for now, if it's okay. There's someone I'd like to see it. Then I'll turn it over to you."

Connor hesitated. "Okay, as long as you turn it over soon."

They headed for the elevator.

"Did they find anything voodoo at the crime scene?"

Connor shook his head. "Not that I'm aware of. Why?"

"I wondered, since someone put the doll in my room."

The elevator slowed to a stop and Connor stepped to one side to let Julie Ann exit first. "The car's parked out front."

Julie Ann walked briskly through the lobby, unaware of the admiring glances from most of the men checking her out. Connor noticed though and fought the impulse to tell them to quit drooling.

On the street Julie Ann paused by his dark sedan. It was still early so the temperature was bearable, but the humidity immediately started to seep through her top. She waited for Connor to catch up so she could climb into air-conditioning. She glanced up and down the street.

Connor noticed her checking out the street. He dropped the luggage in the trunk. Someone must have followed them from the house yesterday. That's the only way they'd know where she was. Was she checking to see if anyone was watching them today?

He needed to be aware of that possibility. He opened the passenger door and lightly touched her curls to make sure she didn't bump her head when she slid into the seat. A warm sensation shot right to his groin.

He pulled his hand back and reminded himself again of the reasons he couldn't get involved with a victim of a crime, especially this one.

"Slide in and I'll get that air-conditioning going."

"Thanks."

Connor drove through the narrow streets, periodically checking his mirror. He found a parking spot halfway down the street from a restaurant he knew.

"Come on lady, you may not need food, but I need a coffee. It could be a rough day." Connor took her arm as they headed to the restaurant.

Julie Ann nodded. "I could use another coffee. I'll be okay today. Everything hasn't really sunk in yet, except that I know it wasn't a robbery."

"What do you mean?"

"I just know."

"Is there something you're not telling me?"

"Not at the moment. I have no proof." She hesitated. "I know my mother and I'm familiar with the area. Nothing makes any sense."

He was a cop. He went with facts. He wouldn't understand how some things felt right or wrong. He probably thought she was a little crazy.

"Trust me. Let me know what you're thinking. Don't try and investigate this on your own. If it really is a murder it could be dangerous. I'll check out anything you find or even things you might want to know." Connor stopped, put his hands on her shoulders and turned her toward him.

Julie Ann regarded him for several seconds.

"You can trust me."

"Maybe, but I don't know you. I don't know that you're not going to sweep this under the rug or that you might even be involved in it somehow. I've heard stories about police corruption in New Orleans and Jefferson Parish my whole life."

"You're wrong, not about the corruption but about me. I am looking into it. And for your information I'm arriving at the same conclusion you are about your mother's death. There appears to be a few things from your history twenty-eight years ago that might raise a question."

Julie Ann's eyes widened. "What? You've been checking into my family? Into my life?"

Connor nodded. "It's my job. It's routine in any investigations. We need to know if there's something in the background that might be a motive for the crime."

"I see. I hope you found it interesting," she snapped. "You talk about trust. You could have asked me about my background, or about my mother."

"Would you have told me?"

"No, but that's because I don't know much." She jerked away and stomped into the restaurant.

"Damn, that went well," Connor mumbled and followed her inside.

Now he needed to figure out how to investigate her birth and birth parents without making her even more angry.

Julie Ann shivered. The temperature in autopsy was cold. Everything was stainless steel and sterile, and the floor was white tile. She should have brought a sweater, but it was so hot outside. It hadn't occurred to her.

"Are you okay? Here," Connor removed his jacket and draped it over her shoulders.

"Thanks." She slipped her arms through the sleeves and wrapped it around her.

Dr. Cormier wheeled out the stretcher and pulled the sheet down to Perrine's shoulders.

Julie Ann stared down at her mother for several moments.

"Do you recognize the person as Perrine Dupré?"

Julie Ann nodded. "Yes, that's my mother."

She reached out and touched her mother's shoulder with one finger.

A kaleidoscope of images flashed through her mind.

Her mom knew she was going to die. She wanted to protect Julie Ann and she had planned on giving Julie Ann something.

Julie Ann stepped back. She took a deep breath.

"Do you want to leave?" Connor asked.

Julie Ann shook her head. She took another step forward and put her hand on Perrine's head. She needed to develop those visions. Love flooded through her.

"I love you too, Mom."

More images appeared, a legal brown envelope, but what? And where? A flash of white and everything faded. Julie Ann waited, but nothing else passed to her.

She bent over and kissed her mother on the forehead.

"I love you, mom. I'll find out who did this."

A faint image of a blonde woman and a shadowy figure passed in front of Julie Ann.

The cold of the room infused her body, even through the jacket.

"Are you ready?" Connor asked.

"Yes." Julie Ann gave her mother one last look before she moved toward the door. She needed to be alone and process what she'd just seen and felt. So many images. Maybe make notes so she didn't forget anything.

Connor parked in front of the house. The crime tape had been removed.

Julie Ann's hands were clenched tightly in her lap. She stared out the window.

"You don't have to go in the house today. You've had a rough morning. It can wait. You could stay with Savannah for a day or two.'

"You met Savannah?"

"I talked to her yesterday. She knows you're coming back today."

"That's nice. I will go across and visit but I want to move into my home today. Right now, I'm waiting for Mom to burst out of the door. And, yes, I know it's not going to happen. My head knows that, but my heart hasn't accepted it." She opened the door, climbed out and carefully opened the gate.

Connor waited a few minutes before he followed her.

She touched the doorknob. A vision passed in front of

her. A man inside stood by the door. There was a flash. Her mother crumpled to the ground.

Julie Ann dropped her hand and took half a step back.

Damn her mother's visions. She'd known he was waiting, and she was going to die. That's why she ran away from the house. So she didn't die inside. *Thanks, Mom.*

After a deep breath, Julie Ann opened the door, hesitated and stepped inside. She stopped to survey the room.

An icy cold blasted through her body. It felt like she had floated outside her body. She could see the room and herself standing there staring at the space by the door where the man had waited. He was fuzzy, not clear enough to describe.

She briskly rubbed her bare arms.

"Are you okay?"

She continued to rub her arms. "I will be. It feels cool in here."

"Why don't we do this later? You can stay at the hotel a few more days, or with Savannah."

"No, I'm fine, really. I'd like to go through the house now. I'll stay here tonight."

"Are you sure? Do you think it's wise? If your mother's death wasn't a robbery you could be in danger. They got to you in the hotel."

"I realize that." Julie Ann whispered.

"Julie Ann! Is that you girl?" The voice came from the sidewalk.

Julie Ann turned back to the door. The solid shape of the older woman limped across the street with the help of a gnarled wooden cane.

"Savannah? Yes. It's me." Julie Ann skipped out the door and down the walk.

"My, you sure are skinny, girl. Don't you take time to eat in New York? Come here, baby." Savannah held out her ample arms.

Julie Ann moved into the circle. Savannah wrapped her tight and held her for a long time.

Julie Ann found comfort for the second time in days.

"I'm so glad you're still living here. I can't believe she's gone. It's not fair. She was such a good person."

"You got that right."

"Oh, this is Deputy Sheriff O'Reilly." Julie Ann extracted herself from Savannah's hug and indicated Conner who stood in the doorway.

"We've met." Savannah dropped her arms and fixed a cold stare on the man.

Connor smiled. "And here I thought we'd bonded yesterday."

"Hmmph!"

Julie Ann grinned and linked her arm through Savannah's. They walked back to the house. Julie Ann helped Savannah up the stairs.

It didn't seem quite so cold inside this time.

"We just got here. Right now, I need to go through the house and Mom's room to see if there's anything missing. They weren't able to determine what was taken in the robbery."

"Robbery my foot, it was murder." Savannah snorted and eased her ample backside onto the couch against the wall. She folded her arms in front of her and fixed a stare on Deputy Sheriff O'Reilly.

"You go ahead, baby. I'll keep an eye on this one."

Julie Ann decided to start upstairs. The stairs were steeper than she remembered. A smile teased her lips when she thought of Savannah and the deputy. He was in for more than he knew.

She stopped at the door of her mom's workroom. Papers from the desk were thrown all over the place. Everything had been pulled from the shelves. Mom would never have left it like this. Obviously, the room had been tossed. Someone had been looking for something, but what? The computer and printer were several years old. No one had touched them. Maybe robbery had been the motive but there was nothing of value in this room. She remembered the brown envelope from her vision.

Inside the room she squatted down and picked through some of the papers and the books. Besides the shelves, they'd tossed the small bookcase and emptied every drawer in Mom's desk. No sign of a brown envelope.

Nothing appeared to be missing in here, but then she didn't know what they were looking for. She'd need to try to figure out what that might be. There wasn't anything to steal. Why would anyone throw her mother's bills around?

She'd sort through everything, but not today. She'd tackle it over the next few days.

Down the hall she opened the door into her mother's bedroom. She stood quietly, looked around the room and took in all the familiar details. The double bed with the homemade quilt her grandmother had made. The antique rocking chair in the corner. It had been awhile since she'd been home. A rush of sadness overwhelmed her. When she was in New York she'd forget how much she missed this place and her mother.

The walls of the small, square room were still painted pale brown. In her younger years Julie Ann had thought the walls were made of milk chocolate. A smile surfaced.

She moved around the room. Her hand touched the dark oak furniture. It showed signs of both age and loving care but still gleamed with a deep luster not found in new furniture.

Julie Ann lowered herself into the rocking chair in the corner and pulled the crocheted afghan her grandmother had made around her. Mom had picked the various plants and dyed the wool herself for the afghan. The wool was various shades of greens, yellows and a few other bright colors. Grandma had then made the afghan for her mom. It matched the quilt.

The rhythmic motion of the chair soothed her. Julie Ann remembered all the times when she'd had a bad dream or was afraid during a storm. She'd crawled into the small four-poster bed under the quilt made up of the brilliant squares of green, purple, red and yellow. Mom would wrap her arms around her and murmur that everything would be okay.

Julie Ann remembered the many nights she'd spent in here. Nights during a thunderstorm or when she'd been sick or afraid, or maybe just plain lonely.

A dark emptiness clawed its way up from her toes. It filled her body completely. She shuddered at the completeness of the feeling of loneliness and desolation. She'd never have any more of those nights. She'd never feel another hug from Mom. She'd never be able to tell her how much she loved her.

The nightstand held a glass, partially filled with water and a paperback turned over where her mother had put it down when she finished reading that last night.

Julie Ann stood up and moved across to pick up the book. It was a Daphne du Maurier novel. Mom had loved her writing and read her books over and over again.

She placed it back carefully on the nightstand. She wandered over to the window and stared down into the back courtyard for several seconds before she slid down the wall onto the floor. She shrank into the corner and wrapped her arms around her knees. A crack appeared in the shell Julie Ann had carefully built around herself the last day or so. The pain squeezed through the crack, shattering the rest of the shell and permeating every pore of her body. Finally, the damn broke and the tears spilled over. The tears had built up since yesterday and burst through. Her body convulsed. Even though she had cried when she got the news, this was different. She sobbed uncontrollably at the realization of how much she had lost. She cried for Mom, for the love she'd lost and for the time she'd lost due to her own ambition.

The sobs echoed through the house.

In the kitchen Connor looked up the stairs and listened

for several moments before he turned to Savannah. "Shouldn't you go to her?"

Savannah regarded him with her dark brown eyes. "No. That baby needs to cry. She can't move on if she don't grieve, proper-like. We wait."

They stayed in the room and continued to measure each other.

Connor paced back and forth. He stared out the window at the street. He stomped into the kitchen out of Savannah's view. He wanted to comfort Julie Ann and wipe away her tears, but he understood she had to grieve. He remembered his mother when his father died.

He gripped the kitchen counter to fight the urge to rush upstairs, He wanted to wrap his arms around Julie Ann and hug her and console her until she quit crying.

Savannah finally heaved herself to her feet and came into the kitchen. "You want tea?"

His hands still gripped the edge of the counter. "Please."

Savannah bustled around and put the kettle on. A few minutes later the kettle whistled.

The sobbing gradually ceased.

Savannah poured tea. "Do you want milk or lemon?"

"Nothing, thank you, just clear."

It seemed longer, but after another five or ten minutes, Julie Ann plodded down the stairs, into the kitchen. Her eyes were red and slightly swollen, her face was blotchy, and her hair was tangled and fell around her face.

Even like that she took his breath away.

Connor wanted to take her in his arms and kiss all the pain away, but Savannah watched him like a hawk, so he didn't move.

"Tea's ready. You want a cup?"

Julie Ann perched on the edge of a chair. "Thanks, Savannah."

"Did you notice if anything was missing?" Connor asked.

"No, I don't think so. I still have to check the last

bedroom and the bathroom. I'll go through Mom's office later, but I didn't notice anything missing. The room's a mess. There are papers and books strewn everywhere so it's hard to be sure, but I'd guess nothing was taken. I'm not sure exactly what Mom kept in there. They were definitely looking for something, but it wasn't a usual break-in. They had something specific in mind. Maybe a document of something. Besides an old computer, and printer there's not much to steal—an iron, her sewing machine and a few of her personal papers, letters and cards. Nothing anybody would want to steal. I'm sure it wasn't a regular robbery. Like I've said before, it doesn't make sense."

"Yeah, why would they break in here and not one of the wealthier apartments in the area? I agree. It's not logical, that's for sure. I know I can't figure it out, not yet. Let me know if you notice anything when you finish checking the house. Right now, I should be getting back to the office. Will you be okay?"

"I'll be fine. Savannah's here."

"Where will you be staying tonight?"

"Like I already told you, I'll stay here."

"Yes, but I thought after you'd seen the house and maybe picked up a few things, you'd want to stay somewhere else."

"You can stay at my place." Savannah offered.

She poured the tea and placed a cup in front of Julie Ann.

"Thanks Savannah, but no, I want to be here. I need to be here."

Savannah nodded and settled down into a kitchen chair with her tea.

"I still don't think it's a good idea. The person might come back." Connor said.

"Why would he do that? There's nothing to steal or if there is, they didn't find it, so they know it's not here. They didn't even touch the TV—probably because it's too old. Everyone says it was a robbery but there's. nothing worth stealing. And the little amount of money here, they didn't touch it. They won't come back. And besides, if they want to get to me, they did that at the hotel. I'm no safer there."

"What you mean, they got to you at the hotel?" Savannah snapped.

"Someone put a voodoo doll of me in the hotel room while I was sleeping."

"They what? You sure you okay? You think there's spell on it?"

"If there is, it's probably one to send me back to New York."

"Don't you joke about that. You know how serious it can be."

"I know Savannah and I'm going to check it out with Ava."

"Hmph."

"Who's Ava?" Connor frowned.

"She's a priestess with knowledge of voodoo. She might have knowledge about the doll."

"Voodoo? You're right. Someone was in your hotel room last night. They could have killed you then if that was their plan. I agree it wasn't a robbery, but I have no proof. And if robbery wasn't the motive, what was it? And now you think voodoo might be involved." Connor stared the two of them.

"If I stay here, I might get a feel for what happened."

"What do you mean, get a feel?" Connor's eyes narrowed. Voodoo, feelings, spells, what were these two thinking?

"If I'm here in familiar surroundings and have Savannah to bounce things off, I might come up with some possibilities. That's all I meant."

Savannah grinned.

"Yeah, well, okay then, don't do anything stupid. If you come up with anything, anything at all you call me— anytime. Or if you hear anything in the house, you call me right away. You leave the police work to us."

"Yes sir, of course." Julie Ann managed a mock salute.

What was she thinking—that he was a cop, but one of the good ones or one of the corrupt ones? "I'm one of the good ones."

"Well, they haven't done much so far." Savannah mumbled under her breath. "Nobody's even been around for more than a few minutes since they found the body, until late last night."

"We're following procedure." Connor's chin jutted forward defensively. He avoided looking in Savannah's direction and focused on Julie Ann. "I'll keep you informed as to how the investigation is going, but you stay out of it. You could get hurt."

"Like my mother?" Julie Ann took a sip of hot tea.

"Exactly."

"Sounds like you agree it's not a robbery gone bad either. What are you going to look for?"

"I don't know yet. I'm going to review all the reports to start with." Connor pulled out his card, turned it over and scrawled a couple of numbers on the back. "That's my cell and my home number. You use them if you need anything—anytime, day or night."

Julie Ann took the card and turned it over. "Thank you."

"I gotta go. You call if you need anything. I still think you should stay at a hotel. Nice meeting you, again." Connor nodded at Savannah and marched out the front door.

Julie Ann followed him to the door. She watched him get into his car and managed half a wave before she closed the door.

He drove down the street.

What did she mean when she said she might get a feel for what happened? Did she think there were ghosts in the house or something? She had kept the voodoo doll. Why? What did she expect to find? Was there more to this than he understood?

Inside the house Julie Ann turned back to Savannah. "I'm going to find out what happened to Mom. She shouldn't have died that way and I'm going to find out why."

"You be careful girl. There's something evil going on around here. I don't know what it is, but you don't wanna to get involved. I notice you didn't explain that sixth sense of yours to the policeman."

Julie Ann managed a weak smile. "I didn't think he was up for that. He got that weird look on his face when I showed him the voodoo doll and again when I mentioned sensing something. He's not a believer. Besides, I don't totally understand that sensing thing myself. I've always tried to avoid using it. Most people think I'm crazy when I say something about seeing or sensing something. Perrine was the one with that skill or power. She encouraged me to work with it and strengthen it. She knew she was going to die."

"You sensed that?"

"Yes, when I came into the house. She ran so she didn't die in the house."

"That makes sense. Now you think Perrine might try to talk to you?"

"Uh huh, I'm hoping she might. Mom would want me to find out what happened. And she'd be happy if I tried to improve my sensing and vision skills. We both know Perrine's not going to be able to rest peacefully until we find out what really happened and why. And I get the feeling there's something she wants me to know. I think it's in a brown envelope—somewhere."

"And you know this how?"

"When I said good-bye to her today, I got flashes."

"Yup, that's Perrine trying to get through to you, sure 'nuff, but I don't want you gettin' in any trouble. She'll never rest if something happens to you."

"I'll be fine, Savannah. Really, I will. I'll be careful. I don't have a choice. Now, how about you whippin' me up some of your special red beans and rice. Nobody makes it quite like you and I haven't had it since I moved to New York."

"You've got it, girl. You come on over to my place and

let me see if we can put a few pounds on those skinny bones of yours."

"That sounds good. And for the record, I think you know more than you're telling anyone. You've known Perrine for a very long time. You know more about my birth mother than Mom ever told me."

"Now baby girl, don' you start going there. That's nothin' but trouble."

"It's time I knew what Perrine would never discuss and you will tell me. There's a good chance it has to do with why they killed her."

Savannah heaved herself up from the chair and wrapped an arm around Julie Ann's shoulder.

"We'll see, we'll see... Let's see what Perrine says first."

"If she says anything, but if she doesn't you are going to tell me what you know. It's time I learned the truth."

"You sound like your mother. We'll talk later."

"I'm holding you to that. Now, I'm going to see Priestess Ava. I need to talk to her. You make those red beans and rice for dinner. I'll be back shortly."

Savannah nodded. "Priestess Ava is a good idea. She'll help you."

They moved to the door together. Something made Julie Ann glance over her shoulder back into the living room. A shadow disappeared into a corner.

Who was it? Was it the murderer? Were the spirits restless? Was it her mother? Or just her imagination?

Chapter Five

After the taxi drove off Julie Ann stood on the street and stared at the small sign tacked over the door of the old wooden house, Chez Voodoo.

She could have walked. It wasn't that far from her house, but the heat continued to be oppressive. Clouds blocked the sun and hung over the city, holding in the heat and humidity.

She had come here with her mother often, particularly when Perrine was the voodoo priestess. She was comfortable with voodoo. She knew it always focused on the positive. It had never been frightening. She hadn't attended a voodoo ceremony since she had moved to New York.

Who would put a voodoo doll in her hotel room? She was sure voodoo had nothing to do with her mother's death, but the doll had upset her. Other than trying to scare her away, what could it possibly mean? Or maybe it was a distraction to throw her off the track. She hoped Priestess Ava might be able to help her with an answer.

Julie Ann pushed open the door and stepped into a small store loaded with books on shelves and piled on counters. A bell rang. No one was around, or answered the bell, so she continued through the door into the next room.

This one held crystals and runes in dishes and in loose piles on tables. More books and CD's filled the shelves.

There was still no one around. Julie Ann knew Priestess Ava often talked to groups in the courtyard. They discussed philosophy and the voodoo religion. She didn't want to interrupt a discussion if there was one.

She walked through the next door into a small hallway and out into the courtyard. It was empty. She turned to her left and stepped through the next door into the church.

A tall, black woman wearing a long white dress with a white apron and a white scarf tied around her head, turned when Julie Ann entered the room.

"Julie Ann Dupré, child, welcome. I'm sorry I wasn't out front to greet you."

She hurried across and wrapped her arms around Julie Ann. "I am so sorry to hear about your mother."

"Thank you." Julie Ann returned the hug and felt the energy flow from Priestess Ava. She soaked it in before she finally pulled back. "That's what I wanted to talk to you about."

"Your mother's death? Of course, although I'm not sure how I can help. Shall we go and sit in the courtyard?"

"That would be nice." Julie murmured.

She liked it out there. Riots of red, orange, yellow, purple and coral colors filled the flower beds, attracting butterflies, birds and bees. Street noises never entered the area. It was a place of serenity and peace. And it always felt cool, despite the temperature.

"I can make tea."

"No, that's fine, really. I wanted to talk to you about Mom's death."

"What about it?"

"Do you think it was voodoo related?"

"Goodness no, I don't think so. Why would it be?"

"I don't know. I'm trying to figure it out, make some sense of it. So far, I have a few pieces, but nothing fits.

The police say it was a robbery gone bad, but there's nothing missing. And I had a vision. She knew she was about to die. She didn't enter the house but ran away. She was shot her three times, in the back."

"You saw this?"

"Yes, but it doesn't make sense. I'm trying to come up with other possible motives. I know a lot of people feel threatened when you mention voodoo."

"True, but I don't think Perrine would have been killed because of it. There are a lot of people in the Quarter that belong to the voodoo church. Besides, why would they target your mother? Why not me? I'm the High Priestess now."

"It was a thought. Also, I found this in my hotel room this morning." Julie Ann handed the voodoo doll to Ava.

Ava regarded it carefully before she touched it. Then she took it by one hand. "This was in your hotel room?"

Julie Ann nodded.

"How did it get there?"

"I don't know. The door and the window were both locked. It was sitting in a chair. When I picked it up, I could see a group, and a man in front of the group. I could see the man, but the group was very blurry and indistinguishable."

"I see. It could be the man put it in your room but there was a group of people behind the plan. This is a voodoo doll, but not one of mine. Someone could have bought it from any of the local shops. It's one made for tourists and then they added the blood. It's a warning and meant to scare you."

"That's what I thought. It worked. It does scare me. I guess if I left all this alone, accepted the police report and went back to New York maybe I'd be safe."

"That's possible. It could be that's what they hoped you would do when you got this."

"But I might not be safe there either. If I don't know why mom died, I can't make an educated decision on what to do. Running away has never been an option in my family."

"That's true. I don't pick up anything from the doll. Whoever purchased it didn't have any powers. There's no spell attached. I will try and find out where it was bought but it's very common. I doubt if anyone will remember selling it. If you do leave New Orleans the people doing this might feel less threatened."

"I can't. For Mom's sake, I can't let this be swept under the rug. I need answers and a motive. Besides, if the motive has something to do with her past, it may be about me. If it is about me, how can I be sure I'm safe even in New York? Or even if I am now, what about in another year? Do you know anything about my past?"

"No, Perrine never discussed it. It was obvious you were adopted but she never shared any information about your parents or where you came from. You are going to stay in New Orleans?"

"Yes, I'm staying at home. I'm hoping I might pick up something there or Perrine might talk to me."

"You must be very careful. Many things in life don't make sense. Stay open minded; listen to your spirits. Perrine may talk to you or send someone else. Have patience but stay alert and watch for any possible sign of danger."

"I'll try to be patient and careful. I hope someone will talk to me. I hope it's Mom."

"You must learn to be still, wait and listen. You can't rush nature or the spirits. And work on developing your own powers. Don't try to hide them or avoid them. You may need them to help protect yourself. Now, what else is bothering you?"

"What do you mean? Isn't the voodoo doll and Mom's death enough?"

"It could be, but I'm feeling there's something more to your search." Priestess Ava took Julie Ann's face in both her hands and tipped her chin up.

Julie Ann wanted to look away but couldn't. She could

feel the tears creep slowly up and then spill down her cheeks.

"I should have been here."

Ava let go of Julie Ann's face. "You're feeling guilty."

"Yes. I should have come home more often. I should have been here, and it wouldn't have happened."

"Now you don't know that. If you'd been here, you might have also had an accident and died with your mother. God and the spirits work in mysterious ways. There is always a plan. Your mother was so proud of you. She bragged about how well you were doing in New York and how your business was growing and what a great entrepreneur you were. She didn't resent you not coming back. She loved your weekly talks and your visits."

"Are you sure? I mean, we were always so close, but..."

"Perrine was a great lady. She loved you deeply, but she believed in that old saying 'Don't put a bird in a cage, let it fly away. If it comes back it's yours, if it doesn't, it never was.' She had to let you go, but she knew you'd be back. She was a very smart lady."

"I know. I loved her so much. I missed her a lot when I was in New York, but I got kind of wrapped up in my business."

"She understood."

"I'm not sure I do or that I can forgive myself."

"You must learn. Your mother doesn't want you to remember her with guilt. She wants to be remembered with love."

"I can see why you're the priestess. You're very wise."

"I learned a lot from Perrine when she was the High Priestess."

"When did you see her last?"

"Actually, it was the day before she died. She dropped by for tea."

"What did you talk about?"

"You, of course. She was so excited that you were

coming home. She said she'd been preparing so everything would be ready for your visit. Oh, she said she had a surprise for you.

"What was it?" Julie asked eagerly.

"She didn't say, and I didn't ask. I wish I had. I'm sure you'll probably find out. Maybe she'd bought you a gift?"

"There was nothing in the house, unless that was what was stolen."

"Maybe you'll find a receipt, or maybe it hasn't been delivered yet. Ask some of her friends, maybe they know."

"I will. Thank you."

"Have you made any plans for her funeral yet?"

"No, I haven't talked to her friends about it yet. Savannah mentioned Charlie wants to do it up in style and have an old-fashioned funeral with a band and a parade from the church to the cemetery."

"That sounds wonderful. Perrine deserves it and the neighborhood will get a chance to mourn her in style. Good for Charlie."

"I need to talk to him about planning it. The hotel said they'd have a reception there. Would you speak at her funeral?"

"I'd be honored. Let me know when and where. Now I'm going to give you a special packet of mine. I want you to keep it on you at all times. It is to protect you against unknown threats and danger."

"Why? Do you think I need it?"

"I don't know, but if you're staying in New Orleans and looking into Perrine's death it won't hurt to make sure you have a little extra protection." Ava slipped into the church and came back a few minutes later with a small ball wrapped in cotton muslin tied tightly at the top.

She held it over Julie Ann's palm and mumbled a few words before she handed it to her. "Now put it in your pocket and keep it there. Keep it on you at all times, day or night. Promise me."

"I will." Julie Ann obeyed and stuffed it in her pocket. "Thanks, Ava. I don't know that I need any protection, but I'll be careful."

"Perrine didn't think she needed protection either. I wish I'd given her something to protect her when she was here."

"Okay, okay. I'm convinced. It stays with me at all times. Thank you."

"You take care now." Ava gave Julie Ann a hug.

"I will. I promise." Julie Ann and headed back out the way she came in.

Ava stood and watched her go.

Maybe I should have made the potion stronger. There's an aura around her that says she's going to have to face some life-threatening challenges.

Connor stared at the folder in front of him and drummed his fingers on the desk. Savannah had been right. The police really hadn't done much to investigate the death. The only police who had been there were Tozer, who had dropped by, and the officer who had been first on the scene. Forensics were there briefly but didn't do an extensive investigation.

The first page, a copy of the original phone call from Savannah was in the file. The second page had a few lines scrawled on it. Other than saying it was a robbery gone bad, Tozer hadn't filled out anything.

A middle-aged, black lady—no one was going to ask about her. They could write her off and no one would ask questions. In a week it would be forgotten. Connor could see the whole thing unfolding and being filed away in a day or two.

Except—someone was asking questions. They hadn't counted on that. A young, white woman from New York wanted to know what really happened to her mother.

She planned on getting to the bottom of it, with or without his help. He knew that. She wanted answers and she was going to find them.

He flipped to the third page of the report. It was written by the attending officer who secured the site and stated where they found the body. She had surprised a robbery in progress and taken three shots all in the back. Perrine Dupré had died instantly where she fell. Forensics hadn't found anything.

The coroner's report hadn't been filed yet.

After Conner had walked through the house, he had called back forensics. The next page was from Frank after he and his team returned to the house and did a thorough investigation. They had turned up two cigarette butts in the courtyard, a heel print in the living room and a partial thumb print on the back door. They also had the bullets Doc Cormier had removed from the body. They were running tests on the items.

Connor's written report put together the information from forensics to make a timeline and state the killer had picked the lock, with gloves on and entered through the front door. While waiting for Perrine he'd gone outside into the courtyard, taken off his gloves while he had at least two cigarettes and on the way back inside, before he'd put his gloves on, he'd left a partial print while locking the back door. The killer hadn't made many mistakes but the ones they found might help identify him. At least they proved it wasn't a random break-in or shooting.

He was running the prints through AFIS, the Automated Fingerprint Identification System. They might not be there, but if he was a professional, they might get lucky.

If Connor hadn't asked the forensic team to take a second look, all of those things would have been missed.

Conner pushed the folder away. He put his hands behind his head and leaned back in the chair. This was murder, not robbery, but they were missing a motive.

His background check on Savannah turned up nothing. She'd lived in the same house with her husband for over forty years. Her husband had died fifteen years ago. She had no children.

She did have a younger sister who lived with her daughter, Savannah's niece, in the Metairie area. A nephew was in the armed forces, serving overseas.

Perrine's background check left a few unanswered questions. Julie Ann had been a year old when Perrine took over raising the child. No report on where the child had come from. No one ever visited the child once Perrine became her foster mother and then legally adopted her. It would have been a private adoption.

He needed to do some digging into Julie Ann's background, find out where she was born and who were listed as her birth parents. He had information about her school record in New Orleans, college in Chicago and her business in New York, but there were a lot of gaps he needed to fill. The gaps in Perrine's background and in Julie Ann's background both appeared in and around the time of Julie Ann's birth.

He considered her reaction to his doing a background check. Would she be open to answering some questions? He'd talk to her and explain he wanted to figure out a motive. She'd said she'd prefer he ask her rather than snoop into her past. Maybe she'd be open to that. She'd also said she didn't know much.

His thoughts drifted back to Julie Ann. Great figure, eyes that you could drown in, lips you wanted to taste, plus she had a head on her shoulders. She ran a successful business in New York City. The combination intrigued him. Of course, anyone involved in a murder investigation had to be off limits. He knew that. And she planned to return to New York once her mother's murder was solved. So no long-term relationship. Not that he wanted one. Did he?

He never planned to get married. He'd seen what it did to his mother. Married to a cop aged a woman and put a lot of pressure on the children. His father hadn't been around for a lot of Connor's growing up. He'd been called out at Christmas and birthday parties. And then he'd been shot. When a police officer knocks on your door a police officer's wife knows why they're there. No, he couldn't marry any woman and put her through that.

Any relationships he previously had Connor made sure they realized up front it wouldn't be permanent. So far it worked out for everyone.

Julie Ann might make him think twice about his decision, but he knew he'd never change his mind. She deserved better than a cop.

Besides, she didn't want anyone to take care of her. She was independent, made her own decisions and her opinion of him didn't appear to be much better than Savannah's.

Okay, man, concentrate on the case, not on the delicious Ms. Dupré.

Connor leaned forward over the desk and opened the second folder labeled Perrine Dupré.

He found out she had been born in New Orleans to black parents. She had no siblings. They had lived in the Pontchartrain area. Her father had worked on the railroad; her mother took in laundry. Then they had moved to the Esplanade Ridge near the French Quarter area when Perrine started school.

Perrine had gone to school and graduated with honors. She'd gotten a scholarship to the University of New Orleans, a public university, where she got her bachelor's degree in business management and accounting. She'd been hired by one of the smaller hotels to manage their finances and worked there until she was shot.

She never married and lived in the house on the edge of the French Quarter with her parents until they died. Her parents had babysat Julie Ann while Perrine worked. If they weren't available, the neighbors helped out. It was that type of community.

The information he found out so far was that Julie Ann had attended local schools, been a good student and graduated with honors. She'd left New Orleans and gone to Westwood College in Chicago, where she got a bachelor's degree in interior design. After graduation she'd moved to New York, where she got employment decorating store windows for the first year, then got a job with an interior design firm.

After a couple of years, she opened her own interior design business, 'Perrine's Interior Design'. From what he'd been able to figure out she had worked hard and built up a solid business. He hadn't found any information on her birth parents yet. He needed to focus his research on that.

Maybe he'd drop by Julie Ann's on the way home, just to make sure everything was okay.

Why she had to stay in that house was beyond him. Didn't she realize she could be in danger? And that comment about getting in touch with her mother, what the hell was that all about? Was she one of those woo-woo psychic people?

He shook his head.

"Oh, that smells so yummy."

"Dig in. You don't want it getting cold."

"I don't need a second invite." Lenny shoveled a spoonful of the rice and beans into his mouth.

Julie Ann followed suit. She perched on a wicker chair at Savannah's kitchen table with Savannah, and Lenny Carrone who lived four doors down from Savanah. She leaned over a humungous plate of beans and rice.

She couldn't believe the amazing flavors. She closed her eyes and savored the taste. If you managed to find a place that served southern food in New York it definitely never smelled this good and never tasted like this.

Silence ensued while everyone dived in and ate.

"You eat up now." Savannah admonished Julie Ann. "You finish that plate. I've got some bread puddin' I'm going to warm it up for you."

"Oh, I'd forgotten how much I missed good New Orleans food. You can't find food like this anywhere else."

She'd spent many hours here as a child, mostly with her mother, but sometimes on her own, helping prepare scrumptious dinners. Savannah had been like her second mother.

"Maybe you need to move back where you can get some decent food and put a few pounds on those skinny bones of yours." Savannah interjected.

Julie shoved another forkful of the mixture into her mouth and managed a weak smile. "I'll be lucky to finish this plateful, Savannah. It's huge. I usually have a salad."

"I can manage anything you might have left." Lenny grinned across at her.

"No wonder you look peaked. Look child, it's going to be a rough week or two for you, what with the funeral and all. You're goin' to need your strength. Now you eat."

"Yes ma'am," Julie Ann turned to the task of finishing the huge plate of red beans and rice. "Mmmm, nothing beats your recipe, except maybe my mom's."

She turned to Lenny. "I don't think there's going to be much left for you."

"Ah, well. I don't need it anyway. I heard you had to identify Perrine."

"Yes, I saw her body this morning."

Lenny reached across and squeezed her hand. "How did that go? You okay?"

"It went all right, I guess. They said I could do it via a television camera, but I asked to see her. I needed to touch her; to say goodbye."

Savannah nodded. "She look okay?"

"They had her covered, so I didn't see where the bullets

hit her. She looked peaceful. I already told you when I touched her, she knew she would die. I also sensed she had left her body. I hugged her and said goodbye, but I know she wasn't there. Hopefully she is somewhere around and heard me. I thought I felt her with me last night."

"I'm sure she was baby. She ain't goin' nowhere until she knows you're safe."

"You think?"

"I know so."

"Does she want me to figure out who killed her?"

"Now, that I don't know. If it puts you in danger, then she probably doesn't."

"But how do I know until I figure out why she was killed? Did you see mom that day?"

"Perrine? You mean the day she died?"

Julie Ann nodded.

"Uh huh, she and I had coffee that morning. Then we spent time out in her garden, checkin' on the plants. She sure loved her garden."

"I remember. We spent a lot of time out there. I'd forgotten. I forgot a lot."

"It'll come back, baby. Perrine always knew it wasn't because of her, you didn't come back. She knew you loved her."

"But I lost so much by staying away. I forgot everything that was special here."

"You set different priorities. It can mean sometimes you lose perspective about the important things in life. When you get older you re-evaluate those priorities and maybe adjust them. Some people never do. Sounds to me like you're starting to mature and understand a lot about what's important in life."

"Sure, but it's after I lose the most important thing in my life. I thought I'd built the perfect lifestyle. New York is so far from New Orleans. When you spent time with Perrine on Sunday, she didn't appear worried or concerned about anything?"

"Nope. I went to church and got home around two. She was jest headin' out, said she had to do some shoppin'. Didn't see her again and I never heard any gun shot."

Julie Ann put her fork down. "Did she say anything during the weeks before?"

"Nope. I know she bought the local paper more often, but I figured she jest wanted to follow the local rebuilding and changes in our district and there's an election coming up." Savannah shrugged. "You eat up. You clean that plate, you hear."

"I'm trying." Julie Ann picked up her fork.

"No, wait, I remember she did say she was going to talk to old Charlie Beauchamp. She called Charlie and wanted him to come over. She said she had to protect you. She needed to make sure you knew. I don't know what she was talkin' about. I don' know what she wanted you to know. She had been kinda, I don't know, maybe worried for the last week or so. You better check with Charlie. Maybe he can help you."

"Old Sweetness—Perrine was always close to Charlie. They've been friends since before I was born. At one time I even thought he might be my father."

"Now that don't make no sense, you're white and Perrine wasn't your actual mother."

"I know, but as a child I used to pretend that maybe Perrine was my real mother and Charlie was my father. I know, it doesn't make sense. I was just desperate to try and have a mother and a father. They were always close. I know he loved her. I don't understand why they didn't get married."

"You poor thing, I never thought how hard it might be on you, growin' up, not knowin' who your parents were. I always thought Perrine loved you enough for two people."

"And she did. I couldn't have had a better mother or been loved more. It's just that sometimes you wonder."

"And she never told you?"

"Nope. She just said my hair was the same color as my mothers."

Savannah went quiet.

"Savannah?"

"I don't know much. Harry and I had lived here a long time. We watched Perrine grow up. When she brought you home, I asked about her raising a white baby."

Julie Ann straightened in her chair. Prickles made the hair on her neck stand on end. "And?"

"Perrine said she and your mother had been roommates in college."

"The University of New Orleans?"

"Uh huh. Your mother had you and was living in an apartment. She was shot in a drive-by. She and Perrine had drawn up a legal document before she was killed, so Perrine could adopt you and raise you if anything happened to your birth mother. It was a private adoption. Perrine said your mother seemed to know her life might be in danger and worried about what might happen to you if anything happened to her."

"What if the drive-by shooting was deliberate? It could have been murder. What if my mother was murdered too?"

"Now, child, I don't know nothin' about that. Perrine said it had been ruled an accident."

"Sure, like someone ruled Perrine's death a burglary gone wrong; just another accident. I know they say there's corruption in the police department, but how high does it go?"

"Now don't you start lettin' your imagination run away with you. It could get you in to big trouble."

"I could already be in big trouble and I don't even know why. Did my birth mother know something she shouldn't? If she was my mother's roommate, I need to do some research. I think I'll spend some time in the library tomorrow, reading over old news articles."

"Julie Ann…"

"Don't worry, Savannah, I'll be careful. Maybe I can find an old yearbook of Mom's."

Savannah shook her tightly wound curls.

"You listen to Savannah, girl. She's one smart woman, besides being a good cook." Lenny spoke up. He'd been sitting back, listening to the conversation.

"What about my grandparents? Did they know my background?"

"I don't think Perrine told them anything more than she shared with me. They accepted you because you were the grandchild they always wanted. I think Perrine was trying to protect everyone."

"And Perrine never mentioned my father?"

"No. She said she didn't know, but there was always something. I don't know what. I felt maybe she knew more than she was sharin', but I never pressed her. I figgered if she wanted me to know she'd tell me. I think toward the end she had decided that maybe you needed to know something."

"I guess it's too late now and I'll never know."

At the knock on the door, Julie Ann stiffened. "I'll get it for you."

She moved quickly out of the kitchen and peaked through the curtain before opening the door.

Quickly she turned the knob and threw the door wide open, throwing her arms around the tall, older black man standing there. He shuffled backwards, adjusting his thin frame to accept the weight of the woman who hung desperately around his neck. He hugged her back.

"Charlie 'Sweetness' Beauchamp, the best damn tenor saxophone player there is. I can't believe you're here."

"Miz Julie Ann, as I live and breathe, I wasn't 'spectin to see you here, but then of course you'd be here after what happened to Perrine. I'm so sorry child that your home comin' had to be this way."

Unwinding her arms Julie Ann stepped back. "I'm sorry, too.

You're still the best-looking man I know. I'm so glad you're here. Come on in, Savannah's serving beans and rice. I'm sure there's plenty left over."

"Mmm, hmmm, that woman can sure cook." Charlie stepped into the room and closed the door behind him. "Now let me get a good look at you."

Julie Ann took a few more steps back and stood self-consciously in front of the man.

"You need to put a little meat on those skinny bones of yours. Don't you eat in the city?"

"What is it with my weight? Everyone seems worried about it. I'm fine. I'm perfectly healthy."

"Mmm, hmmm—still as pretty as ever. It's good to see you girl." Charlie wrapped his arms around her again and pulled her close.

She rested her head on his chest. Memories of Mom and Charlie flooded over her.

"I'm sorry about your mom. That must have been a terrible shock to you."

"It was, but then I think it was for everyone that knew her. Do you believe it was robbery?"

"Is that you, Sweetness?"

"It sure is, Savannah. Am I here in time for dinner?"

"Of course and you're certainly welcome to stay." Savannah stood at the kitchen door. "Come on back here and we'll put another plate on the table."

"We're comin'." Charlie turned back to Julie. "No siree, I don't believe it was robbery."

"What then?"

"That I don't know. Everybody loved your mom."

"I know."

They moved to the kitchen. Savannah motioned Charlie to sit.

He bent down, then straightened and pulled a newspaper from his back pocket. He dropped the New Orleans Gazette on the table and eased himself into a chair. "Sure smells good."

Julie Ann pulled an extra plate from the cupboard and placed it on the table in front of Charlie. She noticed his hair was totally gray now, his face wrinkled in sadness.

Savannah brought the pot over and dished the rice and bean concoction onto his plate.

"I see we got a local boy running for governor, just declared his candidacy." Charlie waved his fork toward the picture on the front page of the paper.

Savannah glanced down at the blurred photo. "Rumors been floating around for awhile that he was positioning himself to run."

"The way I hear it, he's got some fancy people hired to get him into the governor's house. His mama has got the money to make it happen." Lenny nodded. "Good to see you, Charlie."

Savannah put the pot back on the stove and eased herself down into her chair. "You sit back down I've got bread pudding for dessert."

"I can't. I'm stuffed." Julie Ann shook her head.

"You can manage a small dish. You need to keep your strength up for grievin'."

Julie Ann sat down and stared at the bowl Savannah put in front of her.

Charlie bowed his head and mumbled thanks under his breath. "Amen."

He took a forkful of the colorful mixture and popped it into his mouth.

"Nobody makes red beans and rice like you, Savannah."

"Thanks, Charlie, but I know how much you loved Perrine's." Savannah slapped a hand over her mouth. "Me and my big mouth, I'm sorry, child."

"No, it's okay Savannah. I've accepted it. Perrine's dead. She'll never be forgotten. I don't want people to quit talking about her. We all loved her."

"I came by to talk to you about planning an old-fashioned parade and funeral for her. We'll do it up real fine.

I think she'd like that. I mentioned it to Savannah." Charlie put his fork down. "What do you think, Julie Ann?"

"I guess I was thinking of a regular funeral and burial, but Savannah mentioned what you were thinking. It might be nice to make it a celebration. I mentioned it to Priestess Ava, and she thought it was a great idea." Julie Ann replied.

"Perrine wasn't a regular person. She touched a lot of lives. Remember all those jam sessions we had at your place?" Charlie asked.

Julie Ann took a spoonful of the pudding. "This is so good. Yes, I do remember those sessions. Perrine used to pretend she didn't see me when I got up and sat at the top of the stairs to listen to all of you."

"A lot of those people would like to be able to celebrate her life. They'd like to play one last time for her. That's what our New Orleans funerals are about."

"Celebrate her life, it has a nice thought behind it. And people wanting to play one more time for her, I think Mom would like that. Thanks, Charlie, that helps."

Charlie reached across, covering her small hand with his large, gnarled one. "She deserves to be celebrated. We'll miss her, but always remember the good times."

"They were almost all good times when you were with Mom." Julie Ann replied.

"That they were child, that they were."

Julie Ann regarded his face.

He had been in love with her. Why hadn't they got married?

"I've forgotten a lot of those things. And I seem to have blocked out a lot of those good times. I need to spend time in the house and talking to the neighbors. Will you arrange the celebration, Charlie?"

"I'd be honored. Once they release her, we'll let her rest in state at Gallagher's Hall. Then we'll have a big, ol' parade to the cemetery."

"Julie Ann and I'll make the food. I'm sure a lot of the other ladies will want to contribute too." Savannah said.

"And the hotel said they'd like to hold the reception." Julie Ann said.

"I'd love to play in that parade." Lenny added.

"Absolutely, it wouldn't be a parade without you, Lenny. Sounds good, I'll let you all know when I've got things started and y'all can help with details." Charlie said.

"I asked Priestess Ava to speak and she agreed."

"That's good. She knew your mother well. I'm sure a lot of other people are going to want to talk about Perrine, too."

"It looks like everything is under control. Let me know what I need to do. Keep in touch, Charlie. Right now, I'm stuffed I'm going to go excuse myself and go back to my house if no one minds." Julie Ann stood up, hugged Charlie and Lenny and blew a kiss to Savannah.

Savannah caught the kiss. "Are you sure you don't want to stay here tonight?"

"Don't be silly. I don't know anything so there's no reason why anyone would want to kill me. I'll be fine. And I've got my cell phone. I'll plug in that sexy deputy's phone numbers as well as the police emergency call number, although I'm never sure whether to trust them."

Charlie shrugged. "Some of them are good cops, but like anywhere, there are always a few bad apples in the crop."

Savannah nodded. "And don't you go getting involved with no policeman. You're better than that."

"Thanks, Savannah. Don't worry. I'm looking, not touching, but he does provide an attractive object to look at it. I have no intention of getting involved with anyone for another ten years. Maybe after I'm one of New York's top interior designers. Once my career is made, maybe I'll change my mind. We'll see. Besides, I don't think I'll be in New Orleans long enough to get involved with anyone."

"You're not planning on staying here?"

"No, Savannah, I don't think so. I have a business in New York, but I'll be here until we figure out what really happened to my mother."

"Hmmph, Perrine always hoped you'd come back to live here. You going to sell her house?"

"I don't know. It's an option, but it's been in the family for a long time. First, I need to know what happened to Mom. Then I'll think about the house. Do any of you know if Perrine purchased a vault?"

"I think so, but you might want to check with her lawyer, Maury Hinkle."

"Thanks, Charlie, I'll do that."

Charlie pushed his empty plate away. "That was perfection, as usual, Savannah."

He pulled out his harmonica.

"Maybe I'll stay for a few minutes." Julie Ann sat down, closed her eyes and leaned back in the chair. She'd listened to that harmonica for a lot of years growing up.

She drifted off. It had been a long day.

Julie Ann jerked awake. "Sorry, guys, I'm almost asleep. I really have to get to bed. Thanks for dinner Savannah and the after-dinner music Charlie. I'll see you guys tomorrow."

"You be careful now. We still don't know why Perrine was killed. You're at risk too. You see or hear anything you high tail it over here."

"I will." She headed out the door and checked carefully before she crossed the street.

She opened the creaky gate and stopped. The curtains in Perrine's living room moved. A shiver proceeded down Julie Ann's spine. She should have left a light on.

Was there someone in the house? Was she in danger? Maybe it was Mom?

Julie Ann glanced over her shoulder to Savannah's house. She debated going back but decided to go inside, carefully. She inserted the key in the lock and waited. Nothing. She turned the doorknob. No visions.

Julie Ann cautiously stepped to one side and pushed open the door. It swung back. She stepped into the room, turned on the light and looked around. No one appeared to have been there. She closed the door, locked it and dropped the key into her bag. She checked that the back door was locked, then picked up the voodoo doll she'd brought back home and climbed up the stairs to her old room.

Her bag still over her shoulder she opened the third bedroom door. It was her room. She scanned the room. The single wooden bed, with another homemade patch-work quilt, still stood against the wall. The battered, second-hand desk with the straight back wooden chair and the hand-painted yellow dresser all brought back memories. Memories of her and Mom painting the dresser sunshine yellow, Mom reading her bedtime stories every night and Mom trying to help her with her homework at the battered desk, bubbled up inside her.

Dinner tonight with Savannah, Lenny and Charlie had felt like being home with family. They were her family. She'd been raised by them. How had she forgotten she had family here, a loving, caring family? Compared to this community, New York was pretty cold and sterile. She had no family there. Maybe she'd keep the house and come back often enough to keep in touch with her 'family'.

In her room she aimed for the closet. She opened the door and pushed the hangers to one side. Her hands skimmed over the wainscoting about three feet from the floor. It took a couple of tries to find the right spot. It had been while. The back wall swung open to reveal a small room, barely big enough to house two people. Julie Ann slipped through the door and closed it behind her.

It was dark and dusty. Faint moonlight filtered down through a cobweb covered vent in the top corner of the room. It highlighted the tiny dust particles floating down. Against the side wall stood a small cot covered with a gray blanket.

Her old worn panda sat on the cot, propped up against a pillow.

It had been a long time since she had been in here. Mom showed it to her when Julie Ann was about two years old. She called it the safe room. She taught Julie Ann that if she was ever scared or thought someone might be after her, she was to go into the room, close the door and wait for her mother to come and get her.

That never happened, although they did practice it occasionally. Julie Ann always thought of it as a game and mostly she would sneak in and have tea parties with her dolls.

She put the voodoo doll beside her panda.

A few years later she'd asked her mother about it. Perrine said she'd had it built in case of emergencies. Julie Ann never really understood the need for a safe room. No one else had one, but it was fun to play there.

Now she realized her mother had built the renovation for protection. Even back then, after she adopted a child, she was concerned someone might be after them, or after Julie Ann. The renovation had taken a few feet from large closets on each side and a section at the back of the bathroom. The peaked roof gave enough height you could actually stand up. It had been well planned and a lot of work. Her mother had built it for her and Julie Ann's safety, but from what. Or who? It sounded like it might be because of Julie Ann's birth mother. Had she also been murdered?

And the room hadn't helped Perrine because she'd been killed outside, before she could get up here.

Julie Ann sat down on the cot, pulled her panda into her arms and hugged it tightly against her chest. Her other hand fondled the packet in her pocket Priestess Ava had given her.

A floorboard creaked on the stairs.

She held her breath, clutched the panda to her chest and tiptoed to the door. She put her ear against the panels.

Muffled footsteps moved through the room. The closet door opened and closed.

"Damn," a husky voice muttered.

The closet door slammed shut. The footsteps moved off.

Julie Ann continued to squeeze her panda. She held her breath, then let it out slowly so it didn't make a sound. Someone had broken into the house. She hadn't heard them. If she hadn't been in the secret room, they might have found her and done…what? She could only guess.

Were they looking for her? Did they want to kill her, like they had her mother? But why? She didn't know anything.

After several moments of silence Julie Ann dug into her bag, pulled out her cell phone and punched in a number.

CHAPTER SIX

Julie Ann curled up in a ball on the cot and hugged her panda. If she'd gone straight to bed would she be dead by now?

A door opened and slammed shut.

Damn, she'd forgotten to go down and lock it after the person left.

"Julie Ann? Julie Ann, where the hell are you? The police are here. It's Connor." Feet thundered up the stairs.

Julie Ann pushed the panel aside and hurried into the room, yanking the door closed behind her. Connor raced into her bedroom and enveloped her in strong muscular arms.

"You're alright?"

"I'm fine. I hid in the closet and he didn't see me."

Inside the circle of his muscles, secure in his strength, the terror abated. She allowed herself a minute to enjoy the feeling of safety and leaned against the solid chest.

His strong heartbeat pounded in her ear. She was surprised at the rapid beat. He didn't appear to be that out of shape that running up the stairs would elevate his pulse rate.

"I was so worried after you called. I was afraid they might have come back. You're sure you weren't hurt?"

Connor dropped his chin against the top of her head and held her tight against his body.

"No, I'm fine. When he didn't find me, he left. I called you."

"I'm glad you did."

Julie Ann felt warm and safe. They stayed like that for several seconds.

Finally, she pulled away and looked up at him.

He lowered his head at the same time she looked up and simultaneously their lips touched. It began with Connor's lips brushing softly against her own. He tasted like beer and spearmint.

Her own pulse accelerated. She wanted more and slipped her hands behind his neck. She pulled him closer.

Connor immediately responded by pulling her tight against his body, deepening the kiss, his tongue skimming over her lips.

Julie Ann slid her tongue between his teeth. A moan slipped out from the back of her throat. Flames burst hot between her thighs. Her nipples hardened and pressed against his chest. She could feel him growing hard.

"Deputy?" a voice called up the stairs.

"Damn," Connor growled.

"Yeah," Julie Ann whispered in his ear.

He pulled away.

"We'll get back to this." Connor replied.

"I'll be here."

"Yes, Officer?" Connor trudged out of the room.

He wasn't wearing his usual suit jacket. He'd replaced it with a Kevlar vest that revealed his tight butt, encased in form fitting jeans. Julie Ann wondered how it would feel to run her fingers over those firm muscles. She felt the heat rise to her cheeks.

Smarten up lady; you don't get involved with anyone until your business is successful, especially a cop. And he's only here because someone wants you dead.

She started to follow Connor downstairs and stopped. She went back into her room, opened the closet and the secret room and grabbed the voodoo doll.

Downstairs she heard the young policeman reporting to Connor.

"We've checked the house and yard. No one here. Whoever entered the house is long gone."

"Forensics?" Connor snapped.

"They're on their way, sir. Apparently, Sheriff Tozer didn't want them to come out. He felt it would be a waste of time but relented when he heard you had requested them."

"Good. Secure the house, same as you would any crime scene, until forensics is finished."

"Yes, sir."

Connor turned to Julie Ann when she entered the living room. "Okay, I'm taking you over to Savannah's until the crime scene investigators are finished. You should spend the night there."

Julie Ann looked up at Connor. "No, thanks, if they are after me that could put Savannah in danger. I'll be fine here. I don't think they're not going to try again tonight."

"You never know, but you're probably right."

Julie Ann observed how Connor's thick eyebrows furrowed together. His eyes darkened. She knew he struggled to find an argument to get her out of the house.

"I need to be here tonight. It's important."

Connor shook his head. "I don't understand why. The risk…"

Julie Ann raised a finger to his lips. "Trust me on this. I'll be fine."

"Hmmph. Come on, I'll take you to Savannah's. I'll be back when everyone leaves."

"Here, you might want this. I don't need it anymore." She handed him the voodoo doll. "It's a regular voodoo doll that any tourist can buy in the shops around the area. They may have changed the hair color but it's a cheap voodoo doll."

He hesitated before gingerly accepting it with his fingertips.

Julie Ann grinned. "Don't worry, here's no spell attached."

"Thanks. I'll enter it as evidence and have the lab check it over. We're doing background checks on the hotel staff and interviewing people about how this got in your room."

"Let me know if you find who did it."

"I will." He took her arm, once outside he slid his free arm around her waist and pulled her close to his body. He buried his face in her hair. "You know you're driving me crazy."

"Connor, we're on a public street. Someone could be watching, like the people who broke into the house tonight."

Connor jerked back. "You're right. We don't know who they are or what they want, yet. Come on, let's get you inside."

He ushered her across the street and knocked on Savannah's door.

The door opened immediately. "What's goin on? I saw all them police cars. I wanted to come over but figgered no one would let me in? You okay, child?"

Savannah pulled Julie Ann inside and wrapped her arms around her.

Once again Julie Ann felt safe and secure. People were looking out for her. If this happened in New York there was no one there who really cared. They might not even notice if she was missing for a day or two. Did she really want to go back and live there?

"I'm fine, Savanah. Someone broke into the house but didn't find me. I called Connor."

Savannah pulled her tighter. "They're not finished. It wasn't only Perrine. It appears they want to get rid of all the loose ends."

"And I'm a loose end. I wish I at least knew why."

Three hours later Connor rapped on Savannah's door. He saw Julie Ann move the curtain to check and see who was there.

She opened the door.

"I came to take you back to your place, unless you've changed your mind."

Julie Ann shook her head.

"Is Savannah still up?"

"Sort of, she fell asleep in the chair."

Connor smiled. "Okay, flip the lock and we'll let her sleep."

He took her hand and led her across the street. He opened the door. "It's clear. We've checked it out. There's no one here."

Inside he brushed her hair back from her face and ran a finger over her lips. "I have to go back to the office and write a report. Otherwise I'd spend the night."

"I've told you I'll be fine. It's after midnight. I need to get some sleep."

"I'll be back in the morning to check on you, but if you need anything phone me." He bent forward, kissed her gently on the lips and pulled her into his arms.

Julie Ann returned the kiss, but then pushed him away. "Don't make it too early, I need my beauty sleep."

"Okay but keep your phone with you at all times. Make sure I'm on speed dial and if you hear anything, anything at all, you call me."

"Yes, sir," She gave him a weak salute. "Now I'm going to bed."

Connor opened the door. He hesitated.

"Go," she gave him a gentle push, closed the door and locked it behind him.

Maybe she'd get a new lock tomorrow. Too many people seemed to be able to bypass this lock and get in the house whenever they wanted.

She crawled up the stairs. In her room she pulled off her clothes and fell into bed. Her bones ached from exhaustion. She yanked the cotton sheet over her, aware of the light pressure on her body. She closed her eyes. They burned, even when they were shut. She couldn't remember feeling this exhausted.

Seconds after her head hit the pillow, she slept.

She sat bolt upright.

What was it?

What had wakened her?

She was shaking. Her nightgown was damp with perspiration. She sat quietly and listened. There was dead silence. She lay back and tried to fall back to sleep. Her pulse raced, her mind flitted from what Savannah had told her about her real mother, to her talk with Priestess Ava, to Mom, and back to Connor.

She pushed her feet over the side of the bed into terry cloth slippers. She reached for her housecoat, slipped her arms through the sleeves and belted it around her waist. She put Princess Ava's ball in her pocket, grabbed her cell phone, slipped out of the room, and padded down the stairs.

Downstairs moonlight flooded the kitchen. Nothing appeared out of place. She opened the fridge, picked up an apple and rubbed it on her sleeve before she sauntered out into the courtyard.

Perched on a rock ledge she took a bite of the apple and surveyed the floral garden centerpiece. Mom had worked hard at the planting and keeping things growing. The rich scent of May Myrtle enveloped her. The air felt cool and fresh. Who would take care of the garden now Mom was gone?

She looked up at the clear sky. Millions of stars scattered across the deep violet blue carpet. She found the Big Dipper, which was her one accomplishment. Mom had been the one to find other constellations like the Seven Sisters, the Little Dipper and Leo. She'd tried to teach Julie Ann where to find all the constellations, but Julie

Ann had never been able to follow the stars. She did appreciate them though.

She smiled at the enormity of the sky and the silence. She pulled her feet up under her and stared at the universe, remembering all the times she and her mother had sat out here and talked and wondered at the stars.

Back in New York everything had been prepared for an extended absence. Her plants had been given away, most of the furniture now wore dust covers, the phone had been temporarily suspended. She took another bite of the apple. Her original plans had been to stay at least a month with her mother.

Now she didn't know how long she'd be here. It could take a few months to clean out the house, sell it and settle all Perrine's affairs if that was what she decided. Plus, she had no idea how long it would take to find out who had murdered Mom, and probably her real mother. Those were her priorities. *Weren't they?*

She needed to find out about her birth mother and how she'd died. And why? Had they killed her father, too? What could possibly be the reason to kill her family so many years ago and now kill Perrine and attempt to kill herself? What secrets had been hidden from her?

Staring up at the stars, life seemed a little overwhelming now that Mom was dead. She'd let New York infect her when really, everything important in life was here.

A smile flitted across her face when she looked at the home where she'd been raised. The small, two-story house built over seventy years ago, almost touched the sidewalk out front like most of the houses in the neighborhood. It was sandwiched between her neighbors with only a few feet between houses. Martha Wright, a widow in her late seventies, lived on one side with a black cat. She always said it was a lucky cat.

George and Monet Smith lived on the other side. George worked at a bank and Monet worked at the hospital.

Julie Ann usually didn't see much of them when she came home to visit. She hadn't seen them in the two days since she'd been home this time. That wasn't a surprise. George and Monet were probably working. She should check on Martha, though, and see how she was doing. Maybe tomorrow.

With no front yard Mom had made the courtyard the center of their world. They had spent hours out here—reading, listening to the fountain or puttering in the small flowerbeds. Business had pushed all these wonderful memories out of her mind.

She thought about her expensive Soho apartment. She'd used all her decorative skills and tried out new ideas with trendy designer furniture, the latest colors and accessories, but it lacked warmth. Her mom had filled their home with worn furniture, family mementos, warmth and love.

Why hadn't I come home sooner?

Tears started with a trickle down her cheeks that increased to a rivulet. She dropped her face in her hands and sobbed. Gradually the sobs subsided. She rubbed her arm over her wet cheeks and hiccupped.

Out of the corner of her eye she noticed a silvery shimmering figure gliding toward her. Her breathing became rapid. She stared at the silvery form. It stopped a few feet in front of her.

"Mom?" Julie Ann stumbled to her feet.

"Mom, Mom is that you?" She inched toward the figure.

The figure held up her hand, palm forward.

Julie sensed not to move closer.

Through the shimmering shroud, she recognized her mother.

"I'm glad you came home. I'm sorry I wasn't here for you." The voice floated across the space like a soft breeze.

"I'm sorry I didn't come home more often. I should have been here for you all those years." Julie Ann responded. "I'm so sorry."

"Don't be. You were following your dream. I supported you. You were doing the right thing. I am here because I want you to know that I was murdered. You must be careful. Be very careful. It's dangerous that you came back. They might try to kill you, too."

"Who did it? Let me know. I'll make sure they get caught."

"I should have told you sooner. I'm sorry. I was going to explain everything when you came home this time, but I was too late. Pay close attention to your senses. Go with your gut. I love you. I can't stay. Look for..."

Julie Ann felt the warmth of her mother's hug and a kiss on her cheek. The vision faded into the night.

"Mom, come back, please." Julie Ann waited for several moments. She stared into the darkness, squeezed her eyes closed and tried to wish her mother's return. It didn't work. The courtyard remained empty and dark.

What were you going to tell me, Mom? What am I supposed to look for? And where?

She shivered in the evening coolness and finally trudged back inside. She checked over her shoulder a couple of times, just in case. No one was there.

Inside she debated making tea but decided maybe a few more hours of sleep would be better. She had another challenging day ahead of her.

She padded upstairs, climbed into bed and pulled the covers over her head. Still pondering the visit from her mother in the courtyard sleep eventually carried her off into an abyss of darkness.

Would she see her mother again? What was she going to explain? Whatever secrets she'd kept were now going to put Julie Ann in danger.

The sun wove its way across the room and over the single bed. Julie Ann dived under the covers.

"Sleep, I need more sleep," she muttered into the pillow.

But life didn't cooperate. Her mind flashed back to last night.

Was it a dream? Did I really see my mother?

Most people would say she'd dreamed the whole thing, but Julie Ann believed her mother was watching out for her. Somehow, she had managed to come back to her, even briefly.

Sleep had no intention of returning. She should get up and see if there were any signs from her mom in the courtyard. Maybe she'd left the brown envelope there. She gave up, tossed the covers to the bottom of the bed and dragged herself to the shower.

Showered and dressed Julie Ann tromped downstairs to the kitchen. Things had been moved and changed since her last visit. The coffeemaker was new, and the toaster was wide enough for bagels.

There was a fine dust on counters and doorknobs from the forensics team. She'd clean it up later.

After programming the coffeemaker, she popped a slice of bread in the toaster. When the percolating stopped, she poured a cup of strong, black coffee, buttered the toast and carried both outside to the courtyard.

In broad daylight it looked like it always had when she had come out here. She remembered thinking about how they had spent many a pleasant hour chatting away while digging in the dirt, planting bulbs and enjoying the color of the flowers and the deep scent of the begonias. She took a deep breath. She remembered there had been the scent of begonias in the air last night, right before her mother showed up.

She put the plate on the rock ledge, sat down with her mug in both hands and took a sip of steaming coffee. She stared at the place where Mom had appeared. The clouds were gone, sun was starting to warm up the air.

Would she show up again? Maybe she had been dreaming.

No, Mom had been there. Julie Ann breathed in the scent of the begonias and briefly felt a hand on her shoulder.

A sharp bark broke through her reverie. She lowered her coffee mug. A small, brown, mixed breed dog sat a few feet away. It barked again.

"Well, hi there, fella. Where did you come from?" Julie Ann dropped one hand from her mug and wiggled her fingers. The mongrel jumped up and moved closer so Julie Ann could scratch behind the dog's ears.

A smile played with her lips while Julie Ann rubbed his or her head and scratched under its chin. "Good boy, good doggie. How did you get back here?"

She looked around, wondering if there was a hole in the wall somewhere. The only way into the courtyard was through the house or the walkway between her house and Martha's. But there was a wrought-iron gate that blocked the entrance to the courtyard. She could see the gate was closed.

"So how did you get in here?" She rubbed the dog's head. "It wasn't through the house and you may be skinny but not skinny enough to slip through the wrought-iron gate. Did someone drop you over the wall?"

The dog growled in pleasure and rolled over to have its belly rubbed.

"So, you're a girl. I guess us girls need to stick together. I wish Mom was here, too. I thought I felt her again, for just a second, right before you showed up. I can't believe how empty my life is and will be without her."

The furry mongrel raised her head, crooked an eyebrow and looked at her.

"Oh god, I miss her." Julie Ann bent down and wrapped her arms around the dog. The tears over flowed and she wept into the dog's neck. "I, I really…really miss her. She taught me how to live life to the fullest and how to be happy. She taught me to stand on my own two feet and to trust my instincts."

The dog sat patiently while Julie sobbed. Gradually the sobs quieted. Julie Ann finally released her hold on the dog's neck and sat back.

The dog put one paw up on Julie Ann's leg.

Julie Ann gave the dog a hug.

"Mom, where are you? Why did you leave me last night? I need you to tell me who is after us and why." Julie Ann wiped her face and bent down to pat the dog. "You think I'm crazy. Right? But she really was special. She came back last night to warn me. I just wish she'd told me what to watch out for."

The dog sat up on her hind legs and rested her head on Julie Ann's knee.

"You are kind of cute, you know. I can't figure out how you got in here. Are you lost? Maybe I should put an ad in the paper. Do you want something to drink?"

The dog looked up at her and whined, then rolled over to have her tummy scratched again.

"Okay, girl, let's get you some water. Have you got a name?"

Julie Ann searched for a collar but didn't find one.

"No? Maybe I'll call you Marie, Marie Laveau. They say she was my great, great grandmother you know. Not really on my side, but on Perrine's. Maybe she sent you here to protect me, except Perrine wasn't my birth mother so I'm not sure how that works. I know it's a made-up story, but Marie helped the sick and the poor, and you helped me cry again and move ahead with my grieving. So okay Marie L., let's go get some breakfast."

The dog followed her obediently into the kitchen, her short stubby tail wagging in the air.

Julie Ann glanced down at the animal.

"It's probably coincidence, isn't it, you showing up in the courtyard right after Mom appeared, and in the courtyard? And yes, I know I'm being silly. You're a stray dog who probably dug your way into the courtyard."

The dog bounced in front of Julie Ann as she walked

into the kitchen and then slowed down and let Julie Ann pass her. Julie Ann felt a cloud of love touch her when she passed beside the dog.

"Mom?"

Connor rubbed his eyes. He'd been at his desk all night researching the case. In the last forty-eight hours he'd only been back to his apartment to shower and change clothes.

"You look like hell." Bobby Ray Franks stood in the doorway, holding two cups of coffee. "I thought you could use this, but I'm not sure it's strong enough. You know you can go home and sleep after a shift."

"Thanks." Connor waved to a chair.

Bobby Ray shoved a few papers to one side and placed one of the coffees on the desk before he dropped into the vacant chair.

After he took a sip of the steaming liquid he looked across at Connor. "How's it going?"

Connor shook his head. "I don't get it. I've never seen a case more badly mismanaged. What was Tozer thinking? There was a break-in last night and he didn't want to send forensics, or anyone, out to investigate. It's like he doesn't want to solve this case and wants to mess it up as much as possible."

"Maybe he does." Bobby Ray replied.

"What makes you think that?"

"My team pulled the original call. Tozer said no rush, do it whenever we had time. We got there a couple of hours later. We'd only been there, maybe an hour when he finally showed up on the scene. He ordered me to do a cursory check. He said it was a robbery. We didn't need to spend any time on the case. Robberies in that area never get solved."

Connor nodded. "I thought something like that might have happened."

"Maybe someone bought him off?"

"I'd say that's a distinct possibility."

Bobby Ray ran a hand over his bald head. "Can you check his bank records?"

Connor nodded. "It's on my list to try to do it. It's going to be tricky. I don't want to trigger anything that might alert him. If he's clean he'll be mad as hell. If he's guilty and whoever hires him finds out..."

"I can see that being a problem."

"It was lucky no one got hurt in the break-in last night. A murder two days earlier and then a break-in, I doubt if it was another robbery attempt, any more than the first one was. Night shift got the call and forensics followed up. I need to get reports from both. The lab checked the bullets from the shooting Sunday night. They're from a Ruger LC9s gun. It's a match to a bullet fired about seven years ago. A doctor in Baton Rouge was killed when someone tried to break into his office for drugs."

"Interesting. That's not a gun anyone would use to break in and rob someone in this district."

"No, it's a gun more likely used by professional hit men. There was also some rifling on the bullet that indicates he used a silencer." Connor took a sip of coffee.

"Robbers don't usually use a silencer."

"Those were my thoughts exactly. I figured that was the case when no one heard the shot. There's not a lot of space between the houses down there. Even with the thunderstorm a neighbor might have heard gun or a backfire. He didn't know there would be a thunderstorm so he would have had the silencer already on the gun."

"What else have you got?"

"Not much. A lot of mystery and a lot of nothing. We did get two fingerprints. They're running them but no hit so far. I've trying to track down Julie Ann Dupré's real mother. There doesn't appear to be much information. I've pulled birth records from the local hospitals from twenty-eight years ago. It's a shot in the dark. She could have been born anywhere. Interestingly, the birth records for the Baptist hospital from twenty-eight years ago were destroyed in a fire."

"That's quite a coincidence?"

Conner shot him a look. "Yeah, do you believe in coincidences?"

"Not me, man."

"Me neither. I'm trying to track down hospital obstetric staff from that time, but not having much luck yet. I need to check that doctor in Baton Rouge that was shot with the same gun. Was he part of that obstetric team?"

"Another coincidence?"

Connor shrugged.

"What are you thinking?" Bobby Ray asked.

"I have absolutely no idea. Louisiana police have a history of being corrupt. Maybe the mob is involved?"

"If that's the case, you'd better be careful. They take out cops and it's never even investigated."

"Yeah, I know all about that." Connor replied bitterly.

Bobby Ray averted his eyes. "Right, sorry about that, I forgot."

Connor shook his head. "Maybe it's time someone did investigate it."

"You could get in a lot of trouble. Tozer could get you suspended."

"He might, or maybe I might find something that shows he's corrupt and was back then."

Bobby Ray glanced over his shoulder. "Don't talk like that man. You don't know whose listening around this place."

Connor shook his head. "There comes a time when a man can't continue to ignore everything that's going on any longer."

"Have you got something specific in mind?"

"I know you're due to go off duty, but could you send

your team out to that break-in last night? I'm sure no one missed anything, but I'd like a second pair of eyes on the scene, in daylight. Focus on the outside. Maybe check the street as well, to see if anyone noticed anyone maybe watching the house. You know what to look for. We have a murderer out there, maybe one who has been committing murders for several years."

"We can do that if it helps nail a murderer. I'll okay the overtime." Bobby Ray hoisted himself out of the chair and dumped his coffee cup in the garbage.

"The victim's daughter said it was one man who broke into the house last night. I don't care what anyone else says, it wasn't another robbery. I think he meant to kill her. I'll let her know you're coming back for another check. In fact, I'll go out before you get there and be there when you arrive."

"You're going to be there?" Bobby Ray smirked. "Isn't that over and above? Is this why you're not sleeping at night?"

"Get out of here. Let me know what you find."

"Will do. Anything else?"

Bobby Ray shuffled out of office.

"Yeah, watch my back if you can."

"It's not going away. You were supposed to make sure it disappeared quickly and quietly."

"I'm sorry. I thought it would be easy. It was a robbery. A middle-aged black woman in the French Quarter, but the girl returning to New Orleans is causing complications. She's keeping the case open. Another deputy, not on our payroll, has now been assigned to investigate."

"He needs to be stopped, whatever it takes. We can't have them investigating. Next thing he'll be snooping into things that have been buried for years."

"I'll get right on it. It will be forgotten in a few days."

"Good, and next time don't miss the girl. She could turn out to be a big problem."

"I thought we were only going to scare her off."

"That was the original plan, but she's not leaving town. Besides, it's not a good idea to leave any loose ends."

"I get it. There's a dog in the house now. I don't know where it came from, but it wasn't there when I took out the old lady or searched the place. It sort of appeared from nowhere. It could be an added problem."

"That would be your problem. I don't care where it came from, handle it. Also see if you can find out if the girl knows anything and if she's talked to anyone before you get rid of her. Don't mess it up this time."

"I understand. I'll take care of it."

"Make sure you do. You're well paid. Earn that money. We don't want anything that could cause problems."

"I'll take care of everything."

"I expect nothing less. We need to wrap this up quickly. We have other work to do. Have you heard from our partners?"

"Yes, they have a shipment coming in two days."

"Good. Make sure you take care of that, too."

"Not a problem."

"I don't want any more screw-ups. I'm thinking maybe the cop needs to be silenced as well. He's beginning to be a nuisance. Take care of him, too."

CHAPTER SEVEN

Julie Ann carried her coffee into her mother's office/work room. Marie L. trotted along at her heel. Perrine occasionally brought work home from the hotel where she worked as the manager, but as far as Julie Ann knew it was never anything important.

A sewing machine sat on the shelf in the corner.

Julie Ann smiled at the memory. Perrine had made costumes for her for Mardi Gras. The ironing board and iron stood next to the sewing machine, set up, waiting for Perrine's return. The rest of the room had been ransacked. Books had been pulled off her small bookshelf and dumped on the floor.

Why would anyone want to go through her mother's personal papers? What were they looking for? Did it have something to do with the hotel's records?

It didn't make sense. If they were looking for cash, they hadn't taken the money in the can downstairs. Her mother's jewelry box hadn't been touched, not even opened. She'd noticed that when she'd gone through the house the first time. It sat on the dresser in Perrine's bedroom with a few trinkets, a thin gold chain and her grandmother's wedding band. It hadn't even been opened.

They weren't looking for money. It wasn't a robbery. That was proof.

Julie Ann put her coffee on the desk and flopped down on the floor. *Where to start?*

Marie L. snuggled in beside her, dropping her hairy chin on Julie Ann's lap. Julie Ann absently scratched the shaggy head with her left hand as she started to pick up papers, scan them, sort them and put them in piles. The letters went in one pile, paid bills in another, unpaid bills in a third pile and junk mail into the waste basket.

In the first pile were the letters she'd written to her mother from New York. There didn't seem to be many of them. She was sure she'd sent more letters that that over the years. She should have written more often, but they talked every week.

She moved to the next pile, the bills. They appeared to be from the last five years. They were all stamped paid. She found one or two that were due this month. She put them in the third pile. She'd have to remember to pay them.

Marie L. stood up and wandered out into the hall. After a few minutes she returned to Julie Ann.

When she finished going through the papers Julie Ann stood up and placed the piles in the slots of Perrine's desk. She started to pick up the books. Maybe she could find an old yearbook. It might have a picture of her birth mother, Perrine's roommate. That would be a start of her search. Pawing through the books she didn't see anything that looked like a yearbook. The was odd because Perrine had four yearbooks, one from each year she was at university. Julie Ann remembered they were in the left corner of the bookshelf.

Had Mom moved them? Had the person who ransacked the room stolen them, but why steal an old yearbook?

Maybe she could get one from the University or read it in the archives. A knock on the door interrupted her search. "Come on Marie, we'll finish this later."

Julie Ann hurried downstairs and opened the door. Savannah stood there with a covered tray in front of her ample bosom.

"Did you check to see who it was before opening the door?"

Julie Ann hesitated.

"That's what I thought. You start checking, girl. Someone out there wants to hurt you."

"Yes, ma'am," Julie Ann hung her head.

"Have you had breakfast?"

"I had toast and then some orange juice. I think I had another piece of toast."

"I didn't think so. You need some real nutrition." Savannah pushed her way past Julie Ann and stomped into the kitchen. "You get in here, girl, and eat this before it gets cold."

Marie charged after Savannah, sniffing at her ankles, wagging her tail in welcome.

"Well, now, who's this?"

"That's Marie L. She showed up in the courtyard this morning and seems to have adopted me."

"She's kind of cute for a mangy mongrel. You better get her checked out. She might have fleas or something."

"Good idea. I'll do that if no one claims her. I want to put an ad in the paper and see if I can find her owner. And I need to get her some food. What have you got there? Mmm, it smells good." Julie Ann lifted the cover.

Savannah slapped her fingers. "Sit."

Julie Ann obeyed quickly. Savannah placed the tray in front of her and removed the cover to reveal a plate heaped with cornmeal hotcakes smothered in maple syrup and spicy sausages on the side.

"It looks yummy. You shouldn't have."

Marie moved to Julie Ann's side and plopped down on the floor.

"Yes, I should've. You haven't eaten anything substantial, have you?" she glanced at the toast, still sitting in the toaster. "And the kitchen's a mess. Also, coffee isn't going to give you any energy. It's the least I can do for Perrine. Eat."

Julie Ann obediently picked up her fork and popped the first bite of the hotcakes and syrup into her mouth. She sighed in pleasure. She hadn't had a breakfast like this since the last time she'd been home.

"That's better." Savannah poured herself a cup of coffee and plopped down across from Julie Ann. She nodded approval as the food disappeared from the plate.

"When you finish eating, I'll help you clean up the mess from last night."

"Thanks."

At a sharp bark, Julie Ann glanced down. "What? You're hungry too? I don't know if you like sausage. It's spicy." She picked up a small piece and offered it to the dog.

The dog snapped it up, swallowing it without chewing.

"Boy, you must be hungry. Here," Julie offered the dog another piece of the sausage. "I'm definitely going to have to buy some dog food today. I'll bet you need water."

She picked up the small bowl, refilled it with water and put it down on the floor.

"Are you sure you want to keep that stray mongrel?"

"I don't think I have much choice. She seems to have adopted me. Besides, she showed up in the courtyard, pretty much in the same place I last saw Mom last night. I don't know, it might be a sign or something." Julie Ann wiped the corner of her mouth with a napkin. "I can't believe I ate all of that."

The bare plate in front, held only a residue of syrup. "I guess maybe I was hungry."

Savannah had a Cheshire cat smile on her face. "That's better. You'll have some energy now. Did you get any sleep last night?"

"Some. I woke up and couldn't get back to sleep so I went out into the courtyard and sat there for awhile." Julie paused. "I saw Mom."

She watched Savannah's face.

"I'm not surprised. Perrine wouldn't leave this place without seeing you."

"She said she had been murdered."

"We knew that. Did she say who did it? Or why?"

"No, she said I should be careful, and I should look for something."

"She'll stay around until she's sure you're okay. Probably until her murderer is caught."

"But that might never happen. The police aren't even investigating it as a murder, except maybe Conner. I don't think they even looked into the robbery, at least not until I showed up."

"True. And don't you go getting involved with that deputy. He may be cute, but you don't want anything to do with them police types. They're always trouble. And you're right about the investigation. They didn't do a thing until you showed up. If Perrine won't leave until they figure out what happened and you're safe, you don' think…" Savannah looked down at the dog.

"What?" Julie followed the glance to the dog and looked back at Savannah. "What?"

"Nothin'. I jest wondered. It seems odd that you see Perrine in the courtyard last night and this morning that dog's there."

"No. Don't be ridiculous. That's not possible. Is it?" Julie Ann stared at the dog.

In response Marie L. barked and wagged her tail.

"No, I don't believe it. It couldn't be. Although I must admit it did cross my mind when she first showed up."

"You're right, it's probably not," Savannah agreed. She bent down and patted the dog.

They both stared at the animal.

She barked again and wagged her tail. She looked like she was smiling.

Julie Ann finished wiping the kitchen counter after Savannah headed home. She needed to go grocery shopping for food for herself and Marie L. She should also rent a car since she planned on staying for a while. If she needed to do research at the University, help plan her mother's funeral, or who knows where else, it would be easier if she had a car.

The phone rang.

"It's Connor. Are you doing alright?"

"I'm fine, thanks."

"Good. I wanted to let you know we're doing a little more investigation after last night. A small team is coming back out to check for a few loose ends."

"Okay, are they looking for anything in particular?"

"No, but this investigation is sort of a double check. Different officers and staff have done different parts of the investigation so far. We want to make sure we didn't miss anything. Forensics covered the inside of the house last night. Today we want to check the outside and maybe the street."

"I see. That sounds thorough." Julie Ann rubbed Marie's back with her foot.

"You might want to go over to Savannah's for a couple of hours while they're there."

"Thanks for the heads-up, but I think I'll stay here. I have stuff to do. I'll stay out of their way."

"That's your choice. I'm going to come along too and keep an eye on things."

"I'm glad you'll be here. I'll put a fresh pot of coffee on." Julie Ann hung up and hummed while she filled the coffee machine. "Hey, Marie, you're going to meet a very sexy cop. Hopefully he's one of the good ones."

Connor arrived first. Julie Ann watched the tall, dark deputy march up to her door.

She swung it open before he knocked.

"Hi, come on in."

Marie sniffed around his legs and barked.

"Who's this?" Connor squatted and patted Marie, rubbing under her chin.

She licked his hand.

"That's Marie L. It looks like you've passed her inspection."

"Where did she come from?"

"She found me in the courtyard. I have no idea where she came from."

"In the courtyard, how did she get in there?"

"I don't know. I checked but I couldn't see any way she would have gotten in. I guess someone dropped her over the wall or she's a spirit dog."

Julie Ann heard another car pull up outside. She peaked out the window and saw four policemen emerge from a marked police car. A tall, bald man with a spare tire pushing against his uniform shirt buttons emerged and pointed down the street. Two men headed in that direction. With the other officer he climbed the stairs to the front door.

Connor opened the door. "Hey, Bobby Ray, meet Julie Ann Dupré. It was her mother that was the victim here. Julie Ann, this is Deputy Sheriff Johnson. He's one of the good guys. The courtyard is through here, Bobby Ray."

Connor led the way and the two officers followed. Marie barked and trailed along after them. She continued to bark and sniff at the two new policemen.

"Come on, Marie, back inside and let them do their work." Julie Ann motioned to the dog and closed the door.

"What are they doing?" she asked Connor when he came back inside.

"They're checking the courtyard for any signs the intruder might have waited there."

Julie Ann nodded and patted Marie. "He could have got through the side gate. It would have been closed but it didn't have a lock on it."

She watched a man pick up something with tweezers and dropped it into a plastic bag.

"Forensics dusted for prints inside after the robbery, and before you moved in. You probably noticed. They dusted again last night. They need to eliminate the people who should be here. If you can think of people who might ordinarily be here and make a list for me that would be helpful."

"I can do that. I'll get Savannah to help. Besides Savannah, Perrine and myself the only other one I can think of is Charlie."

"That's a good start. Once we eliminate neighbors and friends, we can focus on the other prints. We'll run them through our system and see who shows up."

"This is the fourth time they've been back. Is that normal?"

Connor ran his tongue over the inside of his cheek.

"Well?"

"It can be, depending on the crime. Sometimes we tape a crime scene off for weeks. This time, it's not usual, but then there have been two break-ins in three days. Today, I wanted new eyes and in daylight. They might see something others have missed in the dark." He waited for more questions, but Julie Ann just nodded.

"I appreciate you making sure you do everything possible to catch the killer."

"It should have been done right the first time. Someone slipped up. If we don't re-do it there's no way, we'll catch whoever killed your mother."

"Thank you."

"For what?"

"For doing your job, properly."

Connor turned away. "I'll check and see how they're doing."

He returned to the kitchen. "They're almost finished out there. The dog showed up this morning?"

"Uh huh, and she and I bonded. She checks out everyone who comes in the house."

Connor bent down and patted Marie's head. "Good girl, you keep Julie Ann safe. Are you going to keep her?"

"For now, but I'm going to advertise and see if anyone claims her."

"Until then you could use a watchdog. She may be small, but she looks like she's doing a good job. Why Marie L.?"

"I don't know. It just seemed to fit."

"I see. That wouldn't be short for Marie Laveau would it?"

"Well…yes."

"You believe in voodoo?"

"Yes. Why? Do you have a problem with it? It's not evil like people believe. It's a religion."

"So, I've heard."

"You sound doubtful?"

"I've heard about the spells and the voodoo dolls."

Julie slipped her hand inside her pocket and fingered the protection ball Ava had given her.

"That's for the tourists. The spells are supposed to be used for good only. If someone uses them for evil, it comes back on them. And if you've done your research you know Perrine was a High Priestess in the voodoo temple until she retired."

"Yes, I did find that. She wasn't at the time she died."

"No, she'd retired. Priestess Ava took over, but Perrine still attended the voodoo church."

"I see, and you don't think that had anything to do with her death?"

"No."

"What about the voodoo doll?"

"It's New Orleans. You can buy one of those at any of the shops in the French Quarter. Tourists love them.

I'm guessing whoever bought it thought they might scare me into running back to New York. Or maybe the murderer wanted the death to look like it might be tied to voodoo to throw people off the real reason, whatever that is. But it does show it likely wasn't anyone in the neighborhood and definitely not someone who actually knows anything about voodoo."

"I'll take your word on that for now."

If Connor didn't want to know about voodoo that was fine with her. It was another challenge to any kind of a relationship between them.

"Oh, it was one of the night clerks at the hotel who put that doll in your room. Someone paid him five hundred dollars to do it." Connor said.

"Who paid him?"

"He doesn't know. They phoned him after he came on duty. He agreed to do it. They left the doll and an envelope with the cash in it on the corner of the desk when he wasn't there. He never saw anyone. And the cash has been spent or handled or deposited so we can't check for fingerprints."

"And the night clerk?"

"He no longer works there. I don't think losing his job was worth the five hundred dollars they paid him."

"Probably not. Thanks for letting me know. He must have been the man I saw when I picked up the doll."

Connor stared at her.

"They must have followed us from the house to the hotel." Julie Ann changed the subject.

"That's what I think. You still haven't found anything missing from the house?"

"Not really. I think there might be a couple of letters missing from her desk, but I'm not sure. And why would anyone steal old letters? And her yearbooks from university appear to be missing. But again why would anyone steal a yearbook?"

"I don't have answers for either question. Those things

are not what a break and enter thief would be looking for, or steal. It's not what someone would kill over."

"That's what I thought. I'm still looking for the yearbooks but no sign of any of them yet. The police originally said it was a robbery so why didn't the thief even go through her purse or jewelry box?"

"What do you mean?"

"Her purse was with her when she died, right beside her. From the reports I've read it wasn't touched. Her jewelry box was on her dresser. They didn't even open it. They didn't go through any of the drawers in the kitchen where someone might keep loose change or take the can with a few dollars in it by the front door. Nothing in the house was touched except her books and papers upstairs. Don't you think that's odd, if robbery was the motive?"

"I do, which is why we ruled it out at the beginning, even if some people didn't." Connor scribbled away in his notebook for a few seconds before he shoved it back into his pocket. "You managed okay last night? No more problems?"

Julie Ann hesitated for a minute, thinking about seeing her mother, but that hadn't been a problem.

She shook her head. "No, everything's fine. I'm okay. I managed to get some sleep. And Savannah came over and fed me an enormous breakfast."

"Good. I can take you down to the station after the guys are finished, to get your fingerprinting done, if you like. We need to rule your prints out, as well."

"Okay."

"It might be easier if I'm with you to speed up the process. We could go for lunch after."

"You don't have to feed me. Savannah's doing a good job there. I'm going to gain twenty pounds between the two of you."

"I'd enjoy having lunch with you."

"Really? Well…, okay. I'd like to have lunch with you,

too and have you with me when I get fingerprinted would be supportive."

"Good, then it's settled. I know a great little place to eat. Maybe you should move back to the hotel until you get the place cleaned up again after everyone leaves."

"No, thanks, I'm staying here. I've started cleaning after the last visit by the police. I'll keep going after the next wave of guys leave. Savannah has already said she'd help clean up from the forensic guys. Besides, I can't take Marie L. to a hotel and I can't leave her here."

"It's your decision. Do you want Savannah to get her fingerprints done at the same time as you do? It might be easier on her. I can take you both down. You can invite her to join us for lunch, too."

"Thanks. I think she'd like that. I'll slip over and ask her. How much longer do you think they'll be checking out the courtyard?"

"Not much longer. I'll head to the office for an hour or so and arrange for the finger printing; then pick you two up."

"Sounds like a plan. I'll let Savannah know. We'll be ready and waiting."

He was a good man, inviting Savannah to join them for lunch. Julie Ann smiled. She believed he was one of the good guys.

Now to figure out what her mother meant to tell her when she saw her on Sunday. She looked down at Marie L. "Well, if it is you, help me out here. Where do I find that envelope? And where do you hide the Rocky Road ice cream?"

Marie wagged her tail and circled around Julie Ann's feet.

After inviting Savannah to lunch and explaining about the fingerprinting, Julie Ann made a quick trip to the

Quarter grocery store for a few things for breakfast and lunch, dog food and Rocky Road ice cream, while the police finished up. Rocky Road, her and her mother's favorite. She's always kept a quart in her freezer in New York. It helped her get through exhausting days and challenging clients. It also reminded her how she and Perrine had shared conversations over a bowl of Rocky Road. In New York, that last part had gotten forgotten. She'd thought more about her business while she pigged out on her Rocky Road. She wiped away a tear that escaped down her cheek. Just one more forgotten memory.

When she returned from shopping the guys were loading up their car. She watched them drive away, closed her front door and bent down to pat Marie L.

"Good girl. Look what I've got for you."

She placed the paper sack on the counter and brought out a bag of dog food. "The lady said this was the best stuff for dogs so you'd better like it."

Marie whined and wriggled her bottom on the floor.

"It looks good does it? Okay, let's give it a try." Julie reached back into the sack and came out with two small dog bowls. She dumped a handful of the dry food in one bowl and added a little water. She put it down on the floor. Marie raced over and started eating.

"I guess the lady was right." Julie refilled the second bowl with water and put it beside the first bowl before she moved into the living room. Like in the kitchen, things had been moved; tables, lamps, the TV, windows and doors were also covered in dust. Elbow grease and lots of hot water and soap would get things back to normal. Connor had said it would be okay to wash everything down. They'd taken pictures of everything so she wouldn't be ruining any evidence.

A few minutes later Julie Ann started scrubbing at the dust. The physical, mindless effort felt good. It was soothing to bring the room back to its usual appearance.

The knock at the door caused her to jump. She'd been totally engrossed in her cleaning. She left the bucket on the floor and peeked through the curtains.

She hurried to the door, opened it, and threw her arms around Charlie.

"I'm so glad you dropped by."

"Hey now, that's the best welcome I've had in a long time." He squeezed her tight before he let her go. He regarded her through half closed eyelids. "I heard about the break-in last night. You okay?"

"I'm fine—or at least as fine as I can be under the circumstances. I see the local grape vine is still in working order." Julie Ann grinned. "The police were here last night and again this morning, doing their thing. They're finally taking Perrine's death and the break-in seriously. They didn't before."

"That wouldn't surprise me. It surprises me more that they're taking it seriously now."

"Can I get you something to drink?"

"Coffee's good if you've got some."

"I sure do. Let me put on a fresh pot. It'll only take a few minutes." Julie Ann busied herself with the coffee and the water.

"And who do we have here?" Charlie bent down and patted Marie.

"That's Marie L. She found me in the courtyard and appears to have moved in."

"I see. Marie Laveau, huh? And why that name?"

"I'm not sure. It seemed to fit."

"You know Perrine always said she was a descendant from her?"

"Yes, but I don't know that I actually believe her."

"Always believe Perrine. She never told a lie."

"I know that. I just wasn't sure that she knew it for a fact. She might be a descendent, but come on, do I look anything like a descendent. She might have made a mistake there."

Charlie chuckled. "Perrine didn't make mistakes, but I do see your point. I think she told me one time she was a tenth cousin, six times removed on her great, great grandmother's side of the family."

"Really?" Julie chuckled. "With that history, it would be hard to dispute her claim."

"Like I said, always believe Perrine."

Julie poured two mugs of coffee and pushed one across the table to Charlie.

"Got a shot of whiskey to put in that?"

Julie Ann grinned. "I'm sure Mom has some around here somewhere."

"Try the right-hand door over there." Charlie waved his hand toward the cupboards.

Julie Ann moved over and opened the cupboard. There on the lower shelf was a bottle of Jack Daniels. "You've had coffee here before, haven't you?"

She brought the bottle over and poured a shot into the coffee and left the bottle on the table.

Julie Ann picked up the other cup and took a sip. "How's it going Charlie? Where are you playing these days?"

"I'm back here for a few weeks. I'm playing at Preservation Hall. They're letting me sit in with the band. Then I'm back to Chicago."

"Did you see Mom before she died?"

"Uh huh, I was here several times. We had dinner and some good conversation. Savannah joined us a couple of nights."

"How was she, Mom that is?"

"I knew who you meant. She was good. She was working hard, like she always did. She was excited that you were doing so well in New York and had started your own business. She talked endlessly about how your business was successful and what a great interior designer you were and how you were taking New York by storm. She was so proud of you."

Julie Ann sat quietly.

"Somethin's botherin' you, child?"

"Yes. I let my work take over my whole life. I got my priorities all screwed up."

"Don't be worried about it, child. Perrine understood. Like I said she was very proud of you. She knew how much you loved her. She never doubted it for a minute."

"You're sure?" Julie Ann's eyes widened.

"Absolutely sure, Perrine was a very special person. She wanted her child to develop her wings and fly on her own. She didn't want you to feel stifled and anchored here. She believed that each and every person should do their own thing. She did. And she wanted you to do the same. She did seem a little preoccupied the last few days. I asked her about it. She said it wasn't anything she couldn't handle, but she needed to do it before you came home."

"You don't know what she was concerned about?"

"Nope, that's all she said."

"Tell me about her. You've probably known her longer than anyone."

Charlie took a long drink from his mug. His eyes glazed over as he remembered the years gone by.

Julie Ann sat quietly and waited.

"She became a business manager back when black women didn't get those kinds of jobs. The Angelique Hotel, an old boutique hotel firm hired her to do basic accounting and manage the finances after she graduated. That was where she worked when she brought you home."

"That must have been a bit of a shock to you and my grandparents."

"We all knew Perrine. It was a surprise but not a shock. We knew she was helping someone out. Your grandparents were thrilled. They adored you from day one and looked after you while Perrine worked. The hotel expanded and promoted your mother to an assistant accountant."

"I know she loved working there. She took me to work

with her sometimes so I could see where she worked. Everyone respected and liked her."

"They did and when their accountant retired your mother became the accountant with two people working with her. When she brought you home, everyone could see you were the most important thing in her life. While she loved her job, it always came second to you. The Angelique was a family friendly hotel, so it worked out well. Harvey Angel managed it for years, then the daughter, Theresa took it over. She's still there."

"Thanks, Charlie. You've given me a better feel for her. I loved her and knew she loved me, but I think I've missed some of the things that made her truly special."

"The hotel is devastated by her loss. They've offered to do anything to help, including hosting a Celebration of Life party after the parade."

"I knew that. I hadn't thought about the wake after a parade. That sounds like a nice idea. It would make it more personal. I think Mom would like that. I'll make a point of dropping by to thank them. Charlie, you said you'd help plan an appropriate funeral and celebration. Could you maybe take the lead on that? I'm a little overwhelmed right now."

"Of course. I'll talk to Savannah and a few other people. We'll come up with a plan."

"Thank you."

"I almost forgot. Can't remember if I told you, Perrine called last Saturday, the day before she was killed. She asked me to come by on Sunday night, after she'd talked to you. Said she had something she wanted me to have."

"What?"

"She didn't say, and I didn't ask. I figured I'd be seeing her, and she'd explain at that time. I'm sorry, child. I don't know what it was or if it was important."

"Was she upset?"

"No. She appeared to be fine except she sounded concerned about getting some information to you. It sounded like she wanted me to have a copy of something in case yours disappeared. I gather she felt she hadn't let you know that you might be in danger and why."

Julie Ann took another sip of coffee and wondered what her mother had planned on sharing with Charlie. *Was Perrine going to share the secret she kept all these years? Was that why she was killed?*

Maybe she'd never know.

"Did you see her?"

"No, I played that night and came by after we finished. Savannah had already found Perrine's body."

If Perrine called Charlie on Saturday and wanted to give him something on Sunday night, maybe it was still in the house. After the fingerprinting and lunch, she'd go through the whole house with a fine-tooth comb and see if she could find it, whatever it was. She had a feeling it was that envelope she'd seen quickly in her vision.

Was that what people were looking for and killing for? What could be in it?

"Deputy Sheriff O'Reilly." Connor picked up his phone.

"Drop the case."

"Pardon me?"

"Drop the Dupré case before you have a serious accident."

"Who is this?"

"You have a choice. You can pocket get a nice chunk of change, tax free or have a serious, perhaps fatal accident. Think about it."

The phone went dead.

Connor stared at the receiver. He must be getting close to something if people felt the need to threaten him. Of course, they tempered that with a bribe, in case he happened to be a corrupt cop, or a corruptible cop.

He smiled. Well, he wasn't corruptible, didn't take bribes and he didn't plan on backing off the investigation. So, he'd better make sure his will was in order and be more careful with what he was doing.

Right now, he needed to pick up Julie Ann and Savannah for fingerprinting and lunch.

Tomorrow he had a meeting booked with a Lucy Campbell in Lafayette. He'd tracked her down through Perrine's school records. She'd attended university the same time as Perrine and her roommate, Elizabeth Watson. Lucy had attend several of the same classes as Perrine and lived down the hall from them. Hopefully she'd be able to shed some light on Elizabeth. Was Elizbeth Watson Julie Ann's mother? And if Elizabeth was the mother, did she share any information about the father?

Those were only some of the questions he hoped to get answered. He planned to drive up early in the morning.

After the phone call he'd need to keep an eye out for anyone that might follow him, watch the roads he drove on and maybe even wear his Kevlar vest.

How many people were involved in this robbery cover-up? They appeared to have been part of something bigger for over twenty-five years. Could they watch Perrine's house, Julie Ann and himself at the same time? How far up the system did they go?

A lot of questions and no answers.

He picked up the file and grabbed his Kevlar vest. He stopped by the receptionist at the front desk.

"I'm heading out. I'll be back briefly with a couple of people to get fingerprints done. Then I'm out for the afternoon and most of the day tomorrow. If anyone asks or needs to contact me, you can get me on my cell."

"I'm guessing it's not social." The receptionist grinned up at him.

"I wish," Connor replied. He shifted the Kevlar vest over his arm and left the office.

The Kevlar vest hadn't saved his father, but it did provide additional protection.

He'd always had the feeling that nothing could have protected his father, but there was no proof.

After the phone call he had a feeling that at some point he might need all the help and protection available. It looked like he and Julie Ann could both be at risk these days.

But why? What did these people, whoever they were, want? After twenty-five years what had happened, or what was going to happen, that so many people had to die?

He needed to figure that out, and who wanted them both off the case.

And he needed to get a good night's sleep. He was going on will power and coffee. He needed to have all his wits about him these days, especially if he was on their hit list now.

He'd have a good dinner and a good night's sleep, so he was at his best when he drove to Lafayette in the morning.

Chapter Eight

Connor had dropped them off at home after the fingerprints and lunch. Julie Ann waved to Savannah as she disappeared into her house. Julie Ann unlocked her front door closed it behind her and locked it. Marie raced down the stairs to greet her.

"I bet you were sleeping on the bed, weren't you?" She rubbed behind the dog's ears.

She pulled one of the over-stuffed chairs across the room and pushed it against the door. "Maybe I'm over-reacting but with all these break-ins I don't think so. If I am, I at least feel better knowing I should hear the chair being moved if someone tries to break in. I still need to get that new lock. Come on, Marie, let's make tea and maybe have a little Rocky Road ice cream. That always makes me feel better."

In the courtyard she sipped her tea and swallowed a few spoonfuls of ice cream. It had always been her way of coping with stress. Marie curled up at her feet.

Connor had said he was on the trail of her birth mother. He'd told her that Perrine's roommate in college had been Elizabeth Watson. The name didn't mean anything to her. The woman whom he'd tracked down, had attended the university at the same time as Perrine. She was now living in Lafayette. He planned to drive over and talk to her.

Julie Ann asked to go with him, but he refused. He said it could compromise the investigation.

She wasn't sure she believed that, but she didn't want to do take a chance on anything that might mess up the investigation. It was tenuous at best right now. She'd resume her search for the envelope or whatever her mother might have left. It had to be in the house somewhere. Whoever they were wouldn't have come back if they'd found what they were searching for when they killed Perrine. Unless of course, they were tying up loose ends. With everyone dead it wouldn't matter if they found what they were looking for or not.

"Come on, Marie, let's get to work."

The dog bounded into the house and up the stairs.

"You'd think you knew what I was going to do," Julie Ann mumbled as she followed the dog.

In her mother's office she checked the bookshelf again and all the drawers for false bottoms. She checked for hidden drawers or maybe a safe, tapped the walls from floor to ceiling, measured the distance between walls and pulled the carpet up from the floor. Nothing.

It was getting dark.

She flopped down in the chair at her mother's desk. Her mother's old computer sat in the middle, the keyboard in front.

Her mother used computers daily at work, but mostly accounting and Excel programs. It didn't look like she used this one very often.

Still… Julie Ann powered it up. It felt like forever until the screen came on. She searched through folders. There weren't many.

One was named Julie Ann. Inside she found photos of all her interior design projects, her website and the link to her Facebook page. Her mother had followed her career closely.

"Ah, Mom, I never knew." Julie Ann sighed. Mom had followed her career and loved her. Now she needed to think about her own future. She wanted to consider what her mother would have wanted her to do. She also needed to consider her own goals and priorities, should she survive this. Those priorities appeared to be shifting these days.

Marie whined.

"You're right, girl. It's time for supper."

She powered off the computer. Maybe she'd check her mother's bedroom tomorrow.

In the kitchen she found the plate of rice and beans Savannah had left. Julie Ann heated it in the microwave and poured dog kibble into a bowl.

She played with the packet from Ava in her pocket. Would she get to sleep tonight, or should she be prepared for more company?

Maybe she'd sleep in the secret room, just in case. She could use an undisturbed sleep.

After eating she cleaned the kitchen and climbed the stairs. It was early but she was exhausted. She got ready for bed, called Marie, went through the closet and climbed onto the cot in the secret room.

Maybe she'd go for a run in the morning. It might make her feel better.

Before drifting off to sleep she whacked her forehead. She hadn't thought of checking this room out.

Duh! It was secret. No one, except her mother and herself, knew about it. Where is the safest place in the house to hide something? Where would Perrine hide something if she didn't want it found? In here of course. She sat up, turned on the light and looked around. Nothing stood out, but the light wasn't that bright.

If she tried looking tonight, she'd probably miss something and have to go over the room again. Tomorrow morning she'd do a thorough search in here. Right now she could barely keep her eyes open. Exhaustion seeped through every pore in her body.

She lay down and in seconds she was out like a light.

The next morning Julie Ann charged through the front door and grabbed a bottle of water from the fridge. She twisted the top and gulped down half the bottle. Marie raced around her.

She'd slept soundly. The chair hadn't moved. No one had tried to break-in. It was amazing how much a good night's sleep left her alert and energized.

The run left her feeling even better.

Yes, there might be have been a slight risk, but no one would be expecting her to head out that early. She'd pulled on a pair of light sweats and headed down the Esplanade, through the French Quarter, passed the mini-zamboni and the garbage collectors as they picked up the garbage from the night before on Bourbon Street and washed the streets down. She'd always enjoyed the morning hustle and bustle as they cleaned up the city and prepared to welcome the day tourists.

She'd even run by the police station. Only a few police cars were parked in the parking lot.

The crisp, early morning air had felt cool against her skin as she ran. She needed to get back into an exercise routine. She'd been too busy in New York and there hadn't been places to fit in a quick run. She should also find a gym in the area to work out. Exercise always helped her feel better. It might also help her self-defense skills. Here in New Orleans she could just open the door and start running.

Marie barked and jumped up on Julie Ann's leg.

"What? You need to eat?"

Marie ran toward the stairs and back.

"You want me to go upstairs?"

Marie barked and ran back to the stairs.

"You want me to search the room? Okay, I get it. I'll have a quick shower, and then start the search of the secret room. You can help me find whatever's there."

She took another gulp of water and sauntered toward the stairs, thinking about whether she could consider staying in New Orleans. Did she want to go back to New York? Could she move her business here? What about Connor?

So many questions and no answers. She knew she didn't want to get married and have a family, at least not in the near future. But a long-term relationship might work, as long as she maintained her independence. She'd worked too hard to lose that. On the flip side, could she leave Connor and go back to New York?

She'd never met a man in New York that affected her like Connor. She really did want to sleep with him, but did she want more? And it wasn't just Connor.

Her family was here. Damn, life was too complicated. She started up the stairs. Marie raced ahead of her.

The first thing was to find out who had murdered her mother and what they wanted from her. Hopefully then they'd stop trying to kill her.

A knock on the door interrupted her thoughts.

Julie Ann padded back down the stairs and over to the door. She peeked through the curtains.

Savannah grinned back at her.

"Good girl," she said when Julie Ann slid back the lock and let her into the house.

Julie Ann grinned back at her. "I know. I promised. Come on in. I had a great run this morning. I was going to take a quick shower and start searching in Perrine's work room. I also want to do some searching online for information on Elizabeth Watson. Grab a coffee and come up." Julie Ann headed up the stairs.

"What? You goin' to make me climb those stairs?"

"Come on, Savannah, didn't Mom ever get you to come upstairs?"

"No, she respected my limitations."

"Okay, you wait down here. I'll have a quick shower and I'll come back down."

A short time later Julie Ann pulled on a t-shirt on her way out of the bathroom. She almost ran into Savannah as she reached the top of the stairs.

Savannah struggled up the last step, panting. "I ain't doin' that again."

"You came up the stairs? You shouldn't have. I didn't expect you to. I was coming down." Julie Ann stepped over Marie and helped Savannah into the office.

Savannah lowered herself into the wicker chair in the corner of the office and pulled out a fan. She fanned her face. "I see you got everything cleaned up."

"Uh huh, I finished putting the books back on the shelf. I can't see anything missing except maybe her yearbooks. Definitely not anything that would be of interest to a killer. I haven't found any secret hideaway anywhere in here. I checked everywhere."

Marie barked and ran into Julie Ann's bedroom.

"Perrine will have a hideaway some place. I'm thinkin' she's been hiding whatever the secret is, somewhere for all these years. What you searchin' for now?"

"I'm going to look for anything I can find about Elizabeth Watson. I may have to go to the library to read the old newspaper articles around the time I turned one year old, but I was hoping I could pull them up online." Julie Ann powered up the computer.

Savannah sipped her coffee. "I don't know nothin' about searching on that machine. It's good for emails and not much more as far as I'm concerned. Perrine was smart. She'd have had a hiddy place someplace where no one would think of looking. Some place no one would know about, except maybe you."

"That's what I thought, too."

"I'm sure. Perrine never trusted banks and their safety deposit boxes so it's going to be in the house or with someone she trusted."

Julie Ann grinned. "Do you have anything?"

Savannah shook her head. "Nope, she never asked me to keep anything for her."

"Probably if she felt it could be important, she wouldn't want to put anyone in danger. I already checked this room yesterday and didn't find anything. She did tell Charlie she was going to give him something but died before she gave it to him. I do have a few more places I'm going to check."

Marie came back into the room and barked.

"That dog's acting like she wants you to do something."

"She probably want to eat. I'll feed her after I check the university website."

"This a big house. It could take awhile to check everything out."

"You're right, but I'll keep looking."

She'd check Perrine's bedroom but there was only one place her mother might have hidden something that no one else but Julie Ann knew about. She should have checked it last night. Now she planned on doing it later when Savannah wasn't here. It looked like Marie wanted her to go in there and look, the way she kept barking and going back and forth.

"I'm going to play on the computer. I checked the hospital where I was born. They had a fire twenty-eight years ago in the records department. All the birth certificates stored there were destroyed. You think that was a coincidence?"

Savannah shook her head. "Don't believe in coincidences. Honey, I got a bad feeling about this. As soon as we bury Perrine you skedaddle right back to New York. There's something evil here. For whatever reason it's rearing its ugly head after all these years later."

"I think you're right. I can feel the evil in the air. I'll be careful. I did find the doctor on call who probably delivered me. He died in a boating accident twenty years ago. It's beginning to look like anyone that had anything to do with my birth appears to have been eradicated. I may never know the truth. I find that odd."

"Maybe that's good. The truth may get you killed. I'd say they're already trying to make sure you never find anything out about your past."

"Except that not knowing anything looks like that might also get me killed. It appears my only chance is to find out why they want to kill me. Then maybe I can figure out who wants me dead. If I know who it is, I'll have something to bargain with or I'll at least have a fighting chance of staying alive."

"It appears Perrine and your birth mother both had bargaining chips and looked what happened to them."

"The bargaining chips, or their insurance policy, doesn't appear to be very good. Or it had an expiration date. My birth mother's expiration date was only about a year. Perrine's appeared to be about twenty-eight years. Why, after twenty-eight years? Like I said, it looks like I could be dead either way. I'm not fond of those odds. I'm thinking maybe I need to visit Priestess Ava again." Julie Ann fingered the ball in her pocket.

"You think she can come up with a protection spell?"

"Maybe, or if I can feel the evil, maybe she can feel it too and help figure out where it's coming from."

"Or have an idea how to fight it. Maybe she can work something up that will help you get more information."

"Maybe," Julie Ann focused on the computer.

Mom help me out here. Give me something I can use to fight back.

Traffic on the highway to Lafayette was light. Connor checked his rear-view mirror frequently. After the warning he wasn't taking any chances, but he didn't see anyone following him.

Lunch yesterday had been interesting. Julie Ann had brought Charlie Beauchamp along as well, so he could also be fingerprinted.

It hadn't been the intimate lunch he'd originally hoped but he had enjoyed it. Both Charlie and Savannah had regaled them with stories of the old days in the French Quarter and some of the great jazz musicians who had played there. Perrine and Charlie had been close and after the bars and clubs had closed, the musicians had ended up jamming at Perrine's place. He had to admit he'd found it interesting and didn't regret that Charlie and Savannah had joined them, even though he'd been stuck with the bill.

He took the exit his GPS told him to and followed the directions she gave him. He glanced in his mirror and noticed a black pick-up. Had that been behind him on the freeway?

Connor gave his head a shake. Paranoia was getting to him after the warning. Everyone drove a black pick-up these days.

He stopped the car in front of a well-kept, older bungalow near the end of a quiet neighborhood street. The dusky pink house with burgundy shutters stood out from the other more subtle colors in the neighborhood.

Connor approached the burgundy painted door. The lawn was manicured and the flower boxes under the windows overflowed with multi-colored trailing flowers. He rang the bell. The 1812 symphony sounded inside.

A few minutes later the door opened. A woman in her late fifties, her black hair cut into a stylish page boy, smiled at him. "You must be the New Orleans deputy. I'm Lucy Campbell. Please, come in."

Connor followed her into a large open room. Most of the

non-retaining walls had been removed and turned the room into a large, open-concept sunroom.

"Coffee?"

"Please." Connor replied.

The room was painted a stark white that caught all the light. One side held an easel with a large canvas. Several other canvases were piled in the corner.

"Cream and sugar?"

"Black, please, thanks." Connor indicated the canvas on the easel. "You're an artist?"

"Yes. I dabble." Lucy handed him a mug of steaming coffee and motioned toward a table in the sunroom. "Please sit down. You wanted to talk about Elizabeth? That's a name I haven't heard for years."

"When did you see her last?"

"It must have been almost thirty years ago." Lucy slid into the bright orange chair, and leaned her elbows on the glass tabletop. "She got pregnant at the end of her last semester. She graduated and left. I heard she stayed in the New Orleans area, close to Perrine."

"She had the baby. Did you know who the father was?"

Lucy shook her head. "No, Elizabeth kept him a secret. She said he had money and his family disapproved of her. He didn't want to go public with their relationship, but the family lived in Louisiana. I don't know where she met him or if he was a student. From what she said, he might have been six or seven years older. I don't think he attended the university, but that's only my opinion."

"Could he have been an instructor?"

"Maybe, but I don't think so."

"Had they been together for very long?"

"From what she did say and how she acted, I'd say Elizabeth and this guy had been seeing each other for about two or three months when she got pregnant. She really loved the guy because she'd never slept with anyone else before she met him."

"Did she tell him about the baby?"

"I'm not sure, but I don't think so. After she found out she was pregnant I don't think she had anything more to do with him.

"She didn't see him again?"

"No."

"Was it her decision or his? Maybe he ran because she got pregnant?"

"It's possible, but like I said, I don't think she told him she was pregnant. She knew his family would be upset and probably want her to terminate the pregnancy."

"She wanted the baby?"

"Oh, yes. I don't think she'd planned on getting pregnant but when she did, she was happy about it. If his family found out, she seemed concerned about what they might do if they knew she'd had a child. She would have tried to keep it from them."

"No hint as to who the family might have been?"

"No, sorry."

"Okay. Thanks, Lucy, that helps. Thanks for the coffee." Connor stood up.

"She did phone once, about a year later."

Connor paused. "What did she want?"

"I'm not sure." Lucy hesitated. "She sounded like she wanted to hear a friendly voice. She said she was living in New Orleans and had a baby girl. When I asked how she was doing there was a long pause. Then she said she was managing but she thought someone might be stalking her. Before I could ask anything more, she hung up."

Connor pulled out his notebook and made a few entries.

"I called back, but she didn't answer. I heard she'd died in an accident shortly after we talked."

"Yes, in a drive by shooting."

"Oh migawd. I didn't know she'd been shot. No wonder she didn't want his family to know anything. How is her daughter?"

"She's doing well. Perrine Dupré adopted her."

"Perrine? Another name from the past. She was Elizabeth's roommate. If anyone would know who the father was it would be Perrine. Have you talked to her?"

"Unfortunately, Perrine died a few days ago."

Lucy's hand shook and the coffee spilled on to the tabletop. "Perrine's dead?"

Connor nodded.

"Was it an accident?"

"No, why would you ask that?"

"Because you said Elizabeth was shot. A drive-by shooting doesn't sound accidental. It sounds more like it was deliberate. Especially after Elizabeth told me someone was stalking her. And if Perrine adopted the girl and has now died, even these many years later, I just wondered. It sounds like it could be related."

"We're looking into that possibility. Thanks again. You've been very helpful."

"I wish I could be more helpful. Is the daughter in danger?"

"I hope not. Thanks, again." Connor strode to his car.

He heard the door lock behind him.

Not much, but he'd start checking on it right away. Maybe there was a record of Elizabeth Watson somewhere, a birth certificate, family, maybe even a tax return. He'd do a scan. Too bad she didn't have a more unusual name.

It could be another piece of the puzzle. A wealthy family living in the area thirty years ago with a son around twenty-five or twenty-six years old at the time. He'd make a list of wealthy, powerful families in the area with a son now in his early fifties. Maybe something would click, maybe he'd get lucky.

What were the odds?

Back on the freeway he drove toward New Orleans. A black truck pulled in behind him three or four cars back.

Connor noticed the black pick-up. It seemed more than a coincidence. *Who was following him?*

Suddenly the truck pulled out and sped up. It raced past Connor, slowing down as it passed.

The windows were blacked out. Connor couldn't see the driver. Suddenly the passenger window rolled down. Shots were fired. The truck raced off.

Connors car swerved erratically back and forth. His tire had been shot.

Connor struggled to keep the car straight and pull it off to the side. He tried to get a license plate, but it was smeared with mud. With the car under control he pulled off the highway and stopped. At least traffic hadn't been heavy, and he'd managed to avoid hitting another vehicle.

He phoned to get his tire changed.

They hadn't shot to kill but it was a warning. He was sure the next time, and there would be a next time, they would shoot to kill.

Had they done this so Julie Ann would be more vulnerable? Was someone else targeting her at the same time?

Savannah had gone home.

Julie Ann made a sandwich, grabbed another cup of coffee and hurried to the stairs. She was going to go through the secret room inch by inch. If her mother had hid anything there, she was going to find it.

She glanced out the living room window and noticed Charlie sauntering up the street to Savannah's.

She opened the door to say hi. Marie L. raced between her legs and across the street, barking at Savannah's door.

"Marie, get back here. Marie! What is wrong with that dog?"

"Maybe she's trying to tell us something." Charlie moved faster than Julie Ann would have expected. He reached the door first and pounded on it before Julie Ann had crossed the street.

"Savannah, Savannah Cheval are you in there?"

Marie continued barking and jumping at the door.

Julie Ann thought she heard a door close. She ran toward the back door. Marie raced in front of her.

She hurried down the side of the house and when she got close to the courtyard someone pushed past her and shoved her hard. The last thing Julie Ann saw as she fell into the bushes was Marie biting at a pair of ankles in long gray pants, black loafers and black socks.

"Stop, thief, stop," she yelled.

Charlie raced around the side, but the person had disappeared down the street.

"You okay?"

"I'm fine Charlie. Go check on Savannah." Julie Ann struggled to pull herself out of a jasmine bush. Twigs scratched her cheek when she thrust herself forward onto her knees.

She heard Marie inside the house, still barking.

Was Savannah okay? Why would someone hurt her?

From her position on all fours, she pushed up off the cement walk and hurried into the house. "Charlie? Savannah?"

In the kitchen she found Savannah sitting in a chair. She leaned forward, head in her hands. Charlie handed her a towel with ice.

"Savannah? Are you okay? What happened?"

Savannah raised her head. "I'm okay, girl. Don't you worry. He didn't hurt ole Savannah."

"What happened?"

"Not rightly sure. I was watching my favorite soap. I heard a noise, so I came into the kitchen to check on it. Suddenly, wham, I'm being punched in the stomach and the face."

"Oh migawd," Julie Ann's hand went to her mouth. "Are you sure you're okay? I'm calling an ambulance."

"No, no, I'm fine. I don't want no ambulance. He stopped when he heard Marie barking and then Charlie banging on the door."

"Did he say anything? Did he ask for money?"

Savannah held the ice to her face. Charlie placed a large hand on her shoulder.

"Savannah?"

Savannah glanced up at Charlie before she looked at Julie Ann.

He nodded.

"He didn't want no money. He wanted to know what Perrine had told me, or if she'd given me anything. Then he said to convince you to get out of town."

"Damn, this is all because of me."

"No honey, they would have got to me at sometime because I was friends with Perrine. Don't you go blamin' yourself."

"Who else is to blame? This seems to continue to revolve around my birth mother. I'm calling the police." Julie Ann marched across to Savannah's phone and dialed.

"Connor? Julie Ann, I'm reporting another break-in and an assault. Someone beat up Savannah."

"Damn, is she hurt?"

"She says she's not and refuses to go to the hospital."

"Are you with her?"

"Yes, Charlie and I are at her house now."

"Charlie's there?"

"He was on his way to visit Savannah."

"All of you stay there. I'll have a patrol come by and check the area. I'm on my way back from Lafayette. I'm having my tire changed and traffic is picking up, but I should be back in less than an hour. I'll phone the attack into the office."

"Okay, we'll wait here. He's on his way back from Lafayette and will be here shortly." Julie Ann put down the receiver. "Now, no argument, Savannah, you're going to lie down with the ice. You said he hit you in the stomach. You're sure we don't need to get that checked out."

"Honey, you've seen my stomach. It takes a lot to get

through all those rolls of fat. I'm jest fine. Maybe jest a little shocked."

"Okay, but you're going to lie down until Connor gets here. Charlie, help me get her to the couch." Julie Ann's lips constricted into a tight line.

She'd had enough. They'd murdered Perrine and now beat up Savannah. This was her family. Who knew what else they'd done, or who they'd attack next? Charlie? Lenny?

It was time she took the fight to them if she could figure out how to do that. With or without the police she would find out who was doing this and who the hell her father was.

Everything appeared to revolve around her birth. They knew who her mother was and had killed her. Logically this had to do with her father and finding his identity. What could possibly be so important people had to die if they found out who was her father?

She was going to find out and then she'd make sure they paid for their actions, damn it.

"The next time that damn dog gets in the way I'm going to shoot it."

"That would be brilliant and bring even more attention to you. Everything is supposed to be an accident. For years, up until these last few days we've stayed under the police radar, or we have them on our payroll. Keep screwing up and they might start investigating some of the other accidents over the years and our guys might not be able to keep it under wraps. You're getting sloppy."

"Hey, who knew the damn dog would show up? It's supposed to be in the house across the street."

"And what kind of accident were you planning for that old woman? I don't remember asking you to take care of her."

A pause filled the room.

"I thought I'd get her to convince the girl to leave town and go back to New York."

"You thought? When did I give you permission to think? You're not paid to think. You do exactly what I tell you, nothing more. You understand?"

"Yeah, yeah, I got it."

"Good. Your thinking is going to cause us more problems. It's going to narrow the focus on the girl. Accidents close to her are going to be looked into and maybe considered related. The police will be investigating this last stupid attack. Because of you they're crawling all over that place. I'm going to have to fix it. The money is coming out of your salary."

"Hey…"

"No, you screw up you pay for it. Did you get anything from the old lady?"

"No, she said she didn't know anything."

"Let's hope that's the truth. You understand the next move?"

"Yeah, yeah, I know what to do."

"Good, make sure you follow the directions, no more trying anything on your own. I'm thinking of bringing in out of town talent."

"Don't do that. I'll take care of it this time."

"You'd better. We need this settled quickly. There's not a lot of time left."

Chapter Nine

With the tire replaced Connor climbed back into the car and pushed down on the gas pedal. He didn't usually speed or use his police status without a good reason. But he had a good reason. He turned on both. *What the hell? They were going after Savannah now. And Julie Ann almost got hurt.*

This was spreading to too many people. He needed to figure out who was behind it, and why. And he needed to do it fast before someone else lost their life.

Cars pulled over to the side to let him through. Twenty minutes later Connor zigged and zagged through the narrow New Orleans streets. He turned the siren off.

A black pick-up pulled alongside his car. Connor glanced over at the blacked-out windows. He kept his window up, turned the siren back on and slowed his speed. The truck pulled ahead and then slowed down so Connor's front bumper hit the truck's rear bumper and bounced Connor's vehicle up on the sidewalk. Connor braked and swerved to miss several cars and pedestrians. By the time he had the car under control the truck had disappeared.

It had to be the same truck. There were more people involved in this than he had originally thought. Someone had been at Savannah's at the same time the truck followed him to Lafayette and back. At least his car was still drivable, even with the body damage.

He sped toward Savannah's and slammed the car into the curb in front of her house. He raced to the front door.

Charlie opened it before Connor got there. "Slow down deputy, nobody's hurt. And the villain is long gone."

"But someone could have been hurt."

"That's true, but you still need to take a deep breath and slow down. Come on in."

Charlie was right. He needed a clear head to think. He took a deep breath and counted to ten before he stepped inside.

Marie barked at him, and sniffed his ankles.

Connor bent down. "Hey, Marie, I hear you bit our culprit. Good, girl."

Marie wagged her tail.

Julie Ann hurried into the room. "You made good time."

"I wanted to get here and make sure everyone was alright. Are the police here?"

"Not yet. I guess they're busy."

Connor pulled his lips together. Someone should have been here before this. He pulled out his phone and dialed.

"This is Deputy Sheriff O'Reilly. Let me speak to the duty officer. Harry, how come there's no one at the house where a woman was attacked? I called it in about an hour ago?"

"Sheriff Tozer said everyone was over worked and that it could wait."

"Did he? I see. Well, I'm overriding that order. An elderly woman has been beaten. Police need to protect the public and follow up on the case. It's also across the street from where another woman was killed. Send a team out ASAP and put me through to Tozer.

"Sheriff, this is Deputy Sheriff O'Reilly. There's been a murder and several break-ins and personal attacks in the last few days, all in the same neighborhood and across the street from each other. You may not be interested in a murder or women being attacked, but I am. I'm overriding your orders and making it a priority. I'm also going to let your superiors know about your unprofessional treatment of these cases. I wanted you to know. You can attempt to block my orders but I'm going over your head and up the ladder." Connor hung up before Sheriff Tozer had a chance to reply. He turned to Savannah.

"There will be police officers here shortly. They'll be doing a complete investigation. I need to make another call and get forensics out here. Savannah, are you really alright?"

"I'm fine. He took me by surprise. Other than a few bruises, I'm good. Julie Ann got knocked down. She probably has more bruises that I do."

"Julie Ann?"

"I've got a few bruises and scrapes on my side and knees from the fall and the jasmine bush, but I'm good."

"Charlie?"

"I'm fine. I never saw anyone."

Julie Ann glanced up at Connor. "Thanks for getting here so quickly. Marie saved us all. I didn't see much above the guy's knees, but she got his ankle."

"I'm glad no one was hurt. I'm also surprised that someone would attack Savanah. It seems like a risk without much return. It sounds like they're getting worried and ramping up their efforts. We need to figure out why they're escalating. Why the urgency all of a sudden?"

"Good question. Did you find anything out in Lafayette?"

"Not much. Your mother was Elizabeth Watson. Your father is older maybe by five or six years and from this area. That's it."

"Elizabeth Watson. I'm hoping there might be a picture in an old yearbook. Mom's yearbooks have disappeared. I haven't been able to find any photos online. I may need to go to the university archives. They should have her picture and bio. Maybe I can learn more about her."

"That's a good idea, but don't go alone. I might be able to go with you. Now, I think this time Savannah needs to go to your place. Give the police time to go through her house and yard."

"Good idea. Come on Savannah, pack a little bag and you sleep at my place tonight."

"No, sir. I stay here. I don't sleep in nobody else's bed and I'm not hikin' up those stairs again."

"Don't argue. You don't want to be here when the police and forensics go through the house."

"I'll come over until they leave, but I ain't sleepin' in your house."

"Okay, if you insist. You can have supper at my place tonight."

"I'm making supper."

"We'll do it together. Come on, let's go." Julie Ann gave her a gentle nudge.

"What about you, Charlie" Connor asked.

"I didn't see anything. I don't think they're after me, at least not yet. I think I'll head home. Besides I need to work on the funeral arrangements and the parade."

"Theresa, from the Angelique Hotel phoned to confirm they would host the celebration party after the parade. She said they'd handle that part." Julie Ann said.

"You said they were going to do that. That's a mighty fine offer. I'll contact the lady when I have the date and times set." Charlie turned to Connor. "Deputy Sheriff, do you know when they'll release Perrine's body so we can bury her proper?"

"It should be any day now. I'll check and let you know."

"Thank you, sir. Now I think I'll go home and make a few phone calls."

"You can always come by my house for dinner and make the calls from there." Julie Ann said. "Savannah will be doing most of the cooking."

"Might just do that," Charlie replied.

"If you need anything, or remember anything, you call me." Connor handed him a card.

Charlie nodded and left the house. Connor watch him stroll down the street and saw him scratch his head. Charlie might not say much, but Connor figured he was worried, too.

Julie Ann took Savannah's arm. "Let's go. Come on, Marie."

Savannah shuffled back along beside Julie Ann. "I should bring food."

"I've got food."

"Not enough to cook a good dinner. I've seen your cupboards." Savannah pulled her arm away and started to open and shut cupboard doors. She stuffed bags and boxes into a sack.

"Okay, I think I've got enough for dinner."

"I think you've got enough to last a week," Julie Ann replied.

"Lock your doors and windows, keep your phone on and close, and if you think there's anything odd, call me right away." Connor squeezed Julie Ann's hand.

"Don't worry, I will. Thanks for being here."

Sirens sounded in the distance and a faint revolving red light flashed from down the street.

"I'm hanging around until everybody finishes the investigation. I'm right across the street if you need anything." Connor followed them out the door and watched Julie Ann, Savannah and Marie cross the street and go inside.

The police car pulled up to the house.

Connor cast one last look across the street. Maybe one night in the future it could be him and Julie Ann going into that house, just the two of them.

What are you thinking, man? She loves New York. I'll never leave New Orleans. She's way above my pay grade and has her own business. I don't want a relationship. Cops shouldn't marry. And she believes in that voodoo crap.

Right. No future in a relationship here. Focus on the job.

Yeah, right.

"Taste this." Savannah held out a spoonful of shrimp and sausage pasta."

"Oh, Savannah, that's to die for. I need the recipe."

Savannah released a deep belly roll chuckle. "Now child, you know that other than a list of ingredients I add a dash of this and a sprinkle of that."

"Of course, I should have known." Julie Ann tossed a salad. "I guess Charlie's not going to make it."

"I think he's still mourning Perrine. Give him time."

Julie Ann set the table in the courtyard so they could eat outside. A cool breeze floated over the area. Marie settled under the table so she could catch anything that might drop on the ground.

"Have you seen your neighbors since you've been back?' Savannah slipped a bite of pasta to Marie.

"Not really. I dropped by Martha Wright's for a minute today, to let her know I was staying here for a while. I can't believe she's eighty. She's doing well, but felt awful about Perrine. She can't believe it happened in this neighborhood."

"I can imagine. None of us can. Martha's lived here a long time, back when Perrine's parents were alive. She still manages to get out and do her shopping. We all keep an eye out for her."

"She said a real estate person had come by a few weeks ago and wanted to buy her house."

"Some person wanted to buy up most of the block and build a big apartment complex. He came by and made offers to several of the people around here on this side of the street. Perrine told them no."

"Mom never mentioned it."

"It was a few weeks ago, maybe a month or so. She said she had no intention of selling her parents home. The agent wasn't too happy. I think he had your other neighbors, the Smith's, considering it, but he needed Perrine's house because it's in the middle. He wasn't very happy with her refusal. He tried three or four times to change her mind, but you know Perrine."

"Yes, I do. Once she makes up her mind, she's not likely to change it. I can't see her leaving this house or this area. And I certainly don't see her selling to a big apartment building. I guess if he got three or four houses, including this one, he could make a lot of money on a deal like that."

"Probably, but we don't want no big apartment building in this area."

"No, Mom, would never go for that. Would he be upset enough to use violence to get her to sell?"

"In this day and age, who knows? Money rules for a lot of people."

"He hasn't contacted me so I can't see him breaking inot the house and trying to kill me. Logically, he would contact me and try to get me to sell. Then maybe he might resort to other methods."

"Maybe he sent a letter with an offer and you haven't got it yet?"

"Or I ignored it. I'll check again."

They heard the police cars drive off.

"I'm goin' home." Savannah hauled herself up and carried her plate into the kitchen.

"You don't have to rush off."

"I'm tired. It's been a long day. I'm goin' to soak in a hot bath and go to bed."

"You be careful, especially getting in and out of your tub. I can stay until you get out of the tub."

"I've been managing my tub for fifty years. I'll be fine."

"Okay, but whoever they are, they seem to be upping the

ante and now you're included. Be careful. I'll help you get home."

"I'm fine. The police jest left so the house is good. Your deputy might still be there. I'll lock everything up tight when I get inside. You do the same when I leave. I'll see you in the morning."

Julie Ann watched Savannah lumber cross the street and go inside. She saw Connor come out, check the door behind him and get into his car.

He waved before he drove off.

Once she was sure Savannah was safe, Julie Ann checked all the doors and locks, made a cup of tea and went upstairs.

In the secret room she began her search. She couldn't believe it had taken all day to get back to it. First, she checked all the walls. She tapped and knocked, listening for any difference in the sounds. Perrine had designed the room so she could have included a safe or a hidden cupboard.

After she'd searched for half an hour, she'd found nothing.

She did the same thing on the low ceiling, checking for any possible hiding place. Marie laid on the bed and watched her.

"You know, you could bark or jump up or do something if I'm close."

Marie perked up her ears.

If Marie L. was the reincarnation of her mother, she wasn't being any help whatsoever.

Julie Ann started to check the floors for a loose board or a place where something might be hidden. Once again, the light in the room was not very bright and at floor level it was quite dark. She need to find a flashlight, but it was late, and she was tired. Her eyes kept closing and her brain felt like it was in a thick, mushy fog. It had been a long day. At one point she drifted off, sitting on the floor, her head resting on the bed.

She jerked her head up and stared blankly at the floor. At this rate she might miss something because she was over-tired. Besides, it didn't look like her mother had hidden anything in here. She'd finish checking the floor in the morning when there was better light in the room, and she'd go over the room one more time. She'd been so sure her mother would have hidden something in here. Where else could it be?

After getting ready for the night Julie Ann fell into bed in the secret room. It felt safer there. Marie L. jumped up and curled around her feet. Sleep pulled the cover over Julie Ann's head and she was sound asleep.

Marie L. growled a low guttural sound deep in her throat and stood up on the bed.

Julie Ann rolled over and automatically moved her hand toward the dog. "It's okay. Good dog, good girl. Go back to sleep."

She closed her eyes.

Marie uttered another growl. This time the hairs on the back of Julie Ann's neck stood on end. She could hear a noise downstairs. Footsteps? A door?

Damn, she'd forgot to put the chair in front of the front door, but she'd put a new lock on.

She laid quietly, patted Marie and shushed her. She could hear a creak on the stairs.

She reached for Marie, but the dog jumped off the bed and ran toward the stairs.

Julie Ann hesitated then moved to the door and pulled it tightly closed. She climbed back on to the cot. She wrapped her arms around her legs, listened and waited. She couldn't believe someone was back again, especially after the attack on Savannah. The stakes appeared to be getting higher. Perrine had died but obviously that wasn't enough. *What did they want? What were they afraid might be exposed?*

She heard Marie growling and barking.

A man's voice shouted, "Go away and get out of here. Damn dog, go."

The barking continued.

Julie Ann heard steps come into the bedroom. The closet door opened and then slammed shut. The man swore and stomped off into Perrine's room. Marie continued to bark and follow him. Julie Ann could tell where he was by the sound of his feet. She wasn't sure but it sounded like he might have a limp.

Maybe he had a bite on his ankle.

She sat quietly and shivered as she listened to the sound of someone wandering through her home, sure that it was the same man who had killed her mother and probably attacked Savannah. She was sure he had a gun. The better to shoot her with. She offered up a silent prayer that he didn't decide to shoot Marie.

Why was he back here? This was the third time. He hadn't found anything on his previous visits so the only reason she could think of for this one was that he wanted to kill her. But why? She didn't know anything. There was no motive she could think of and so far, no one else had found a motive for any of the killings.

What were they missing?

Maybe Connor was right, maybe she should move to a hotel.

No, she wouldn't let them chase her out of her home. Besides, she was safer here anyway. If they wanted her dead, they could find her in a hotel. They had the first night. And she might not have the same safety she had here, in Perrine's secret room. She listened to the steps move downstairs and out the door. Marie barked at his heels.

There was silence, then a scratching at the closet door.

"No, Marie, go away." Julie Ann whispered.

Marie continued to whine and scratch. Julie Ann jumped up, opened the door and let the dog in. "Shh, be quiet."

Marie jumped up on the cot and snuggled next to Julie Ann. Julie Ann patted her absently, "Good dog, good girl."

Everything had gone deadly quiet. She should call Connor, but he needed his sleep, too.

She waited for another few minutes. There still wasn't a sound. "Okay girl, let's check and see if he's gone."

Julie Ann slid the door open and slipped out into her bedroom. She stopped, pressed her back against the wall and listened.

Silence.

"Okay girl, we're going downstairs to make sure he's gone, so no barking."

The house was in total darkness. Julie Ann crept out into the hall and down the stairs. Silence echoed through the house.

She flipped the light switch. The soft yellow light flooded the room. There was no one there. The front door had been closed and locked. He'd picked the lock. She'd get another one with a sliding bolt.

Julie Ann noticed a scrap of paper caught under the front door frame.

He must have dropped it when he left.

She scuttled across the room and grabbed it. It was folded in squares. She opened it and read it. Blindly she reached for a chair and collapsed into it, the note clutched in her hand.

I can't continue. The guilt is too much.
I don't want to live without her.
This is the only way I can escape.

Julie Ann

The sun was casting a morning glow over the street. Connor covered the steps to the front door in two strides, his fist hitting the door before he'd even skidded to a stop.

Julie Ann had phoned and said someone broke in and wanted to kill her. He hadn't asked any questions. He'd panicked and sped to get here as quickly as possible.

When she didn't open it immediately, he felt the hand of the devil grab his stomach and twist. He pounded on the door.

"Julie Ann? Are you there? Julie Ann, open the damn door."

The door opened.

"Shh, quit shouting. It's early. You'll wake the neighbors. I don't want to worry Savannah. She already had a bad day. Get in here." She grabbed his arm, pulled him into the room and closed the door. "I was coming down the stairs when you knocked. You're driving a different car."

"I had a fender bender on the way back from Lafayette. The car's in the body shop. I'm driving a police vehicle for a few days. Are you okay?" Connor pulled her into his arms and clutched her to his chest.

Julie Ann rested her head against his chest and slipped her hands around his waist. "Your heart is racing."

"You scared the hell out of me, again. I told you not to stay here. They could have killed you. One of these times they're going to be successful."

"They could kill me wherever I stayed. They didn't find me here."

"This time," Connor mumbled.

"I know. You'll catch them."

Connor shook his head. He'd never felt like this about any woman before and the thought he could lose her terrified him. He couldn't have a relationship with her, but he couldn't live without her.

"He didn't…hurt you?" His voice broke. His hands moved up and down her back.

"No, I hid in the closet. He didn't see me. I'm fine, sort of. A little shaken up. He planned to kill me and make it look like a suicide."

"Oh god, are you sure? I know you said that when you phoned, but what makes you think that?"

She dug the note out of her pocket. Her hand shaking, she handed it to him.

He slipped on gloves, took it and read it.

Connor felt the color drain from his face and his pulse rate escalated. He realized what the note meant, and how close he had come to losing her.

They wanted to kill her. He didn't have a damn motive yet, but for some reason they viewed her as a threat. It had to have something to do with her birth mother and her father, but why after all these years. He looked across at her. She was pale but appeared to be handling it quite well.

He pulled out a plastic bag and carefully put the note inside, sealed it and initialed it along the closure, before removing his gloves.

"Maybe we'll get fingerprints off the note."

"Probably not. They don't make too many mistakes."

"You're sure you're okay?" Connor placed his hands on each side of her face. He leaned down and kissed her, gently. His kiss deepened. She slipped her hands behind his head and returned the kiss.

He could feel himself getting hard. He needed to stop right now and call the police. He tousled her hair. "What am I going to do with you?"

"Sleep with me?" She smiled up at him.

"No. I need to convince you how serious this is. We need to figure out how to make sure you're safe." He scanned the room. Everything appeared in order. Nothing looked out of place.

"We need to get the police and forensics back out here. They're getting to know this house very well. I'm getting a thick file on you and this area, but no answers." Connor punched in the number and talked to the duty officer. "He said don't touch anything. They'll send out the next shift as soon as they check in. They should be here in less than hour."

He prowled around the room and poked his head into the kitchen.

"Did you hear him say anything?"

"Not really, mostly he swore at Marie. She wouldn't leave him alone. She was protecting me and distracting him. I think it was the same man who attacked Savannah."

"What makes you say that?"

"I could be wrong, but I think he had a limp. At least it sounded like a limp when he stomped around the upstairs. It might be from when Marie bit him earlier."

"Did he have an accent r anything?"

"Not that I heard."

"Any idea what he wanted this time?"

"Other than killing me, I don't know. I didn't come out and ask him, but I'm pretty sure that the suicide note pretty much says it all. I don't know anything. Perrine never told me whatever they think I know. Both Savannah and my neighbor on the right side, did mention that some real estate person was trying to buy these houses. He wants to knock them down and build an apartment complex. Perrine said no way and without our house the deal wasn't going to work. She was blocking the deal, but I don't think anyone is going to kill over that."

"You never know, Money is a powerful motive. I'll check it out." Connor pulled out his notepad.

"But would a real estate agent leave a suicide note? That doesn't fit." Julie Ann padded across to one of the large over-stuffed living room chairs and curled up with her legs underneath her. Marie begged to be picked up. Julie Ann pulled her onto her lap and scratched behind her ears.

"You read it?" Connor asked.

"Of course."

"You're okay after reading it?"

"No, I'm not okay. I'm scared as hell. Someone wants to kill me and make it look like a suicide. Mom's murder was supposed to look like a robbery. Everything is supposed to look like some kind of an accident, not murder. No one is supposed to be investigating any of this."

"That seems to sum it up, but why? Did you hear anything else when he was in the house?"

"Not much. When I realized someone had broken in and was moving around downstairs, I slipped into…the closet. I heard him move around from room to room. Marie was barking and probably nipping at his ankles. He kept yelling at her. I thought he might hurt her, but I guess he didn't want to risk shooting a dog, although if he's the same shooter who came in on Sunday and killed Mom, I thought he had a silencer. I heard him swearing, but that was all. When I knew he'd gone I came out and found the note stuck in the front door frame. He must have dropped it on his way out. It makes it pretty obvious why he'd come here."

"You're probably right. It's obvious someone wants you dead, but they don't want it investigated. If you were depressed over your mother's death and committed suicide no one would look into it any further."

"That's what I figure. I wish I could understand why they needed to kill Mom and now me. If it's over a real estate deal, why suicide?"

"That I don't know but maybe if it's a suicide they'd think the estate might be settled quicker? I have no idea."

"It doesn't make any sense. But if it's something about my birth mother or my father, what's changed in the last twenty-eight years?"

"Again, I have no idea. You can't stay here. You've got to move."

"No. I'm staying here. If I move to a hotel or somewhere else, they can still find me and try to kill me. Someone was in my room that first night at the hotel. How did they even know I was in town and where I spent the night? They seem to have inside information about everything that's happening and what we're doing. Also, I don't want to put anyone else at risk. If I stayed with Savannah, they might kill her too. Look what they did to her today. At least here, I know the house, and have a chance when he comes in. And I've got my guard dog. It was Marie that alerted me and woke me."

Connor reached over and patted the dog. "Good doggie, good girl. I'll take the note in and have the guys in the lab analyze it and check it for prints. Then I can come back."

"No. I'm fine. You don't need to do that. He visited Savannah yesterday afternoon and now me tonight. He struck out both times, so he's probably had it for now. They probably need to regroup and come up with a different plan. I'm okay, really."

"Are you sure?"

"Yes."

"Okay, then I'll have a police car drive by your place every hour and maybe park in front if they don't get any calls."

"That sounds good. Thanks for coming over so quickly." Julie Ann stood up and Marie jumped to the floor.

"Not a problem. I told you to call me, anytime. I don't want to lose you." Connor crossed the room in two steps and ran a finger along her jaw line. He tipped her face up, leaned down and brushed his lips over her soft mouth.

When she responded Connor deepened the kiss. He slipped his tongue inside her mouth and tasted the warmth and desire. He pulled her into his arms. Her soft body arched again his. He felt the heat permeating his groin area and drew back. He dropped his arms.

Damn, he desperately wanted to make love to her, but not under this situation. Someone had tried to kill her. She was a victim and vulnerable. Besides, she wasn't a one-night stand type of woman and he wasn't a relationship type of guy.

Julie Ann stared up at him. "I don't understand."

"When this is over, I'm not going to pull back. I want you. But I don't want it to be because you're looking for, or need, protection." He whispered in her ear.

Julie Ann forced her soft, pink lips into a pout.

"That won't work. I want you, but not because you think your life is in danger or I'm some white knight."

A sigh slipped from her lips and relaxed them into a smile. "Okay, you win, but one day I'm not going to let you escape."

"One day I won't leave. Now take your cell phone, your dog and go back to bed. I'll have a patrol car pass by every hour."

"Thank you, but the sun is coming up. I think I'll get up and do some research online. See if I can find anything about Elizabeth Watson." She raised herself on her toes and kissed his cheek.

It took every inch of his strength to walk away. She'd got under his skin. He wanted a life with her. And that couldn't happen. There were too many obstacles in the way of a relationship.

"I'll take this to the lab. Call me if you hear or see anything unusual. Police and forensics will be back here shortly."

"Have you turned up anything from the previous forensics yet?"

"No. It's a little too soon. It usually takes a couple of days."

"I thought I'd ask. Maybe I'll go for a run after the police arrive."

"Do you think a run is wise?"

"Hey, do you think he's going to be expecting that? Besides, he won't know my route and I doubt if he can keep up with me. I'll be fine. They'll be picking up the trash soon and there will be all sorts of people on the streets. I went for a run this morning and it felt great."

"I don't like it."

"I'll be careful. Besides, I also know self-defense." Julie Ann jumped into a karate pose. "You don't want to mess with me."

A sigh escaped and Connor ambled toward the door. "I'll call you later to make sure you're okay."

"I'll be fine. Thanks for coming over. You must be getting tired of my calls."

"Never. Maybe we should wake Savannah and get her to come over."

"No, absolutely not. I don't want to concern her. She's already worried because of my mother, and she took that beating yesterday. I don't want to make it any worse for her. I'll be fine."

Connor stood at the door, looking at the skinny girl with tousled blonde hair and dark brown, soulful eyes, wrapped in a purple terrycloth housecoat, with her bare feet sticking out under the hem. Her toenails were painted a bright pink. She was beautiful.

"I'll be at the police station if you need me. I'm only a few minutes away. Be careful."

"I'll be fine. Don't you ever go home and sleep?"

"Yeah, for a shower and I catch a few winks. I'll drop by later."

"You don't have to."

"I want to, and I might have some news."

"Okay. If I'm not here, check at Savannah's."

"I don't want you to leave the house, except to go to Savannah's. Or if you go for that run, please be really careful. You could be in danger anywhere you go. They seem to have a way of knowing exactly what you're planning. Promise me you won't take any chances."

"I'll be careful."

Connor marched to his car. He surveyed up and down the street before he opened the door. He tried to see into the shadows.

Was someone watching from a doorway?

Do they know I'm here? Am I going to be their next target? Is there an accident waiting for me, the same as my father?

And like every time his mind went back to his father's

death, he wondered where had his father's partner been when he got shot? That had always been the unanswered question. It was time he pushed for those answers.

In the coffee room Connor poured a cup of thick, black, sludge which the office jokingly called coffee. Someone had probably made it the day before and it had been sitting there ever since. Stirring in the whitener he added four sugars. Deep in thought he carried the coffee down the hall to his desk.

He ran into Sheriff Tozer striding toward the squad room. The coffee sloshed over onto the floor.

"What's this?" Tozer held out the suicide note Julie Ann had found in her house last night after her unwanted visitor.

"That's the copy of the suicide note the killer brought with him when he entered Julie Ann Dupré's house last night."

"That's what she told you."

"What do you mean?"

"It's typed. She could have typed it herself and called you with some whacky story about a stranger being in the house. Did you see any sign that anyone had been there?"

"No. He was gone when she called."

"That's convenient."

"Right. She should have come out while he was there and got shot like her mother. Another accidental break-in."

"It could have been. All you really know is her version of a possible incident. She could have made up the guy and typed the note to throw suspicion off herself."

"Why would she be trying to throw suspicion off herself? She hasn't done anything illegal. She wasn't in New Orleans when her mother died. I gave the original note to forensics, to have them check and see if there was anything that might help identify who typed it or where it was typed and that would include anything that would point to Ms. Dupré."

"It's a waste of time. They won't find anything. It's probably fake."

"I'd like to hear what forensics say. And the woman was in New York when the murder happened. She didn't do it. She can prove it." Connor retorted.

"Have you checked her flights? And we don't know it was a murder. I'm sticking with death in the commission of a robbery until you or someone else proves differently. Maybe the girl wants attention. You know, get a cop to hang around her and protect her."

"Read the report and you'll see both forensics and the coroner have doubts about a robbery gone bad, based on facts and evidence. They have provided enough evidence to initiate the investigation of a murder." Connor bit his tongue. He couldn't believe the garbage spewing from the Sheriff's mouth.

What happened to innocent until proven guilty? Waiting for evidence? Or protecting our citizens? Were most of the cops in the precinct corrupt?

He thought about the offer he'd received on the phone.

It wasn't worth making more of an issue of it with Tozer, but he hadn't heard anything stupider for a long time, and this from the man in charge of the investigation and the precinct. Doubts had played with Connor's opinion about Tozer for a few years. Now he was pretty sure his concerns were valid.

Sweeping this death under the carpet was obviously what the Sheriff wanted and planned on doing. Connor had no intention of letting that happen. He wanted the truth, whatever it was. He needed to find someone above Tozer who wasn't corrupt. Maybe the new Lieutenant Governor. He ran on anti-corruption.

"Don't fall for some blonde's little game. It's a robbery and that's what you need to focus on. You've wasted too much time on this case already. Wrap it up today and that's an order. It's not like the old lady had much worth stealing."

"No, she didn't which is what makes it look even more like something besides a robbery."

"It doesn't matter. We have more important cases. Close it and move on." Tozer turned.

Connor reached his hand out. "I'll take that note. I was the one who gave the original to forensics. This one is part of my report. I'd hate to break the chain of evidence or lose it. And I'm going to continue the investigation until we catch the people involved. You can write me up if you want."

Tozer glared at him.

Connor stared back. His hand extended.

The sheriff finally slapped the paper in Connor's hand and stormed down the hall to his office. He slammed his door.

Connor gripped the note and set the coffee down on his desk. He took a deep breath. He'd do his own thing, even if he got fired. Every case deserved a thorough investigation. Where was the pressure to bury this investigation coming from?

Jerry Bruckhauser caught Connor's eyes and shook his head. "It's hard to believe they promote people like him—a total moron. If the people in this town knew who was supposed to be protecting them, they'd really panic."

Connor grinned. "Yeah, I know. Even I find it scary sometimes. It's like the Peter Principle says, they promote to their level of incompetence."

"That definitely fits in this case. He's certainly incompetent. Don't let him get to you."

"He won't, not anymore. I'll go up the ladder until I find an honest person if I have to." Conner stared down the hall at the closed door.

Tozer had been his father's partner. When his father had

been shot in the alley during a drug deal gone bad, Tozer had been with him, except that for some reason or other he wasn't actually with him. He hadn't gone into the alley with his partner.

He'd filed the report and said Devon O'Reilly had gone into the alley first, without following procedure and adequately checking out the area before he approached. He'd been shot immediately. Tozer said he heard the shots and phoned it in. The suspects had escaped out the other end of the alley.

Tozer's involvement had always been a little fuzzy. Why hadn't he gone in with his partner? He should have been covering his partner's back. Why hadn't he gone into save his partner when shots were fired? And why would he make a phone call if he hadn't checked on his partner's condition?

The investigation into Devon O'Reilly's death had been cursory. The result said Devon O'Reilly made a bad judgement call. In other words, it had been swept under the rug. It was beginning to look like that was part of the pattern. How far back had Tozer been on the take?

Connor never believed his father had died as Tozer reported. It went against all the evidence and the type of cop Devon O'Reilly had been. His father had always been a stickler for going by the book and he wasn't a hot dog. Even back then they had Kevlar vests. Why wasn't his father wearing his vest? A lot of things didn't make sense.

And it was Tozer again. Back then, the drug deal went bad. Recently, the robbery went bad. Lots of excuses and no one did a thorough investigation. Who should really be investigated?

Connor had tried to get someone to take a deeper look into his father's death, but he'd been shot down. Maybe he'd take another look at it, now, after he wrapped up this case.

Connor headed to forensics.

Frank Reynolds glanced up from his computer screen.

"Tozer tried to keep the copy of the note I gave you. He thought it was the original."

"I wondered what Tozer was going to do with it. He stormed in here saw the copy on my desk and grabbed it. Said it didn't need to be checked out. It was a dead end. I still made him sign it out."

"Good. I'm guessing he thought it was the original and planned on losing it. Anyway, I got it back. You have the original. I have a copy as a back-up, in case something happens to the original. Finish checking it out, will you, and see if there is anything on it."

"Will do. Sign it back in so we have a record."

Connor filled in the form and returned to his office. The file sat in the middle of his desk. He pulled out the report from the lab. He still didn't have anything solid to go on. He knew someone had been there last night, but who? And why?

He had pulled the phone records to see who Perrine might have talked to, recently. He grabbed the phone, punched in a number and waited.

While he waited, he thumbed through the file. He reread the interview with Lucy and the background on Perrine. From Lucy's information his research had come up with three prominent families in Lafayette with males in the right age bracket.

James Craig, the family had made their money in cotton. Now they dealt in the stock market and investments. Craig had just completed law school back then. Now he worked with the family business. There didn't appear to be any major lifestyle changes recently.

Henri Raposa came from a long line of lawyers and used car dealers. The family owned and operated several dealerships in Lafayette. Henri had completed his business degree at Harvard and returned to Lafayette to take over the operation of one of the car dealerships. He was married and about seven years older than Perrine.

Beaufort Dufour, the Dufour's' had old money behind them and a political history. Douglas Dufour had been mayor of Lafayette, as well as a council man. His father had been a state senator. And Beau was now running for Governor of Louisiana. He'd declared a few days ago.

Rumors were the family was involved in racketeering including extortion, drug dealing and money laundering, but it was all rumor. Nothing had been proven. Beaufort had also graduated from law school back then and gone to work with the prestigious law firm of Trouper, Macready and Trouper. He was six years older than Perrine.

None looked like candidates for murder, but there were the rumors of illegal drugs and other stuff drifting around the Dufour's. He'd dig a little deeper and pull information on all the activities of all the men for the last twenty-eight years and see if anything popped.

Maybe he'd dig a little more into the rumors about the Dufours. Someone in the Crimes Against Persons division might have some knowledge of any suspicious drug or extortion activity. If not, maybe he could contact the FBI white collar crimes unit.

He'd check all the names for possible arrests or other contacts with the law that might match the evidence. There might be fingerprints somewhere or maybe a DNA record on file for any of the men. He'd also ask Julie Ann for a DNA sample in case they needed to check for a parental match.

Raposa was a used car dealer. Was he honest? Was there something in his business practices?

Dufour was running for Governor. Would that be reason enough to try and kill off anyone who might know about a secret in his background? Maybe. He'd also look into DuFour's' campaign and see if he could find anything there.

He could always request a DNA sample from each of the men if he couldn't find one on file already, but he didn't want to spook anyone. Besides he'd need a court order if they weren't willing to do it voluntarily and he didn't have any evidence to support that request.

Something told him he might be getting close. He had three potential suspects. If any of them had anything close to a motive, they might be the one who put a contract out on him. Someone had already threatened to do that. From the actions of the black truck, someone already had.

Chapter Ten

Julie Ann sat in the center of Café Du Monde. The sun reflected off the bright colors of shops around Pier Quai 22. She felt the temperature climbing along with the humidity. People, both locals and tourists, were crammed into the Café, so body heat also increased the temperature. She checked her watch.

Connor had told her not to leave the house. After the latest attempt on her life and the suicide note, she shouldn't be here. But it was a very public place and she'd already made this appointment earlier and didn't want to cancel. She'd go directly home after she left here.

Laura had been a friend and classmate back in high school. She might be able to help identify a motive for Perrine's death. It was a stretch, but Julie Ann was desperate. Besides it would be nice to see Laura again.

Laura had managed to squeeze her in this morning. With luck Julie Ann would make it back before Connor found out she'd left the house.

Besides, how much safer could she be than here? Every tourist in town stopped by to try the famous beignets, and so did many of the locals. It was always busy. Nobody could take a shot at her unless they took out about twenty other people.

After she ordered her coffee and beignets, Julie Ann sat back and sipped her coffee. This was something else she had missed, the Café, the tourists, the shops and the park around Jackson Square. New Orleans had an exciting, colorful atmosphere like no other place. She'd forgotten how enjoyable a coffee could be in this area. New York had their sidewalk cafes where people drank their lattes, but it wasn't like the Café Du Monde, and they didn't have beignets. Plus New York tourists were different than those in New Orleans.

"I'm so glad you called." A tall, blonde woman wriggled her way through the crowd.

"Laura, you look wonderful." Julie Ann stood.

The women hugged.

Laura Ashley slipped into the chair across from Julie Ann and waved at the waiter. "You look good. A little tired. I'm so sorry about Perrine. How are you holding up?"

"Thanks. I'm hanging in there. I still can't believe I'll never see her again. They say she died in a break-in, but it doesn't make any sense. I'm trying to figure out why anyone would want to kill her, which is one of the reasons I wanted to see you. I wanted to talk about school and pick your brains."

"Not sure there's much there to pick but go ahead." Laura grinned.

Julie Ann picked up a beignet, shook some of the sugar onto the napkin, and sank her teeth into it.

"Mmm, this is heaven. I'd forgotten how delicious they were."

You had to eat them while they were hot or they lost their taste, so Julie Ann finished quickly and wrapped a small piece in a napkin to take back to Marie L.

"Do you ever remember anyone, besides my mother or your mother, visiting the school or talking to us?"

Laura followed the same process when her beignets arrived. When she finished, she wiped the sugar from her lips. "No, not really, that was a long time ago. No wait, my mother once commented that a man on the other side of the street from the entrance to the school appeared to be watching us. She didn't say whether it might be you or me, or even our mothers, so that's not much help. It could even have been someone's uncle, whom she wouldn't recognize, waiting for their niece."

Julie Ann wiped her hands with another napkin to get rid of the rest of the sugar. "Did you see him? What did he look like?"

Laura shook her head. "Not really. I think I glanced over and there's a vague memory of a blurred figure; medium height, about thirty, maybe. I think he might have been blonde. I didn't pay any attention and it was a long time ago."

"That's a start. He'd be in his late forties, or maybe fifties, now. That's better than nothing."

"I'll ask my mother if she remembers anything more," Laura offered.

"Thanks. I'll take any crumb of information at this time."

"You never said why you ran off to New York? Are you planning on moving back now?"

Julie Ann took a sip of her latte. "I think I've died and gone to heaven. This beats all those New York lattes. First, I didn't run to New York."

"Right, I remember. Where did you go?"

"Chicago. I wanted to be an interior designer and the universities around New Orleans didn't offer any relevant programs, or didn't back then. I went to Chicago because they have one of the best design programs. When I graduated, I got a chance to work for one of the top interior design businesses in New York. You don't turn an opportunity like that down."

"No, I guess not. I always thought you'd come back here and work. You loved New Orleans and your mother was here."

Julie Ann sighed. "I know. I don't regret taking the job in New York and working there. I started answering phones, making coffee, cleaning up at night and occasionally delivering swatch books to clients. I listened to the designers as they met with clients, talked to each other about designs that worked and didn't, and how to meet a client's vision. I got a lot of experience, learned a lot and eventually managed to open my own small design studio. I do regret not coming home more often. I meant to, but I kept putting it off. I'd think as soon I get a promotion, as soon as I get one more sale, then I'll take time off and I'll spend it in New Orleans. It never happened. The longer I was away, the more I forgot how much I loved this city and how unique it is."

"I love the city and its culture. I can't imagine living any place else, especially New York."

"You've done well here, with your movie critique position. What about your family?"

"After I graduated from university, I married Greg Walters. We've known each other since kindergarten. You met him a few times."

"I remember. He was a nice man and kind of cute."

"Not sure how cute he is now." Laura grinned. "We have three children, two boys eleven and four and a daughter age seven. I guess I can see how it happened with you. I debated heading for New York, but the south is in my blood."

Julie Ann sipped her coffee and listened to the street musician playing his horn just outside of the café. "The music is another thing I forgot about. I envy your decisions. I've never met anyone I'd want to settle down with, at least not yet." Her mind drifted back to Connor, but there were too many obstacles in the way of that relationship. Besides, she might not live long enough to ever make a long-term commitment.

"I decided to start my own business and when I finally adjusted my priorities and decided to make time to come back and spend it with Mom, she was gone."

Laura reached across and squeezed Julie Ann's hand. "We all make decisions, some good, some we regret. You did well in New York. I've seen articles on the new up and coming interior designer."

"Somehow that doesn't seem as important anymore. I forgot how much I loved this city. You made a smart decision. I pushed all my memories away to a back corner and convinced myself that I loved New York more. Now I'm back I realize I miss the music, the history, the beignets, the color of New Orleans, the culture of the south and the people, especially old friends."

"If you decide to hang around, we'll get together more often. Look I have to run. I'm previewing a movie this afternoon."

"That's right; you're a famous movie critic, now. One or two of your reviews actually made it to New York."

"It's a fun job. I get to see all the movies for free." Laura kissed Julie Ann on the cheek. "You call me, and we'll do dinner before you head back to the Big Apple. Promise?"

"I promise. And if you or your mother think of anything else, let me know." Julie Ann watched Laura muscle her way through the crowd to the street.

People hurried past, other stopped and stared at the people in the café. They were probably tourists trying to decide if they wanted to brave the crowd and come inside.

Julie Ann noticed two women sitting at a nearby table. One was a large boned woman, maybe in her forties, with her dark hair cropped close to her head. It was cut maybe half an inch all over, more like black fuzz. It accented her large, hawk like nose.

Why would the woman choose a style like that, Julie Ann wondered? The woman should have something longer and styled to take away from the angular look of her face.

"I'm not sure, but I think this area is more sensitive since the radiation," the woman commented.

Julie Ann overheard the sentence as it floated across the

tables. The woman placed her hand above her right breast.

Oh great, Julie Ann, she's probably got cancer and had chemo. How could you be so wrong? Her hair is growing back. When you think of it that way—her hair looks beautiful. Is this what New York has done to me? Living in that city I've got wrapped up with wealthy clients, style, art, and prejudging people.

She shook her head. Now she thought about it, some big city people had a snobbish attitude, basing opinions strictly on appearance, status and first impressions. New Orleans didn't appear to have as much of that attitude.

I need to get back to my native non-judgmental roots.

A man in his early thirties, wearing a multi-colored Jamaican hat, played Coltrane on his trumpet outside the door of the Café.

Julie Ann closed her eyes and tried to remember all the times she'd listened to jazz. Sometimes it was in the clubs. Other times Charlie and his friends dropped by her house after the clubs closed. Some nights they jammed until the sun came up.

Julie Ann had laid in bed and hummed along, playing in time to the music with her fingers on the end of her bed. Sometimes she sneaked up and sat at the top of the stairs and listened to them jam.

Those had been good times. New York had hypnotized her with glitz and glitter and excitement. Her priorities had changed. Her visits back home had been sporadic and short, not long enough for her to reconnect with her love of New Orleans. Looking back, she'd missed a lot of time with things she loved. The biggest loss had been sharing those things with her mother. You never expected to lose someone so early. You think you'll have them for years. The loss had been a wakeup call.

Julie Ann finished her coffee. She elbowed her way through the crowd, out of the café and onto the street.

Who was the man Laura had mentioned? Who had he been watching? And why? Was he involved in her mother's death? Or had he been someone's uncle or relative, picking up a niece or cousin, like Laura had suggested?

She strolled by Jackson Square, or as it had been originally named, Place d'Armes. She stopped to admire the large statue of General Andrew Jackson on his horse in front of the landmark St. Louis Cathedral. The bright white cathedral with its cone-shaped spires sparkled in the sun.

She stopped to read the headlines of the local paper when she passed a grocery store. She picked up the paper, tucked it under her arm and went inside. She needed some more Rocky Road ice cream. She'd eaten quite a bit in the last few days. She paid the clerk and continued toward Burgundy Street, past small boutique stores. One looked empty.

Julie Ann stopped and put her hands up on the glass so she could squint in the window.

It was a small space but there was a display window, room for a reception desk and some tables and displays. It looked like there was a door into a back room. She wondered what was back there. How much storage was there? What would the rent be on a store this size, in this location? Could she use this space to set up an interior design studio? There was potential and it was a good location.

What am I even thinking? I'm not staying in New Orleans. I already have a business in New York.

She walked away. Then paused and came back for one more look.

I could walk to work every day. I could even pick up a beignet to nibble on while I opened the studio. I wonder how many design firms are in New Orleans. Get a grip, girl. You don't want to stay here. But it is a cute space. I could do a little research. It wouldn't hurt.

She kept thinking about the space as she sauntered down the street. A skinny woman, with dirty, dishwater blonde hair, about her age headed toward her. The woman's head was down. She didn't make eye contact with anyone. She was a few feet in front of Julie Ann in her dirty, faded pink sweats and a baggy t-shirt. She glanced up. There was something familiar about the woman. Julie Ann stared at her.

"Monique? Monique Patterson? Is that you?"

The woman stared blankly at Julie Ann.

"Monique? It is you, isn't it?"

"Do I know you?"

"Julie Ann, Julie Ann Dupré. We went to school together."

"We did? Oh, yeah, that was a long time ago. Were we friends? I can't remember. You moved away." She shuffled her feet and started to edge past Julie Ann.

"That's right, I moved to Chicago to go to school. And yes, we were friends." Julie Ann didn't move to one side.

"Yeah, but you left." Monique stopped, but didn't look up. "I heard about your mom. Sorry."

"Thanks."

"I gotta go." Monique mumbled.

"Sorry, what did you say?"

"Nothin'." Monique tried to edge past Julie Ann.

"I had coffee with Laura Ashley, from school. We should all get together for lunch or a drink."

"I don't think so. I don't have a lot of time. I got things. Gotta get going."

Julie Ann put out her hand and touched Monique on the arm. "Where are you living now? Are you married? Children?"

Monique jerked away. "No. Look, I gotta go."

She pushed past Julie Ann and shuffled down the street.

"I'm back at my old house if you want to get in touch with me." Julie Ann stared after her.

Monique didn't reply and never looked back.

What had happened to her?

The Monique she remembered had been attractive and

happy, excited about life. She'd planned on becoming a nurse, if Julie Ann remembered right. When she'd touched Monique's arm today, she felt like skin and bones. She looked and acted like a drug addict. How had she sunk to that?

Some of her friends back then had stayed in the area and done well. Others obviously had not. She should have kept in touch. She made a mental note to try and track Monique down after the funeral. Maybe she could help her.

At the corner she checked traffic and stepped into the street. The vision of something racing in front of her made her jerk back.

A second later a car gunned its engine, pulled away from the curb and accelerated.

Julie Ann heard the engine roar and jumped farther back from the curb. It sped past her.

"Are you okay?" A woman beside her grabbed Julie Ann's arm tightly and pulled her back.

Heart pounding, pulse racing, Julie Ann glanced at the young woman with a toddler in a stroller, who was still clutching her arm.

"I'm fine. Thank you." She swallowed and managed a weak smile. "I'm from New York. We have to watch for things like that all the time. It's all those crazy cab drivers." She touched the small packet in her pocket as she stumbled along the sidewalk. If she hadn't had that quick vision of seeing something speed by, she might not have been able to jump out of the way.

It hadn't been an accident. She was sure of that. Coming from New York had proved valuable this time. She spent a lot of time dodging traffic there. This time she heard the car accelerate after she put her foot on the street.

No, it wasn't an accident. Someone had tried to run over her. If they had succeeded it would have been ruled another accident.

How did they know where she was? Were they

following her? She looked around. Everyone looked normal.

Connor would be furious when he found out she'd gone off on her own. She hadn't planned on telling him and had hoped to get home before he checked on her. Now she had to confess what she did.

Maybe she could avoid saying anything, but she knew she needed to let him know. It might be important to the case and finding the killers. She'd take her lumps when he vented about her stupidity and ignoring his advice. It had been stupid on her part not to listen to what he'd said.

He'd ask about the vehicle. She stopped and leaned against a shop window, clutching her newspaper and ice cream. What did she remember?

The vehicle, it had been big, a truck, black with tinted windows, definitely tinted windows, because you couldn't see the driver, and big tires. The license plate was partly covered in mud, but it was from Louisiana. She ran over it in her mind again. That was the best she could do.

They had tried to kill her at her home and now on the crowded street. It hit her that someone else might have been hit, as well, if they stepped off the curb at the same time she did. She could be responsible for other people's deaths, like the woman with the toddler. Or like Savannah, yesterday. She started to shake. She might not be the only person who died. She needed to make better decisions to make sure she didn't cause any collateral damage, or someone else's death.

Striding down the street toward home she thought of how people seemed to be able to break in through her front door at random. She needed another new lock on her door. She replaced it once, but it was an inexpensive lock and hadn't helped. There was a hardware store a block over, if it was still there. She'd get something sturdy with a sliding bolt, one for the front door and one for the back door.

The hardware store was still there and the woman behind the counter was helpful in picking out the best lock for Julie Ann's doors. For the rest of the walk home, at each street corner she carefully checked all directions before she stepped off the curb.

She made another short detour to a car rental place. It might be safer to rent a car than to walk around the city. At least they couldn't run her over or hurt and other pedestrians. She'd rent it for a week, long enough to get most of the funeral arrangements and any other errands done.

Even in the car her heart raced. The rate gradually subsided, but the icy blanket around her tightened. The shivering continued until she reached home, even with the heater on. She parked the car next to the curb in front of her house. She opened the car door and climbed out. She checked over her shoulder to make sure no one had followed her or watched the house from the street.

Opening the front door, she stood to one side and let the door swing open and hit the wall.

Marie jumped off the couch and raced toward her.

"Good girl. Did you miss me?"

Inside she locked the door and leaned against it. Now she was safely home, the incident in Jackson Square didn't appear to be quite so serious. Maybe it had been an accident. No, she knew better. Someone wanted her dead and other people could have been injured.

How had they known where she was?

Even Connor hadn't known. She hadn't told anyone. The only other person who knew was Laura and Julie Ann was one hundred percent sure she wasn't involved.

The room looked the same as it always did, but things were different now. There was no Perrine. There was no warm, comfortable feeling in the room. It felt cold and frightening. People broke in to kill her.

Would there be more attempts? Will I survive the attempts if there were more? Will I live to go back to New York? Do I want to go back?

The music, the food, even the French Quarter pulled up all the wonderful memories and emotions she'd buried so deep. The love for the area broke through. Maybe she'd go back to New York and rebuild Perrine's Interior Design and work on transitioning it to New Orleans. She'd adjust her priorities. A successful business in New York wasn't number one anymore.

Julie Ann put the ice cream in the freezer before she flopped down in the chair and picked up the receiver. She didn't have a landline in New York, only her cellphone. Perrine preferred the landline. Marie L. jumped up beside her and licked her face.

Julie Ann shook her head, allowing a little giggle to escape as the rough tongue grated against her cheek. She punched in Connor's number.

He'd be angry. She wasn't sure how angry. She had ignored what he said because she thought she might learn something about her past. It hadn't worked out that way. Another stupid mistake on her part. Maybe he'd never forgive her.

She needed to trust him and listen to him. Trust worked both ways but she hadn't been trustworthy.

"O'Reilly." Connor grabbed the desk phone on the second ring.

"Connor? It's Julie Ann."

"What's wrong?" He tightened his grip on the phone.

"Nothing, I'm fine. I had a little accident."

"What kind of accident?" Connor snapped.

"Connor calm down. I'm home and I'm fine."

He drummed his fingers on the desk while he waited for her to continue.

"Someone tried to run me down."

"What do you mean someone tried to run you down? How could that happen if you're at home?"

There was a long pause.

"Julie Ann?"

A sigh slid along the wire and through the receiver. "I went to meet a friend at Café Du Monde."

"You what? I distinctly told you not to leave the house alone."

"I know. I'm sorry. I already made this appointment with an old friend. I wanted to see if she remembered anything unusual about our time in school. And I mean, really? It's Café du Monde. It's a very public place. When Laura had to go to work it was almost noon. We left the café and split up. The streets are busy and crowded. I felt it was safe. No one's going to shoot me or kidnap me from there. Obviously, I was wrong. I'm sorry."

Connor counted to ten. He opened his mouth, shut it, and then counted to ten again.

"Connor?"

"I'm here. And yes, obviously you were wrong. Tell me what happened."

"I stepped off the curb to cross the street at St. Phillip. I heard an engine gun. I jumped back onto the curb as it raced by me."

"Oh, hell, you were damn lucky. You could have been killed."

"I know. It wasn't total luck, not completely. I'm from New York, remember? The traffic is bad there. You always have to listen and watch that the taxis don't run you down."

Connor shook his head. "Did you notice the type of car or get a license plate number?"

"Not really, it zoomed by really fast and I was jumping backwards out of the way. It was black, tinted windows, a truck. I think it had four doors. That's about it. The license plate was from Louisiana, but they'd smeared mud on it. I think the first two letters might have been VF."

"Not much to go on but I'll run it anyhow. We'll

probably get about eight thousand hits. Did you notice anything else, bumper stickers, dents, anything?"

"I don't think so. I'll keep thinking about it."

"Were there any witnesses?"

"A woman beside me, that's about it. She was more focused on me. I don't think anyone else noticed."

Connor let a sigh escape. Another attempt and again, he had nothing to go on.

"You will stay in the damn house now, right?"

"Yes, sir. Am I allowed to go across to Savannah's?"

Connor shook his head. "You should probably stay in the house, but if you go to Savannah's, be very careful. Someone could be watching you. They might even be sitting in a car."

"I hadn't thought of that. I promise."

"Hmph," Connor snorted.

"No really, I won't go anywhere. Are you coming by to check on me?'

"Maybe."

"Don't be mad. I've learned my lesson. I know they are serious about killing me and they're following me. They appear to know where I am most of the time. I get it. I can't figure out how they know where I go. I mean, even you didn't know where I was, but they did."

"Right, so keep that in mind. I'll come by in a couple of hours. I have a lot of work to do. I need to follow up on lab reports, my interview and some other stuff. I'll try and make it by dinner time. Maybe we can eat out." Connor suggested.

"That sounds good or I could cook. See you soon, and I am sorry."

Connor hung up the phone.

He needed to find someone to keep an eye on her. He had a friend who worked as a private investigator. He'd see if Pete might have a few spare hours where he could guard Julie Ann Dupré. Who ever wanted her dead was getting more aggressive. Next time they might be successful.

What was that Julie Ann had said, 'they appear to know where I am most of the time?'

She was right. What if they knew what Perrine Dupré was doing and planning? She talked to Savannah and maybe Charlie about sharing information. There was only one-way people would always know what the Duprés were doing.

Was the house bugged?

Julie Ann curled up in the big chair. She took a spoonful of Rocky Road ice cream right from the container and opened the paper she bought. Marie circled and lay down in front of the chair.

The front page was about the upcoming election and the candidates. She didn't plan to be here to vote and she wasn't on the voting list, so she flipped through the pages, weather, baseball scores and a couple of sales. Her mind kept thinking going back to the car racing toward her. The flash of the vision had pulled her back.

It was the same sense that told her mom what was behind the front door, so she didn't go inside. Perrine had talked about this sixth sense. Many people had it when they were very young, but it dies as they grow older and don't use it. Perrine always said it was like a flower. You had to talk to it, treat it well and give it extra special care so it would grow and bloom and get stronger. She encouraged Julie Ann on how to use it, but when she'd moved to Chicago and then New York she'd forgotten to take care of that sixth sense. It had shriveled and almost disappeared.

Since she'd been home it felt like it was slowly wakening up. Her fingers wrapped around Ava's ball. Closing her eyes Julie Ann took several deep breaths and concentrated on being in the moment. She could feel her mother beside her.

Life in New York had been mostly work. She had people she worked with in her life and a few casual friends.

She seldom went to the theater or ate out. She hadn't even done much cooking. Mostly she'd grab something from the deli on the way home or order in. She had ignored her sixth sense and hadn't fed her soul.

She unwrapped her legs and folded up the paper.

After a few more scoops of Rocky Road, she put the lid on the container and returned it to the freezer. She should go up and finish checking out the floor in the secret room to see if Perrine had hidden something there.

Maybe Perrine had kept whatever it was at her office at the hotel. She glanced at her watch. It wasn't two o'clock yet. Someone should still be in the hotel office. She reached for the phone and punched in a number.

"Angelique Hotel, Theresa Angel speaking."

"Theresa, it's Julie Ann Dupré…"

"Julie Ann, I'm so sorry about your mother. It's a terrible loss for all of us. How are you coping?"

"Not too well, but there's a lot of support in the neighborhood."

"I'm sure there is. She was a special person. If you need anything you let us know. Perrine was like family."

"Thank you and thank you for the offer to host her celebration party."

"It's the least we can do. Just tell us when and we'll take care of it."

"Thanks. Charlie is doing most of the planning. He said he'd contact you when he had more details. I wanted to know if I could come down and look through her office. She may have left me a document and I can't find it at the house."

There was a long pause.

"Theresa…"

"I wasn't going to say anything because I thought it would only upset you, but someone broke into the office here on Tuesday night and ransacked Perrine's office. They took her computer, but it doesn't look like anything else was taken. They searched through all her files and books.

Things were tossed everywhere. We've been cleaning it up and checking to see if there is anything missing."

"Oh my god, did you report it?"

"Yes, and the police came out but said it looked like someone searching for drugs. They didn't think it had anything to do with Perrine's death. They said it was a coincidence."

"Of course, they did." Julie Ann mumbled. "I'm so sorry. Hopefully they didn't do any damage to the hotel or the hotel records."

"No, Perrine had a main back up off site for everything. We've checked to make sure we have copies of everything."

"That's good. Thanks, Theresa. I think I'll still come down. I'd like to take a look through her office anyway. I'll probably be down later this afternoon if that's okay."

"Of course. You know where her office is."

"Yes, thank you." Julie Ann hung up and looked at Marie. "They ripped Mom's office apart looking for something. I wish I knew what it was and if they found it. I guess it's back to searching the secret room."

Marie whined and put her head between her paws.

"You don't look very happy. Not what you were expecting, huh? Me, either. I'm beginning to think Mom maybe never left anything for me. Maybe she changed her mind or had a premonition or something and thought she'd be able to protect me if she didn't share her information. I don't know. Come on, Marie, a little help here."

Marie whined again and went to the stairs.

Julie Ann looked up the stairs.

A sigh slipped out at the thought of sitting in the little room upstairs and going over the floor again. She was beginning to think there was nothing to find. Maybe she'd go across and see if Savannah wanted to go to the hotel with her. She dropped the paper on the table, slipped on her shoes and walked toward the front door.

There was a knock.

Julie Ann jumped. Who was visiting now? Connor?

She peeked out the window. Savannah grinned at her.

Julie Ann opened the door.

"Hey, Savannah, I was thinking about you."

"I thought I'd come across and check on you. You got any tea?"

"Sure do, come on in. I'm grounded. I have today's paper if you're interested."

They headed into the kitchen. She filled the kettle and put it on the stove.

"How come you grounded?"

"I went for beignets with Laura Ashley."

"How come you do something that stupid? I thought you were smarter than that."

Julie Ann shrugged.

"Girl, you need to be more careful. I read Laura's column every week. She writes good reviews. If she doesn't like a movie, I don't watch it. How she doin'?"

"She's doing well. I wanted to ask her about our time in school together."

"Learn anything?"

"Not really, but I wanted to see her and reconnect anyway. I hadn't talked to her for years. I wasn't sure if anything occurred while I was in school, but I thought I'd check out that aspect and talk to Laura."

"And?"

"I asked Laura if her mother had noticed anyone hanging around watching me back then. She said her mother had seen a man one day, who appeared to be interested in us."

"That was a long time ago."

"I know. So maybe whoever is involved today, was part of something a lot of years ago, or maybe not. She wasn't sure if the person was interested in me, or maybe her, or maybe another student. Anyway, after I left Laura, I ran into Monique Patterson on my way home. Man, she's changed a lot. She looks like hell and she wasn't very friendly."

"Monique Patterson?" Savannah looked pensive. "Oh, I remember her, sweet little thing. She came to your house a few times. No, I think she had a rough life. As I remember she married badly, shortly after you left town. He was a jerk who beat her regularly. They didn't have much money and he liked to spend it on himself. When Monique didn't have the money for his habits and his drugs, he beat her. Eventually he sent her out to work as a stripper to make some money. I'm not sure if she ended up working the streets after that. He may have got her hooked-on drugs, too, around that time. I haven't heard anything about her lately. I'm not sure where she ended up."

"Oh my god, that's awful. I had no idea. I can see why she wouldn't want to talk to me. I feel so sorry for her. Is she still with the guy?"

"I think so. Seems I heard he had a few ties to some criminal gang. Don't worry about her. If she wanted, she'd have left him and wouldn't have become a stripper."

"Some people have a hard time leaving a bad situation. The unknown can be even scarier than a bad situation. At least with the bad situation you know what to expect, even if it might kill you. I wonder what happened to her family. I thought they were always pretty supportive. And she wanted to go into nursing."

"I think the parents divorced. Her father left town. Can't remember what happened to the mother. The grape vine in this neighborhood is pretty good, but it doesn't always pick up or share everything."

"That's too bad. I guess she lost all of her support. Perrine never said anything."

"She probably never thought about it. Come to think of it, it's odd that Monique knew about your mom. I mean she don't sound like she reads the paper or watches the news, not that there was anything on the news."

"I didn't think about that. You're right, it is odd. I wonder how she knew."

"That husband of hers or maybe some of her other sleazy contacts, maybe they heard something, and she heard them talking?"

"I suppose that's a possibility. I hate to think she's sunk so low that's what happened. Poor, Monique. I wish there was something I could do for her."

"Don't you start thinking like that. You'll wind up in more trouble with those type of people."

Julie Ann let out a sigh. "You're probably right."

"Uh huh, so what about the reason you've been grounded. It wasn't for meeting Laura or Monique."

"No, not exactly. Someone tried to run me down in their car." She poured the tea and shoved a cup across the table to Savannah.

"That don't sound like no accident."

"No, it was deliberate. I told Connor about it."

"And…"

"He'd told me not to leave the house."

"I don't blame him for grounding you. You sound like one of those too stupid to live heroines in some of the books I read. The ones that go down into the basement, by themselves when there's a serial killer after them." Savannah plopped down into a chair.

"Ouch. Don't rub it in. I know I should have stayed in the house. I deserve it. I thought the area was busy and I'd be safe."

"You thought? And I thought you were smart. I'm beginning to think we were both wrong. I'm beginning to wonder about you."

"Come on, Savannah, I made a mistake."

"You seem to be making a few mistakes. One of them could be a final one."

"I'll be more careful, Savannah, but I need to find out what really happened to Mom."

"No, you don't. That's not your job, especially when you're now the target. Can't you get it through that thick head of yours? They want you dead, too. You're not going to make Perrine proud of you if you're dead. Ever think of that?"

"I…no, I guess not. I'm so upset with losing her. I want to fix it."

"Well, you're not going to fix it. You can't bring her back and you can't make up for lost time. I'm guessing she's hangin' around somewhere trying to protect you and right now she's down right ticked you appear to be trying to follow her into the grave. She'd want you to protect yourself and make her proud of the daughter she raised, not be an idiot who walks out in front of them and says, 'shoot me'."

"I didn't do that."

"Hmph."

"Well, I didn't, at least not quite like that."

"Don't know, but it sounds pretty close to me. She doesn't want you to fix anything. Especially when it can't be fixed. I can pretty much guarantee that. You need to get that through your thick head. It's the police's job, even if most of them are corrupt. And one of them appears to be an honest cop. He is trying to find out what happened."

"Connor, I know."

"Then leave it to him and quit putting yourself at risk."

"Okay." Julie Ann glanced at the paper on the table. She flipped through it again, trying to think of something to change the conversation.

There was a picture of Beau Dufour at a benefit dinner on the society page. His wife stood off to one side, smiling at him. His mother stood behind.

There were more layoffs at one of the computer technologies companies. She flipped over a couple of pages and noticed the headlines, 'Retired Nurse Shot in Own Home'. She pointer it out to Savannah.

"This sounds a lot like what happened to Mom. They say

it might have been a robbery gone sour. Sound familiar? I think I'll call Connor to let him know. It's probably nothing, but it seems odd, two similar killings in a week."

Savannah reached over and turned the paper around so she could see the article. "It says here she used to work in the records department of the Baptist Hospital. I believe that's where you were born. I'm sure I remember Perrine saying you were born at the Baptist. Is that weird or what? Of course, I could be wrong or maybe it's a coincidence?"

Julie Ann stared at her. "Yes, I think that's where I was born. I checked but the birth records from the years around when I was born were all destroyed."

"What you thinkin' child?

"I don't think you're wrong. That means there is a connection. I don't know what it is exactly, but it sounds like the Baptist Hospital is the key. I'd say there's a definite connection between Mom's murder and this woman's murder. There's also a connection to me. Two robberies gone sour. I don't think so. I don't think O'Reilly's going to think so either. At least we've got a thread to follow, although not much of one."

"Now you stay out of it. There's no we, to follow anything. Don't you go lookin' into it. It's got nothin' to do with you. You tell that deputy sheriff and leave all that stuff to the police."

"Yes, ma'am. It's too bad about the records. It would be nice to have an actual birth certificate. And maybe my father's name might be on it."

"You might not want to know."

"Savannah, Mom will always be my mother. She raised me and loved me. But sometimes I'd like to know who my real parents are, even for medical reasons. What's my family history for disease or heart conditions? I have no idea. I was going to have a serious discussion about it with Mom when I was home this time. She'd finally agreed to talk to me about it. I thought we might even talk a little about it that Sunday night, the night she got shot."

"She knew you were going to ask her about your past?"

"Yes. I told her I wanted to know everything she could tell me. I explained about the medical concerns. She understood. She said she needed to think about what she could share and said she'd do the best she could to answer my questions. She did say there were good reasons for not sharing the information, that she'd done it to protect me. That's probably what got her killed. It's like someone knew she was going to share my history."

"Honey child, no one would have known what Perrine planned on doin'. It was a coincidence. There's probably another reason for her death."

Julie Ann was quiet for a minute. "Unless they had her phone tapped, or maybe a bug somewhere in the house. I already mentioned to Connor it was odd that these people always seemed to know where I was. It's like they can see and hear everything I decide to do."

"All this time? That hardly seems likely." Savannah shook her head.

"I agree but I'll ask Connor to do a sweep for bugs, just in case. It won't hurt."

"It's Connor now, is it?" Savannah chortled. "You two appear to be getting cozy. So, you thinkin' of maybe comin' home and stayin' here?"

Julie Ann shook her head. "I'm not thinking anything these days except how to stay alive and trying to figure out why people are getting killed."

"Maybe you should jest go back to New York. That's what they want you to do. Catch the next plane outta here and go home where you'll be safe."

"If I'm a loose end for something, why wouldn't they follow me back to New York? Here in New Orleans, I have you and Charlie and Priestess Ava and others. You're like my family. The police department is looking into it, reluctantly, but the NYPD wouldn't even listen to me. It's not in their jurisdiction, unless someone kills me there. Until I find out why they want to kill me I'll never be safe. I'll never quit watching over my shoulder, wherever I am."

"Hmph," Savannah topped up the tea.

"I'll call the deputy. In the meantime, want to make a trip with me? I promised Connor I wouldn't go out alone."

"Where you want to go?"

"The University of New Orleans."

"Now why you want to go there?"

"I haven't been able to find any of Mom's yearbooks. I know she had them because we used to look at them together. They were on a shelf in her office. We'd laugh at the clothes and some of the group shots. Either she put them some place I haven't found yet, or they were stolen. Why would someone still old yearbooks?"

"I don't know. They didn't want you to see somethin?"

"Maybe. The archives should have copies. I'd like to see a picture of my birth mother and look at the men in the classes ahead of them."

"I think you're asking for more trouble."

"Aw, come on Savannah. I need a chaperone or bodyguard. Take your choice. We'll take my car. I rented one on the way home. I thought I might be safer in a car than on the sidewalk or crossing the road. It won't take long to get there by car, and it'll go faster if there are two people looking through them."

Savannah shook her head. "I think you should call that deputy first."

"I'll call him but I'm not going to mention the University. He'll say no. I'll call the university and check on the archives and what hours it's open. If we don't go today, it probably won't be open until Monday."

"We jest go straight there, look at yearbooks and come back?"

"Yes, ma'am. I'll pull my car in front of your house. You get ready. It'll be a fun trip."

Julie Ann hoped she was right. She didn't want to put Savannah in any more danger.

A short time later Savannah climbed into the passenger's seat.

"I want to make one more stop."

"Now what?

"The Angelique Hotel. I want to check Mom's office and see if her yearbooks are there. I know she had them somewhere, because I remember looking through them. The hotel also got ransacked but nothing was taken except Mom's computer. I thought I'd check and see if maybe her yearbooks were there, if they weren't stolen."

Fifteen minutes later they were in Perrine's office. There were no yearbooks. Julie Ann opened and closed drawers and checked the filing cabinet. Most of her mother's work had been on the computer the last few years so the files were minimal.

They were about to leave when Julie Ann stopped to look at pictures her mother posted on a wall. There were several of Julie Ann at different stages of growing up and of her in New York. At the top was a group photo. It looked like Perrine's graduation class. Julie Ann touched Savannah's arm and pointed to the picture.

"There's Perrine in the middle."

Savannah smiled. "And you look like the woman standing next to her. I'd say that woman was your mother."

Julie Ann bent to get a closer look. "I do look like her, don't I? I think you're right." Julie Ann carefully removed the picture and took it with her.

An hour later they were at a table in the Earl K. Long Library. It was a windowless room with metal shelves and microfiche around the walls and down the aisles. The yearbooks sat between them. Julie Ann picked up the first year. Savannah took one of the others.

Julie Ann quickly found her mother's picture and then Elizabeth Watson's. Julie Ann touched Savannah's arm and pointed to the picture.

Savannah smiled. "Yes, you look like her."

"I do, don't I? Now if I could only find some information on her." Julie Ann flipped through more pages. After spotting a few pictures of the photography club and the choir she turned to the fourth-year students. She ran her fingers over the photos and read the bios underneath. They were alphabetical. She didn't recognize any names. Nothing stood out.

Savannah showed her pictures of Perrine and Elizabeth in year three. Julie Ann smiled.

"Maybe see if there's anyone in there from this area. I might be able to contact them and ask them about Elizabeth." Julie Ann whispered.

They looked through a couple more yearbooks. Julie Ann pulled out a notebook and jotted down some of the names and contact info from the years her mother attended the university. She could search them on Google and see where they were now.

She recognized a few of the men's names. One worked at a local bank. Another taught at Loyola. There were a few others she noted.

It was closing time. They tiptoed out of the room and hurried across the campus to the parking lot. She needed to get home before Connor showed up.

On the drive back she kept checking in the mirror, but no one was following her, or they were doing a good job of staying out of sight.

Maybe they didn't know about her car yet?

Chapter Eleven

Connor put down the phone. He hadn't received the official report from the lab, so he'd phoned to see if they had the report.

They had a match to one fingerprint. It belonged to a hired killer named Sammy One Shot. Connor shook his head. Where did they come up with these names? The guy must have named himself.

Bobby Ray was running the name to see where One Shot was now.

The voodoo doll hadn't turned up anything. Like Julie Ann had said, it was one of the basic tourist jobs, available at any voodoo store. No fingerprints, and the blood was red paint. The same paint used on car models and available in any hobby store.

DNA hadn't come back yet.

He'd phoned the Baptist Hospital and requested a staff list for obstetrics from twenty-eight years ago. They didn't have one. It had been destroyed in the fire. The woman he talked to said one of the obstetric staff, Karen Jackson had just retired. She might be able to help him.

He placed a call to Karen Jackson at the number the hospital had shared.

"Mrs. Jackson?"

"Yes."

"I'm Deputy Sheriff O'Reilly, from the New Orleans police department. I'm trying to find information on staff who worked in the obstetric department of the Baptist Hospital about twenty-eight years ago. I was given your name as a possible resource."

"Oh, my goodness, that was a long time ago. I hadn't been working there very long back then."

"I'm looking into a birth around that time. The woman's name was Elizabeth Watson. She gave birth to a baby girl. Anything you remember about the staff working there at that time, or maybe even the birth. would help."

"Let me think. Amy Lewis worked shift work with me. Sally something was there around that time. Doctor Rosemoor, Doctor Edwards and Doctor McGrath were the doctors who usually worked there.'

Connor scribbled the names on a pad. "That's great. Do you have any contact numbers for them?"

"No, we never kept in touch, when people left. Except for Amy. We stayed in touch for a while after she retired. She moved away several years ago, went to Florida. I haven't heard from her for years. Dr. Edwards died about twenty-five years ago. I think it was an automobile accident."

"A car accident?"

"Yes, we were surprised when it happened. He was quite young. Apparently, he was crossing the road and the driver of the car didn't see him. They said Dr. Edwards' blood alcohol level was high, so he probably walked in front of the car. We found that a little odd because he didn't drink."

"What did the investigation show, do you remember?"

"I don't think there was one. It was ruled an accident."

"Interesting, thank you."

"Oh and someone mentioned that Sally may have died in a break-in recently. I'm not sure if it's the same person. I don't remember her last name. She may have married it and changed it anyway."

"I can check that out. You've been very helpful. If you remember anything else, please let me know." Connor gave her his phone number and hung up.

He tapped his pencil on the pad of names Karen had shared. Accidents and break-ins seemed to be a common thread among people involved in Julie Ann's birth many years ago. That and a connection to the Baptist Hospital. None appeared to have been investigated or followed up.

Who filled out the reports on all these events?

He started a search on the computer. An accident from that long ago might not have been added to the online files. It could still be stored down in the dungeon in one of the old boxes.

He checked obits for Dr. Edwards and found one. He got the date of the accident and hiked down to the archived files.

An hour later he had the accident file in his hand. There was little investigation. A blood sample had been taken from the doctor, but not the driver, which was really odd. because you didn't usually test the victim's blood for alcohol. And then the result of the victim's blood test was missing which was also unusual. The driver was a Fred Ackerman, salesman. That was it. The investigating officer was Deputy Sheriff Harvey Tozer.

Tozer again, and another sloppy non-investigation.

Had he been bought off back then? It looked like it. If he'd been corrupt over twenty-years ago how many cases had he made disappear and swept under the rug?

Connor didn't even want to think about it. If Tozer was corrupt that long ago, were they going to have to revisit all those cases? And if he had been bought off back then, who did he work for?

Connor sat at his desk and stared into space. He thought of his father's death. Tozer was his partner. Had his father figured out Tozer was crooked? Was that why he died, not because it was a bad bust? Had Tozer been paid to make it happen?

Connor felt the anger boil inside. Had he lost his father due to a crooked cop on the take?

Tozer needed to be investigated. But who would do it? Who else in the department might be corrupt? Connor contemplated how to go about investigating a crooked cop. *Who could do it? The police commissioner? The mayor? Were they corrupt too?*

If Connor started to investigate cases going back over twenty years, he could be dead in a week and it would probably be another accident. Right now, he needed to concentrate on his present case. He could investigate Tozer later.

He did a search for break-ins and deaths in the last few weeks. Sally Rhodes name came up. She was sixty-one, a retired nurse. And he bet she worked at the Baptist Hospital twenty-eight years ago. Were any of them still alive, except for Karen? Would she be another victim of an accident?

He needed to solve this case and quickly to make sure no one else died—accidently.

"O'Reilly's not backing off. He's working this case overtime and starting to get close. He's got lab results that could prove troublesome and we can't get rid of those."

"He didn't listen when I threatened him, and he's not interested in a bribe. There's nothing worse than an honest cop. I've keeping tabs on him, and the girl."

"That's not doing a lot of good. He's become a liability. We need this stopped right now before the two of them cause irreparable harm. Things are gearing up. We have a tight time frame and if anything leaks out…"

"It won't. I've taken care of most of the potential leaks. It would be their word against yours and who do you think people would believe?"

"Good point, but we have a shipment coming in soon."

"There won't be a problem. It'll be as smooth as the others. I also made sure all the documents I've found have been destroyed."

"Good. I hope you found them all. What about the Dupré woman? She said she had documentation."

"We've searched everywhere. There's no sign of anything. Once we get rid of the girl no one's going to be interested in any old documents."

"Except maybe an honest cop."

"Don't worry; we'll take care of O'Reilly. We'll tie up all the loose ends. I have a plan in place to get the girl. She doesn't appear to know anything yet. She keeps asking questions, but her snooping could make a few other people start to get curious."

"We don't want anyone asking questions. Take care of all the loose ends. Don't mess it up this time or you may be one of the loose ends we take care of."

"I won't. I'll get her this time. She seems eager to do anything to find out what happened to her mother. I think I can get her to come to me."

"When you do, bring her to me, alive. I want to talk to her and make sure there are no more loose ends before you kill her."

"Okay. I may even be able to get the cop at the same time."

"Even better. Him I don't need to see. Take care of him. Let's get everything tied up and back to running smoothly. Do it quickly."

Connor strode into the small, out of the way coffee shop and scanned the room to see if Julie Ann had arrived. He'd asked Pete to pick her up at home and drop her off here. The less they were seen together the better it might be for her. He was pretty sure he was on their hit list now.

He picked a busy café where they could sit inside to prevent any drive by accidents.

He spotted her curly, blonde hair, partially hidden behind a newspaper and inched his way through the crowd to a small table where Julie Ann sat reading the paper.

When he reached the table, she glanced up. He wanted to bend down and kiss those delectable lips but restrained himself in case they were being watched. He slid into a chair opposite her and flashed a smile.

She closed the newspaper, carefully folded it and put it down on the table beside her.

"Coffee; cream and four sugars," He glanced up as the waiter approached. "Did you want anything else? More coffee?"

"No, I'm fine, thanks. If I drink any more, it's going to start spouting out of my ears. There." She pointed to the article on the nurse.

Connor picked up the paper and skimmed the article. It was the woman he'd already investigated.

"Interesting, but why do you think they're related? Other than the theory about the robbery gone bad?"

"Apparently I was born in the hospital where this nurse worked. She was retired, but she might have been working there when I was born."

"And that would be important. Why?"

"Perrine wasn't my birth mother, as you know. My birth mother, Elizabeth Watson, gave birth to me at that hospital. That nurse worked there about that time and if we tracked her down, she might have been able to give us information on my birth. Maybe she'd have information that would explain why everyone involved turns up dead."

"Yeah, I agree. It makes sense. I've been checking anything I can find around that time frame. The birth records and the staff list from that time frame were destroyed in a fire. I did talk to a nurse who worked there around then. She told me the doctor, who I'm guessing delivered you, was killed in a car accident a few years later. And she mentioned this nurse." Connor tapped the paper.

Julie Ann stared at him. "This is becoming more and more of a larger conspiracy, isn't it? It's not even Perrine anymore. And it looks like it's all about my birth."

"That's what I think." Connor took a sip of coffee and put it down quickly. "Hot! You might have a point with the nurse's death. Her death looks suspiciously like your mother's. It could be by the same person. I've also checked the hit and run that killed your birth mother. The police never followed up any of the leads. I'm trying to do it twenty-five years later, but it's a pretty cold trail. I'll look into this nurse's death, too."

"Elizabeth and my mother were roommates and good friends. I think Elizabeth asked Perrine to look after me if anything happened to her. It sounds like she suspected something might happen to her, but what? And why?"

"If we figure that out, we'll probably solve the case."

"Elizabeth and Perrine had a legally binding agreement drawn up so Perrine could adopt me if anything happened to Elizabeth. Elizabeth died in a drive by shooting twenty-seven years ago. After she died Perrine brought me home, legally adopted me and raised me."

"Do you know who shot her?"

"No."

Connor pulled out his phone. "Jerry, can you do something for me, please? See if you can pull up a drive by shooting from twenty-seven years ago. The vic was an Elizabeth Watson. Thanks, I'll hold."

Connor sipped his coffee. Julie Ann reread the newspaper article.

"Yeah, I'm still here. That was quick. I see. That's it? Who was the investigating officer?"

"Shit, that's what I was afraid of. Thanks, Jer." Connor clicked off.

"What did you find out?"

"There was a drive by shooting. It was ruled accidental. The report said the people in the vehicle were aiming for a drug dealer in the crowd and hit Elizabeth by accident. The car and driver disappeared and were never found."

"Another accident? We're starting to get a long list of accidental deaths that are somehow related."

Connor nodded. "Don't get mad, but it's routine to investigate finances. At the same time Elizabeth died Perrine received a small anonymous donation. It was a one-time payment."

"What are you saying?"

"I'm not sure. Maybe someone wanted to help with the cost of raising a child?"

"My father?"

"It doesn't seem likely. Lucy didn't think Elizabeth had told the father."

"Can you trace where the money came from?"

"After all this time, it's highly unlikely. I am wondering if there might have been some other criminal activity going on at that time, maybe with your father. Maybe Elizabeth stumbled on it and died because of the information she found out."

"That's a possibility. So Elizabeth was another accident and mysterious death that was never followed up. When you start to list all the people involved who have died in various accidental deaths, that alone looked suspicious."

Connor nodded. "I agree. I'm making that list, but even with a list like that, I'm not sure who I could give it to, and have it investigated."

"Can't you go over your boss's head?"

"I can but I'm not sure who's honest. I'm trying to figure that out."

"I asked talked Savannah what she knew. She said Perrine had planned to tell me something about my history when I came home this time. I was concerned about my birth parents' medical records. I also hoped I could convince her to tell me more."

"She planned to tell you something about your birth parents?"

Julie Ann nodded. "And she was killed that week. I'm still wondering if the phone is bugged and they taped our calls."

"That's a possibility of course, but it seems like a bit of a stretch. I did think of it, but have they been listening for twenty-eight years?"

Julie Ann shrugged. "It's a thought. Maybe they have and for twenty-eight years she never told me anything. Anytime I asked about my birth mother she said it was better I didn't know. This was the first time she was going to share any information."

"It's worth checking out." Connor made another call. "Does Savannah have a key to your house?"

Julie Ann nodded.

"Can you call her and ask her to let a police technologist into the house? He'll go to her house and get the key. He'll show proper identification."

Julie Ann nodded and called Savannah.

"Once again, I was going to suggest dinner at a nice restaurant, but I'm thinking it might be safer if we don't travel in public too much. Let's order something to eat here. The burgers are good, or the poor boy sandwich. I think they even have salads."

Julie Ann picked up a menu. "You keep saying 'we'. It sounds like they might be after you, too. Is there something you're not telling me?"

Connor hesitated.

"What? They are? Why? What do you know?"

"Whoever is after you doesn't want me investigating. The case was supposed to get swept under the rug. Another accident, case closed, and life goes on. As you and others have mentioned, there is corruption in the police department. I'm not sure who or how high up it goes.

"But I arrived and insisted on knowing what happened. And you started a legitimate investigation."

Connor nodded.

"Now they want you to back off?"

"Yes. They want the case closed and marked a break-in and accidental shooting. They even offered me a bribe. It was a combined threat and bribe."

"Which is why you said you don't know who's corrupt. Maybe you should pass the case on to someone else?"

"It won't make any difference. If I pass it to an honest cop he'll be in danger. If someone else is corrupt, it will disappear and never be solved."

"But at least you won't be in danger."

Connor reached across and squeezed her hand. "Even if I closed the case, we don't know that you would be safe. I'm not sure they wouldn't follow up on their threat to me, as well. We're in this together. We'll be fine. Let's eat."

Julie Ann rolled her fingers around the packet in her pocket. Maybe Priestess Ava could make one for Connor, too.

Their order arrived. Connor took a bite out of his burger. His phone rang. He had to wait a minute until he finished chewing.

Julie Ann chuckled watching him try to swallow quickly.

Connor clicked on the phone. "O'Reilly. Yeah? Okay, thanks Dooley. I appreciate that."

He turned the phone off before he looked across at Julie Ann. "That was the tech I asked to do a sweep of your house after you mentioned the phone might be bugged. You hit it. He found a bug in the phone. Apparently a very old bug so it's been there a long time. He also found another one in the kitchen, in a light switch and one in that office upstairs."

"So, people have been monitoring Mom for a long time. Until they heard her say she'd see what she could do about sharing my history, she stayed safe. I got her killed." Julie Ann buried her face in her hands. "If it hadn't been for my selfishness, she'd still be alive."

"You don't know that. It appears they have been killing people for many years. We don't know what triggered those deaths. Maybe something has changed. It might not be what you and she were going to discuss."

"Thanks, but I'm sure it's me. I don't know why the information she might have shared could be so devastating to someone. I mean I was talking about learning people's medical health records. There didn't need to be names."

"Dooley removed the bugs, so they aren't monitoring you, for now. I'm going to guess once they realize we found them, and removed them, they'll try and replace them. I'll have someone watch the house."

"Or maybe they'll just kill me." Julie Ann grimaced.

"We're not going there. If I have to, I'll move in with you."

"That won't be necessary. I'll be fine. I've got Marie L."

"Yeah, Dooley said she barked the whole time he was there. She kept biting at his ankles."

"See, I have my protector."

Connor shook his head. "Look, I know you think you can manage this on your own, but the risk is escalating. There have been several attempts on your life. Even you should realize one of these times you could actually get hurt. You're getting a roomie until we catch whoever is responsible."

"But…"

Connor put a finger to her lips. Being in the same house and not touching would be one of his biggest challenges.

"No buts, I'm moving in. It's the only way I'll feel you're safe. When we finish eating, I'll let you off at your place, stop by the station and drop off your DNA sample, hit my place, pack a few things and be back at your house. You shouldn't be alone too long. Want me to bring any food?"

Julie Ann stared across at him. "I might not let you in."

"I can pick the lock. Don't be so stubborn. They're going

to try again. You know it and I know it. We just don't know when. Let's go, I need to get your DNA sent off for testing and get the results into the file. We may need it for a match at some time."

"No food, but a bottle of dry white wine, maybe a Pinot Grigio, would be good. Okay, let's go do the DNA."

He pulled out a test tube, opened the top and passed her a swab. "Run it over the inside of your cheek and put it into the test tube."

Julie Ann followed his instructions and then pushed her shrimp salad away, stood up and edged her way to the door. "Oh, I forgot to mention, they searched Perrine's office at the hotel."

"When?"

"Tuesday night. They took her computer."

"Did the hotel file a complaint?" Connor dropped a few bills on the table for the food and followed Julie Ann.

"Theresa said they did, and the police came and did a cursory investigation. They said it was a coincidence that it was Perrine's office."

"I'm sure they did." Connor sighed. "I'll check it out and have forensics recheck the office."

Connor drove her home, watched to see she got inside safely and then drove to the station. He had a knot in his stomach. He didn't want to leave her there alone even for a few minutes. He looked up a number on his phone.

"Savannah, its Deputy Sheriff O'Reilly. I just dropped Julie Ann at home. She's going to be alone for about an hour. Can you keep an eye on the house until I get back?"

"Sure can. I'll sit by the window and watch her house. She did put on a new lock this afternoon."

"That's good news. She didn't mention it. Thanks." Connor started to hang up. "Savannah, would you mind if I sent a deputy over to your house to check for bugs?"

"Bugs, I don't have no bugs. I'd know. I clean regularly."

"No, not those kinds of bugs. I mean the listening kind

where people put them in your phone or somewhere else in your house so they can hear everything you talk about."

"Why would you want to do that?"

"Because we found some in Perrine's house."

"How long had they been doin' that?"

"A long time and they went after you the other day. I'd like to check and make sure they haven't put any in your house."

"Hmmph, I guess you can do that."

"Thank you. I'll have Deputy Dooley come by again tonight and do a quick check. He's the same policeman that came by and got the key to Julie Ann's."

"Okay, but if he makes a mess, he cleans it up."

"I'll let him know." Connor smiled and hung up.

They'd broken into Perrine's office, obviously still looking for whatever it was they wanted. They hadn't found anything, so they took the computer to see if it was on there. He'd guess it was Tozer who said there was no connection and made it a short investigation. It was time he started a full investigation of the sheriff, his finances and his connections for the last twenty-five years.

That would probably get a quick response from the organization or people behind the corruption. He needed to try and stay under the radar for a few days until after he finished investigating Perrine's death. Once he started to investigate the list of old deaths, he'd need to get some information on Tozer quick. Otherwise he probably wouldn't be around to finish that investigation.

And who could he trust in the department and the legal system to cover his back?

Julie Ann let herself into the house. A shudder wrapped around her and squeezed. It took her breath away. Was someone here? Were they watching the house? What next?

She locked the door and moved the chair in front of it. Then she closed the curtains and peeked out into the street. There didn't appear to be anyone in the area. Still she had a feeling. Somewhere something wasn't right. Maybe it was because Connor was also in danger now.

Danger and death appeared to be lurking around every corner these days. Marie L. rubbed around her ankles and barked.

"Good girl," she bent down to pat the dog. Marie was better than an alarm. As long as the dog came to greet her, she knew no one else was in the house.

She slid the new deadbolt into place. How the hell would she cope with Connor living in the same house? She wanted him in her bed, but not right now. She had to find out her background. What about her birth had caused so many people to die? And so many years later people were still being killed. Why? Did her father know about her? Was he behind the killings?

Suddenly it occurred to her that when Connor moved in, she wouldn't be able to use the secret room in the closet. She trusted him, but not completely. She wasn't sure why she didn't want to tell him, at least not yet. Maybe because it's the one secret she and her mom had together. Perrine hadn't even shared it with Savannah. Julie Ann didn't want to give it up, not yet.

She'd finish going through the room now. She'd find whatever Mom might have hidden there, if she had put anything in the room.

"Come on Marie L, let's go see if we can find that envelope or whatever people are killing for."

The dog raced up the stairs ahead of Julie Ann. In her bedroom she pulled back her clothes and pushed the button.

Marie raced inside and jumped up on the cot. Julie Ann followed more slowly, examining the small room.

Her fingers moved slowly over the wall, tapping lightly around the small area.

No change in sound.

She moved to the floor and crept around it on her hands and knees tapping and checking for loose boards. Nothing.

She flopped down on the bed beside Marie and looked around the room. If her mother had hidden anything it had to be here, but where? Marie jumped down and crawled under the bed.

"What? You're feeling neglected? Come on back up."

Marie stayed under the bed.

Julie Ann got down on her knees and looked under the bed. There was nothing there and she'd already checked the floorboards. She lay back down on the bed and looked around the room.

Marie jumped up on the cot and dropped her head on Julie Ann's lap.

"Maybe there is nothing. Maybe hoping to find anything about my history is a pipe dream."

The phone rang.

Julie Ann jumped up, dumped Marie on the floor and hurried downstairs expecting it to be Connor. She picked up the receiver.

"Hello?"

The Dupré file had been moved. Connor noticed it as soon as he entered the office. "Hey Jer—you see anyone hanging around my desk?"

"Yeah, man. I caught Tozer snooping through your folders a little while ago. I don't know what he was looking for but when he saw me watching, he left."

"Thanks." Connor pursed his lips.

What the hell was going on with Tozer? What else was there about this case that had him snooping around the file? Had the people who paid him to cover things up asked for something specific?

He'd have to make sure he kept the Dupré file with him from now on. In fact, he'd make a photocopy of all the documents and keep the original file off site, in case someone tried to tamper with the one in the office. He certainly didn't plan on sharing any new information with anyone, especially Tozer.

Ten years ago Harvey Tozer had been in charge of the case that got Connor's father shot. To start with, the fact he was investigating his partners death had seemed like a conflict of interest. Connor still felt that his father's death could have been prevented, but he'd been stonewalled every time he'd tried to find out what the hell had really happened.

He remembered that night when his father had gone out with his partner on a tip about a drug deal going down. Devon O'Reilly hadn't been himself that night.

Connor remembered his mother asking if something was wrong. His dad had shaken his head, but he appeared worried about something. Then, in the early hours of the morning, the knock at the door came.

His mother had stumbled out of her room, her housecoat wrapped tightly around her. She opened the door. Connor had stood in his doorway. They both knew as soon as they saw the police officer. Connor had grabbed his mother and held her when she broke down.

He started to draw a diagram on a white board. In the middle he wrote Julie Ann's name, drew a line and wrote Perrine. In brackets her date of death and cause, plus investigating officer. Another line to Elizabeth Watson and again in brackets, date of death and cause plus investigating officer. He kept adding other names, most who were dead.

Birth records were gone, hospital staff lists were gone, the birth mother was dead, the doctor who probably delivered Julie Ann was dead, the nurse who may have assisted the doctor was dead, and Perrine was dead.

Everything had been ruled accidental and all the cases and the investigations had been headed by one man.

What were people trying to cover up? The identity of Julie Ann's father? Was he involved? Was there involvement in drugs?

He dropped Julie Ann's DNA sample at the lab and checked on the other DNA sample he'd submitted but no results on any of them yet.

He called a friend who worked in banking. "Eddie, I have a request. If you don't like it just say so."

"What is it, Connor?"

"I want to do an investigation of someone's finances gong back about twenty-five years, without them knowing about it or raising any suspicions. Is it possible?"

"Wow, and is it someone from outer space as well?"

"Too difficult, huh?"

"I was kidding," Eddie replied. "It's not impossible. It depends on a lot of different things, but it could take a while."

"Do you know someone who could do it for me?"

"Yeah, me. I could look into it. Who are we talking about?"

"Sheriff Harvey Tozer."

There was a long pause."

"Wow, that will be complicated."

"It is. Look, if it could get you trouble don't do it."

"Let me see how it goes. I'll get started. We'll see where it goes."

"Thanks, Eddie. I owe you big time."

"And don't think I won't collect." Eddie hung up.

That was a start. He'd examine Tozer's back cases as soon as he solved the Dupré case. Next he had to stop by his place, pack a few things and take a cold shower. Sleeping in the same house as Julie Ann and not in her bed would take all the moral strength he could muster.

His phone beeped he had a message. It must have come in while he was on the pone with Eddie.

"Hi, Connor, it's Julie Ann. I'm not home at the moment. I should be back in an hour or so. Monique Patterson called and asked me to come by. We went to school together. Savannah knows her. Apparently, Monique's a drug addict. She works the street and has a loser boyfriend. She needs money for a hit and said she'd sell me information on my mother's death and my father for a couple of hundred bucks, but I had to come alone.

She's in the lower Ninth Ward on Claiborne Avenue. Yes, I know I shouldn't believe her but if there's a chance to find out anything it's worth a few hundred dollars. I'll be careful."

Connor pounded the desk with his fist. Jerry looked up.

"I'm in front of the address she gave me. She said it was her house, but it looks like a rundown dump. I feel something might be wrong, but I have to see if she really has information about Mom's murder. I know I promised not to leave the house, but if I can get information on my father or Perrine's death, I have to take a chance and check it out. I'll be careful and I won't go into the house. If I stay outside, I should be okay. Marie is with me. She climbed into the car and wouldn't get out, so I let her come. I told Monique I wouldn't come inside, and she'd have to come out to get her money. I wanted to let you know where I'd gone. I'll wait outside until you get here."

He could hear the dog barking in the background. He put in an urgent request to have a police car immediately drive along Claiborne Avenue and watch for an abandoned vehicle or maybe one with a single woman and a dog sitting in it.

His phone rang again. "O'Reilly."

"Deputy, its Savannah."

"What's wrong?"

"Julie Ann left the house. She came out, got in her rented car and drove off. The dog jumped in the car when she opened the door. I don't have a good feeling about it."

"I don't either. She didn't say anything to you."

"Nope, she didn't see me. She just left."

"She rented a car?"

"Uh huh."

"Where did she rent her car, do you know?"

"No, but she was on the way home from Café du Mond. She might have walked by Enterprise on Canal Street."

"Car rentals usually have a GPS so they can track the car if necessary. What kind of car did she rent?"

"Do I look like a car person? It was blue, maybe mid-size. I have no idea the make."

"I'll check it out. She left me a message and an address. Right now I'm on my way to the address she gave me. I'm going to hang up and call you from my cellphone."

He waved to the receptionist as he raced by her desk, phone in hand.

"Savanah?"

"Hello, yes. That man you sent out said he did find a bug in my kitchen."

"Shit, thanks, Savannah. The message Julie Ann left about where she was going said she was going to buy information from an addict." Phone in hand Connor climbed in the car, hit the accelerator, turned on the flashing red light and raced toward the Lower Ninth Ward. Terror enveloped him. Her call had said she was already at Monique's house.

"You find that girl and don't let nothin' happen to her. We've had enough death around here."

"I'll do my best, Savannah." Connor clicked the phone off.

The area Julie Ann had mentioned was an area familiar to the police. High crime, drug dealing prostitution, you name it. Definitely not a safe place for Julie Ann to go. Damn her, she did one stupid thing after another. She followed her heart not her head and it was going to get her killed.

She said the woman had called her. Maybe there was a phone record. He punched in Jerry's number.

"Jerry, it's O'Reilly again. Can you check a phone number for me?"

He read off the number and waited.

Jerry came back online. "It was from a burner phone. They can't trace it."

"Thanks. Not what I wanted to hear. Can you see if you can trace its location? Thanks. I'll be calling back."

Connor turned the corner on two wheels. He spoke into his phone to dial the Enterprise number.

"Yes, this is Deputy Sheriff O'Reilly. Did you rent a vehicle to a Julie Ann Dupré? Good. What make and model and does it have a tracking system on it? Good, I need to track the car. She could be in danger. Check it out and let me know where it is." He gave his badge number.

The counter person came back online. "According to the GPS information she is in front of 2012 Claiborne Avenue."

"Thank you." Connor clicked off. He was almost there. He turned off the lights and siren.

He phoned the information to the patrol car.

"It's Deputy Sheriff O'Reilly. I need you to find a blue Ford car with Enterprise stickers on it in front of 2012 Claiborne Avenue. Keep the woman from going anywhere until I get there."

"Deputy Sheriff O'Reilly, we spotted the car. It's empty. No one's around."

Damn her, she'd left the car. What the hell was she thinking? You'd think she had a death wish.

Had they already killed her? Could he find her in time? And where was the damn dog?

Chapter Twelve

Julie Ann pulled her car to a stop. This was not a neighborhood she was familiar with except by reputation. She told Connor she wouldn't get out of the car. And she had no intention of even opening the door.

The dilapidated, tiny houses all looked like they would fall down in a good wind. The paint had peeled off the wood sidings leaving a standard gray wood color throughout the neighborhood, where there were buildings. A lot of vacant lots stood between the houses with trash spilled over into overgrown weeds and brush. Old cars without wheels and doors, fridge's, stoves and rusted bed springs all filled up the various yards and empty lots.

Marie barked and growled from the seat beside Julie Ann.

"I agree, but you shouldn't have come. I don't want you to get hurt."

Marie barked again.

"Yeah, I know, too stupid to live. I've read books like that and yet here I am."

Julie Ann checked the number she had written down. It matched the number on the house in front of her except the one number had fallen down and not been replaced.

She hesitated. She didn't want to miss a chance to get information on her mother's death. Monique had said to come alone. No cops. If she was watching she might wonder who she was waiting for. Maybe she was waiting inside the house.

She told Monique that she wouldn't come inside. Monique would have to come outside to the car to get her money and she'd have to give Julie Ann the information before she got the money.

Julie Ann waited. There was no movement. She was not going to to the house.

She took her phone and called the number Monique had used to contact Julie Ann earlier. It went to voice mail.

"I'm out front in the blue car, Monique. I have the money. If you want it, you'll have to come to me."

Julie Ann looked over her shoulder and checked the area. No signs of life. No movement. Not a lot of hiding places.

She made a decision and opened the car door. Maybe if Monique saw her and that she was alone she'd come out. Marie jumped out and raced around the car, nipping at Julie Ann's ankles when she tried to step out of the car.

"Marie, stop that. I'm not going anywhere."

She slid one foot out onto the rutted asphalt. She felt eyes watching her. Monique?

Shivers chased each other up and down her spine. Something felt very wrong.

She sat back down in the car, and punched Connor's number into the cellphone. The call went to voice mail.

Maybe the reception was bad, calls weren't getting through, but they did go to voice mail.

"Connor, I'm outside the address. There doesn't appear to be anyone here. Monique may have decided to get the money another way. I'll wait outside but I hate to think I've missed her. Please hurry."

Marie barked frantically.

Someone grabbed Julie Ann's arm and yanked her out of

the car. She dropped her phone and started to kick and punch.

"Hurry up and knock her out."

"I'm trying but she's all over the place and she brought the damn dog."

Marie barked and bit at ankles.

Julie Ann kicked and screamed. "Don't hurt the dog."

She felt a sharp stabbing pain in her arm. Boy, she'd made another wrong decision and screwed up royally this time.

"Please…dog…"

Drowsiness filled every cell of her body. Legs felt rubbery. Her arms dropped to her side. So tired… She wanted to lie down. Her eyes closed. Darkness enveloped her.

Lights and siren on, Connor raced toward the address Julie Ann had left in her message. Cars pulled over as he sped by. He swerved around those parked in the middle of the streets. He drove through the residential area. The houses became more dilapidated and run down. Concern tighten inside of him. Nothing good happened down here.

Damn her. If she suspected there might be something wrong, why didn't she drive away? Women! Julie Ann had made one bad decision after another and it looked like she'd made another one. Why the hell couldn't she trust him to look after her and figure out the reason they were after her?

This area was a hot bed of drug dealers' and users. Who the hell was Monique, besides being an addict?

People could have seen Julie Ann talking to her on the street. It was about the same time they had tried to run Julie Ann over. If Monique was a user and an addict, she probably worked the streets as well. They could have picked her up and got her to call Julie Ann for the cost of her next hit. After that she probably crawled off to a hole somewhere high as a kite. And the perps waited for Julie Ann to show up.

The patrol car had said they had found the car, but no one was inside.

Damn it, she hadn't stayed in the car. She said she'd wait in the car until he got there, but no, she had to go and check out the house.

He saw the car when he pulled up in front of the address Julie Ann had given him. It sat empty. The driver door open. The patrol car with two policeman was parked halfway down the block.

He held up his badge and motioned then to follow him. The three moved cautiously toward the house. Connor motioned for one of the patrol men to cover the back of the house. Gun in front of him he moved cautiously to the door. He moved to one side and the patrol man moved to the other side. Connor rapped on the door with his gun and called out. "Police! Monique? Julie Ann? Open the door."

Silence.

He knocked again.

Still silence.

"Looks empty," the patrol man commented.

Connor crouched down, twisted the knob and the door swung open. When he stepped inside the stale smell of pot and cabbage, met his nostrils. Boxes and newspaper cluttered the hall.

"Cover me." Connor said over his shoulder. He crept carefully down the hall.

"Clear."

The other patrol man came in through the back door into the kitchen at the same time Connor entered the room.

In the kitchen a body sprawled across the floor.

Connor scanned the room for any sign of Julie Ann or the suspects. The room didn't look like anyone lived there. He bent down to check for a pulse.

None. She was dead, probably from an overdose. The body was still warm, so she hadn't been dead long. Probably about the time Julie Ann got there.

He motioned for the patrol man to check the other room while Connor moved through the rest of the house double checking that no one was inside. He returned to the body.

The young woman could have been about Julie Ann's age, except her life had prematurely aged her. The scars on her arms shouted addict. Obviously, she died from an overdose. The rubber tourniquet was still knotted tight on her upper left arm. A syringe lay a few inches away. His guess was this was the Monique who had called Julie Ann. And after she made the call the suspects, whoever they were, probably shot her up with an overdose.

Connor pulled out his cell and put in a call to Jerry Bruckhauser.

"Hey Jerry, I've got a dead body, OD victim. I'm not sure if it's accidental or murder. My bet's on murder. I need you to take the case. I don't trust Tozer."

"No problem. I'm on my way. What's the address? Secure the site and I'll take it from there and get forensics over to check it out. If Tozer asks, I'll say he must have been in the bathroom and you said it was urgent."

"Thanks, Jerry. I owe you. Julie Ann Dupré is also missing. Can you put out an APB?"

"Shit, sure. What about you?"

"I'm staying away from the office, and Tozer. I'm going to try and find her before she turns up dead. It looks like they kidnapped her and took her alive. There's a chance they might keep her that way for at least a few hours. And apparently her dog came with her, but I don't see any sign of it. I don't know, they might have taken it too."

"Stay put and check the area until I get there."

"Hurry." Connor clicked off and pulled on his gloves. He moved carefully around the kitchen.

Who had got to Julie Ann and where had they taken her? Why had she got out of the car?

And how come after several attempts on her life, they kidnapped her and didn't kill her at the same time they'd killed Monique? He was pretty sure that would be the woman's identity. He'd have forensics check for any prints but if it was a drug house, there'd be a lot.

He had to find Julie Ann and quickly. He couldn't lose the only woman he'd ever loved. Of course she didn't want to live in New Orleans, and he wouldn't leave. There wasn't any chance for a relationship, but at least if she was alive, he might have a slim chance of working out some kind of arrangement.

There wouldn't be any street cameras, not in this area. He'd get the patrolmen to search the area, talk to the neighbors, if there were any, and see if anyone saw anything. He didn't think many of the houses were occupied and if they were it was probably on an hourly basis.

He had no idea where to look. Back outside he walked around Julie Ann's rental car. No visible dents or marks. The driver's door was open. There were grasses and weeds around and under the car. He bent down and examined the area pushing dry weeds to one side. The ground was mostly rocks and gravel, but it looked like there might have been a scuffle. *How did they get her out of the car?*

He expanded the search and walked around again. A shell of an old car sat about thirty feet away, no windows or doors, no wheels, the steering wheel was gone. Lots of footprints in the area, which was to be expected, but some looked new and there were fresh cigarette butts. Were they the same as the one's from the murder site? He picked up and couple and put them in an evidence envelope.

Had someone hidden in the car, waiting for the chance to grab her?

He tried to create a scenario in his mind. If Julie Ann had seen anyone, she wouldn't have opened the door. But maybe they were hiding in that old car. Maybe Marie wanted to go out and when Julie Ann opened the door, they grabbed her.

The ground was too hard for tires tracks. There was no blood at the scene. And only a few paw prints.

Who had kidnapped Julie Ann? And where would they take her? And where was Marie?

Visions of empty lots where there should be houses. Empty houses. Grounds covered with weeds and tall grass. They tumbled through her head. They were the last thing she could remember. Her head hurt.

There were footsteps. Everything in her head kept spinning. She felt nauseous. Julie Ann tried to focus and stop the spinning. Her arms and legs pressed against smooth leather.

Where am I?

She tried to open her eyes. They refused to open. She felt sick to her stomach. She tried to remember what had happened.

The dilapidated house. Monique? She'd gone to talk to Monique.

"Has she come around yet?" A gravelly male voice asked.

"No, not yet." Another male voice replied.

"How much did you give her? You sure she'll come out of it?"

"There's no risk. I've used it before. She's skinny. It may take her a little longer, but she'll come out of it. Fentanyl affects people differently."

"Yeah, it kills people. She'd better come out of it. I need to question her."

Julie Ann lay quietly, listening to the voices. They faded away. She didn't recognize them.

A door closed.

Were they the people who had tried to kill her? If so,

why hadn't they killed her yet? Who the hell were they? What did they want to talk to her about?

She'd stupidly walked into a trap, all because she had to know about her mother's death and her father. Connor kept telling her to stay inside and let him follow up the leads, but no, she knew better. Now she could lose her life because of it.

She'd given Connor the address where she'd gone to meet Monique. Connor could be in trouble, too.

She had so much in her life to be thankful for, but instead of making intelligent decisions she kept putting herself and other people at risk. Her curiosity had killed Mom.

Now, here she was a prisoner and they'd probably kill her and what had she found out about anything. Nada—not a damn thing. Why had she opened the car door? She should have kept it locked and waited for Connor. Damn it, Julie Ann Dupré, you're Perrine's daughter and a successful New York businessperson. How could you let yourself make so many bad decisions? If you die, Perrine and everyone else died in vain. *When the hell would she learn not to be so stupid?*

She left a message for Connor, but he wouldn't know where they'd taken her. She didn't know where they'd taken her.

And what happened to Marie? Where was she? Please, don't let them shoot her.

Connor could be in danger if he came out after her without back-up. Another possibility that her decision could hurt someone else, actually both Connor and Marie. What an idiot she was.

She forced her eyes to open and stared up into a fluorescent ceiling fixture.

Her head pounded. Focus girl, you got yourself into this position. Now what are you going to do?

She fought through the dizziness that spun around her

and struggled to sit up. They hadn't tied her up, so obviously they didn't see her as an escape risk.

What did they need to talk to her about?

Once the room stopped spinning, she checked out her surroundings.

She appeared to be in a small office, sparsely furnished. A large desk sat in the middle of the room. A filing cabinet stood in the corner. She sat on a small leather couch against the wall. The room only had one window, a small one about four feet above her head. Too high and too small for an escape. Her purse and cell phone were missing.

Julie Ann struggled to her feet and staggered to the door. She twisted the knob. Locked.

She stumbled back to the desk and collapsed in the wooden chair behind it. Opening the middle drawer, she found two pencils, a few paper clips and a small notepad. The next drawer had a small pull of chewing tobacco and what looked like mouse droppings.

She shut the drawer quickly and tentively opened the bottom drawer. Empty. Nothing she could use as a weapon.

A sigh escaped. She was definitely screwed. She should have paid attention to her gut instincts and driven away. But no, she had to find out about her father. After all this time, what was so important about finding out about her birth mother and her father? He hadn't cared about her up until now.

It wasn't only about finding her father. It was also because he might be the motive for Mom's death, or maybe he was the one who killed her. Whoever they were had listened to all the conversations with her mother and when Perrine had said she'd share some information she'd been killed.

It was Julie Ann's fault. She was the typical too stupid to live person she'd watched in B movies on TV.

She heard a key in the lock and hurried back to the couch.

"If she's not awake, give her something. I need to talk to her now before someone starts looking for her."

Steps moved across the room and stopped by the couch.

A slap resounded as it hit her cheek.

"Wake up!"

Julie tried not to wince from the slap.

"I said, wake up!"

The second slap to the face made her flinch.

"I thought so. She's faking. She's awake."

Hands grabbed her arms and pulled her to a sitting position.

She opened her eyes. Two men stood in front of her. She didn't recognize either one.

"What do you know?"

"About what?" Julie Ann glanced from one to another.

"Don't play stupid. If you want to get out of here alive, you'll cooperate. What do you know about the Dupré death? What did she tell you before she died?" The thin pasty-faced man in the expensive blue, pinstriped suit snarled.

"I was in New York when she died. I don't know anything about it except what the police have told me."

"And what would that be?" he asked.

Julie Ann licked her lips. They hadn't blind-folded her, so they weren't worried about her identifying them later. It meant that no matter what she said, they had no intention of letting her live.

"Just that she interrupted a robbery and got shot."

"So why are the cops still investigating?" The man with the gravelly voice asked.

"I don't know. You'd have to ask them."

Another slap resounded throughout the room.

"Don't try and be a smart ass. You're playing nookie nookie with the cop that's investigating. You're both talking to people you haven't seen or heard from in years. You're looking for something. What is it?"

"I'm trying to find my father."

The pasty-faced man with the blond crew cut and mustache shot a glance over his shoulder.

The other person, a tall, older man, maybe in his fifties with a slight paunch, shrugged. He motioned pasty-face to keep questioning.

"Who's your father?"

"I don't know." Julie Ann replied. "My mother died, and the name of my father apparently died with her."

"Good." The older man nodded.

"You haven't found anything in the house to give you any information?"

Julie Ann shook her head.

"She doesn't know anything. Get rid of her, but not here." The other person left the room.

Pasty face pulled a gun from a side holster he wore. "Stand up."

Julie Ann sat, staring at him, her mind whirling. He was going to kill her now. What could she do to stop him?

"I said get up." He held the gun pointed at her head.

Slowly, pretending dizziness, she tried to stand up. She needed to figure out how to get away and fast.

"Don't play stupid. The fentanyl's worn off. You're fine. Go through that door." He waved the gun in her face.

Julie Ann trudged toward the door.

"Open it."

She put her hand out and grasped the knob. She turned it slowly. When the door opened, she dashed through and slammed it behind her.

She heard a shot as she raced down a hall and out into an empty warehouse.

She could see a door at the end of the room and raced toward it. Another shot whizzed by her head.

Three more shots.

She ran.

Footsteps pounded after her. "You won't get away." He huffed.

The next shot grazed her arm. She didn't pause.

Please don't be locked, she prayed.

She reached the door and turned the knob. The door opened. Julie Ann raced outside into an alley. She kept running as fast as she could.

More shots fired. She'd lost count. She could still hear footsteps pounding down the alley, but they sounded farther and farther away. She sprinted for the street. Rounding the corner she ran into a gun pointed right at her heart.

"Going somewhere?" the woman asked.

Connor took several deep breaths. Jerry had Monique's house secured. Connor hadn't found much except another cigarette butt in the bushes by the front porch that matched the ones by the skeleton of a car.

The butts came from an expensive, cigarette, only sold in certain specialty shops. According to Jerry, there were five in the New Orleans area.

Jerry was a cigarette aficionado.

Connor had called all five stores and got a list of names of the people who purchased that specific brand. All were men. Nineteen from the New Orleans and eight from outside the city.

He scratched the ones outside the city off his list. He matched the rest of the names to the list of families from Lafayette that he'd found had a possible connection to Elizabeth Watson. One man worked for the Dufour family in the capacity of a chief of staff, or someone who appeared to manage the family affairs. He could be the clean-up guy. When a problem occurred, he made it go away. Had he made Perrine Dupré go away?

His gut told him Lafayette would be too far away. The killer wouldn't want to risk driving her that far. He scratched that one off the list.

Connor walked slowly down the road. He checked out both sides, looking for any signs of which direction they'd gone or maybe some discernible tires tracks that might help identify the vehicle involved.

He spotted paw prints. Connor squatted down. They could belong to Marie, but what was she doing out here? And if they had taken Julie Ann and not Maire, where was she?

He continued to walk along the road. Another spot, a few hundred feet along, he found more paw prints. It was like, if it was Marie, she was jumping from one spot to another, or maybe even flying.

Get a grip, Connor. It's a mutt dog, nothing more. A lot of the ground was gravel and rock. Maybe she just found spots of dirt that far apart. That would make more sense.

Connor strode back to the house and his vehicle.

Two police officers were working outside going through the weeds and garbage. He didn't recognize them. Jerry said they'd been recently assigned to his department.

Inside the car Connor opened up his laptop and went online to research the Dufour family in more detail.

Beau Dufour was booked to speak at the New Orleans Chamber of Commerce tonight as part of his campaign for governor. According to the online information he usually stayed at the Hilton when he had campaign bookings. He punched in the number for the Hilton.

They were reluctant to admit that Dufour was registered there. After giving his badge number they checked him out and called back. They admitted that Beau Dufour was booked into the hotel.

Connor leaned back against the seat. Even if the killer was Dufour, he wouldn't take Julie Ann to the hotel. Too risky.

Back online he searched property registrations for anything the Dufour family might own, closer to New Orleans. They had their large house and estate on the edge of the city, but they wouldn't take Julie Ann there. Too messy.

He kept searching.

Bingo. There was a deserted warehouse about ten minutes from the drug house.

He wrote down the address and started the car. As he roared down the street he spoke to his phone. "Dial the number for Detective Jerry Bruckhauser."

When Jerry picked up, Connor yelled. "I think I know where she is. It's a warehouse on Levine street near the docks, 2721 Levine Street. Leave the house with forensics and the street guys and meet me there. And call for back-up. We're going to need it. I think the Dufour family are behind this."

"The Dufour's? Isn't he running for governor?"

"Yup, that's the one."

"Oh, man…on my way." Jerry hung up.

Lights flashing, siren screaming Connor raced to toward the dock area.

He had to get there before they killed her. When they got what they wanted he knew they wouldn't leave her alive. They believed in tying up all the loose ends. Julie Ann was definitely a loose end. So was he.

He wasn't about to let them tie up either one of those lose ends.

Chapter Thirteen

Driving into the dock area Connor turned off the siren and lights. He glided the car quietly between the large containers and warehouses, checking the numbers on each one. Behind a large corner one he pulled in and turned off the engine.

He switched off the overhead light so no one could see him when the door opened.

Once out of the car he pushed the door closed but didn't shut it tight. He didn't want any sound to give him away.

Were they close by? Was Julie Ann in the warehouse?

He checked his back up gun, in case he needed it and returned it to his back holster. After a visual check of the warehouse area, he made his way toward the water and the dark outline of the Dufour warehouse. When he rounded the corner, he saw two shadows up ahead. One appeared to be holding a gun on the other, but he couldn't be sure. He blinked a few times. He swore he could see a small dog crouched against the wall. *Marie? What was she doing here? Give your head a shake O'Reilly, it's just a shadow.*

He edged closer. The shadows disappeared through a warehouse door. And the dog disappeared. He shook his head, pulled out his cell, hit Jerry's number and whispered,

"I'm at the dock. I think they're holding her in the warehouse at the address I gave you. It's registered to the Dufour family. I'm going in to look around."

"Connor, stop. Wait for back up. You could make it worse or get yourself killed. I'm only five minutes away. Back up's not far behind."

"No time. They're going to kill her. They won't let her go. Time is running out. Five minutes could mean the difference in her survival."

He clicked off before Jerry tried to talk him out of going inside. Jerry didn't realize how much Connor had to lose if he didn't go in and find her. If he waited for back up it might be too late, for both of them and their future.

He moved along the wall slowly, checking the area as he did, until he reached the door they'd disappeared through. He twisted the knob slowly, hoping it didn't squeak. The door opened.

He slipped inside, closed the door and flattened himself against the wall. His eyes adjusted to the darkness. He was in a large empty room. Open ceiling, a few windows at the top either blacked out or covered with dirt, stairs up to a second level, pipes and vents, but no boxes, nothing stored and no one around. The people he'd seen had moved somewhere else. A tiny streak of light cut through the darkness from under a door at the far end of the room.

Connor waited and listened. Nothing. Pressed against the wall he crept slowly toward the door. At the door he stopped, pressed his ear against it and listened.

Silence.

Was the door thick enough to cut out all sound? What was on the other side? Was Julie Ann there?

He debated the risk. Maybe he should have waited for Jerry. He dialed Jerry's number and left his phone on.

"Connor?"

"I'm in the warehouse. Haven't found anyone yet. I'm leaving my phone on." Connor whispered.

Carefully he turned the knob. The door squeaked as it turned on the hinges, Connor held his breath and flattened himself against the wall. He waited.

Nothing.

He kept to one side and peered through the crack. He could see what looked like a hallway with three doors. Mumbled voices appeared to come from the door on the left. *Was that where they had taken Julie Ann?*

He opened the door enough to slip through and edged into the hallway.

A dog barked.

He spun around.

Everything went black.

Connor's head felt like a three- day hangover.

What the hell had happened?

"You stupid fool. How could you let her get away?" The woman snapped.

"She slammed the door in my face. I couldn't catch her. She ran like a blasted deer."

Who were they? One of them was a woman.

Connor tried to get his fuzzy brain to focus. His head pounded. His eyes wouldn't open.

"I can't trust you to do anything right. You're a screw up and becoming a bigger risk than I need." She continued.

"Wait. You can't mean that, after all I've done."

"Yes, after all you've done. Past tense. I think you're outgrowing your usefulness. You're getting old. Maybe even a little feeble. If I hadn't been there, she would have escaped and been able to describe all of us."

"I would have got her."

"I doubt it. You've missed too many times. Besides, now you're becoming a loose end."

"No, no, I'm not. I'll handle this."

"No, this time, I'll handle it. I want it done right. Thanks to you messing up we'll have two bodies to get rid of instead of one. And we need to make them look like accidents. How do I make it look like an accident? I need to figure out a new plan." She sighed.

"I'll take care of it."

"Is that all you can say? No, not anymore. This time it has to be done right. The cop is going to make it more difficult. People won't sweep his death under the carpet or accept it as an accident. He's done too much damage bringing attention to us already. Are they both tied up?"

"Yeah."

"Good. I need to think about this and come up with a new plan." She opened the door and her voice came from the hall.

The door closed.

Connor opened his eyes. The room was dark. He tried to move his hands. The rope cut into his skin. His feet were bound out in front of him. At least they hadn't gagged him, but who would hear a call for help in a large empty warehouse.

He remembered the dog bark.

Had it been Marie trying to warn him? Come, on Connor, get a grip. You're talking about a dog.

Had they taken his cellphone? He wasn't sure. If they had, did they turn it off? Did they throw it away? Where were Jerry and the back up?

They'd said two people to get rid of.

"Julie Ann? Are you in here?"

"Connor? Is that you?"

"Yeah, I'm afraid so, trussed up like the traditional turkey and feeling like one for getting caught."

"At least you saved my life for now. They would have shot me if you hadn't showed up. I'm not sure what they want from me."

"So much for great timing. I'm glad I stopped that, anyway." Connor thumped closer to where he heard Julie

Ann's voice, using his feet and his butt. "Keep talking so I can find you."

"Do you know who they are? I gather the one man has done most of the killings. It sounds like he's the one who shot Mom. Not sure about the other man, but the other person was a woman. I ran into her."

"I'm not sure who they are. I think they're part of, or are employed by, the DuFour family. I'm guessing the one man is Freddy March, although he prefers Frederick Marchon. He has a record for robbery and assault which began in his early twenties. Then he got hired on as a so-called manager, or clean up guy, for the Dufours, a wealthy family in Lafayette. They're into politics and do whatever it takes to climb up that ladder. When they need someone killed or bought off, Freddy does most of the dirty work. Although I think the second man could also have done some of the killings. He might be an ex-con called Sammy One Shot."

"Who?"

"Never mind. No idea who the woman is. The rumor is the Dufours might also be involved in money laundering. The younger Dufour is running for governor."

"Yeah, I've seen something in the paper and a few signs around the area. Most people seem to think he's an honest man. He's promising to clean up crime in this area and clean up corruption in the police department and justice system."

"That sounds impressive, but I'm not sure you can believe him. It sounds like his family has a history of corruption. Are you okay? They didn't hurt you?"

"My arm's a little sore. They shot at me when I tried to escape. A bullet grazed my arm."

"How bad is it?"

"Not bad. I didn't even bleed much. It's a little sore."

"We'll get it checked when we get out of there." Connor bumped into something soft. The scent of summer flowers reached his nostrils. "I'm so sorry I got you into this."

"It's not your fault. I'm the jerk that went to Monique's house."

"That had to be the dumbest thing you've ever done. Why didn't you call me and let me take you there?"

"I thought about it, but the possibility of finding out who killed Mom sort of clouded my brain. Monique admitted she was a drug addict and needed a fix. She said she needed money quickly and she knew something about Perrine's murder. She said she didn't trust cops and to come alone and fast or she'd find a trick on the street and get the money that way. I screwed up."

"You sure did, big time. It could get you killed. As a junkie she'd sell her kid for a hit. They probably got her to call you and draw you down to that area for a shot of heroin. She was selling you out."

"I never thought about that. I guess it's too late to say I'm sorry."

"Not if we can get out of here alive."

"How is Monique? Did she tell you where to find me?"

"Monique is dead. They killed her with an overdose of heroin."

"Nooo. Because of me?"

"They used her to get to you. She was dead as soon as she agreed to help them. They probably promised her a couple of free hits. As soon as she made the call, they killed her with the overdose. She was dead by the time you got to the house."

"Poor Monique. I'm so sorry." Julie Ann swallowed a sob.

"I thought you said you weren't going to go into the house."

"I didn't. I'm not that stupid. I told her I wouldn't come inside the house. I said when she phoned that she had to come outside and meet me at my car. I parked out front and waited. When she didn't come out, I phoned. She didn't answer so I left a message saying I was there and waiting for her. The door opened so I opened the car door and stepped outside, right beside the car. Marie barked. That's all I remember."

"They were using the burned-out vehicle beside you for cover. When you got out of the car, they moved behind you and knocked you out."

"Damn. Another dumb move. I should have paid more attention to my surroundings. I guess I should have left the detecting to you. How did they get you?"

"When you went missing, I did some research on my tablet and found the Dufours owned a warehouse in the dock area. I let Jerry know the address and what I was doing. Hopefully he's in the area by now. He was bringing back-up." He felt a dog licking his ankle.

"That's weird. I can feel a dog in here."

"I took Marie to the meet with Monique. I didn't actually take her. She jumped in the car and wouldn't leave. I didn't want to waste time trying to get her back into the house, so I let her come with me."

"How did she get in here?"

"I have no idea, but she may be trying to protect me."

Connor shook his head. It didn't make sense. How would the dog get into this room? He didn't want to even think about that possibility. This dog was way beyond anything Connor could fathom.

"If you say so. Look, try to wriggle down so you can reach my left arm and slide your fingers inside my sleeve."

Julie Ann paused, then proceeded to do as he'd asked.

He felt the tips of her cool fingers, extending from the duct tape around her wrist. At the touch, fire shot through him.

Not now you idiot, you've got work to do.

"Good, now slide your fingers up just a little farther. Can you feel the metal?"

"Yes."

"It's the handle of my back up knife. They got my guns but luckily didn't find the knife. If you can get hold of it and move it downward so I can grab it, we might be able to cut the rope."

Julie Ann moved the tips of her fingers around the handle of the knife, wiggling it slowly down his arm.

Connor sat frozen, not wanting to have it slip. He felt it inch its way down to his wrist.

"Okay, now what do I do? If I try to pull it out, I could drop it." Julie Ann asked.

"Then we start all over. Let's hope it takes that woman, whoever she is, awhile to come up with a plan to get rid of me. Go ahead, see if you can grab it."

Moving her fingers carefully Julie Ann tried to get a secure grasp on the handle.

It clattered to the floor.

"Damn."

"Don't worry about it." Connor responded. He wriggled and stretched out to get lower. His hands moved over the floor. The fingers searching for the metal.

A wet nose pushed the knife next to his hand.

Connor froze for a second.

It couldn't be…Whatever. He wasn't going to analyze it right now.

He grabbed the blade firmly between his large fingers. "Got it. Okay, wriggle your butt over here, then turn so I can try to cut through your ropes."

Julie Ann shifted herself away from him and then seconds later, backed into him. "How's that?"

Connor moved the knife until he felt the blade against the hemp. "Can you sit up a little taller?"

Julie Ann lifted herself up an inch or so.

"Good." He started sawing slowly with the blade. His fingers carefully marking the area.

"So the man running for governor is part of this?"

"I'm not sure about Beau himself, but his family is certainly involved." Connor paused. "I think Beau Dufour might be your father."

Julie Ann went perfectly still.

Connor kept sawing. He felt the fibers begin to separate.

"Do you know that for sure?"

"Nope, but a DNA sample will prove it."

"Or disprove it," she added.

"Or disprove it. Damn." The knife slipped to the floor. Connor slid lower, his finger searching over the floor.

"They're going to be back soon."

Once again, a cold nose appeared to push the knife into his hand.

"Let's hope not too soon. Got it." This time Connor didn't even question what happened. He grabbed the knife and resumed his sawing.

"What makes you think Beau Dufour might be my father?"

"The data I've put together so far. He fits the information I got from your mother's friend in Lafayette where Elizabeth was raised. He was on my short list to research more."

"You never mentioned it before."

"I didn't want you to get your hopes up or do something that might threaten the investigation. Besides, I have three possibilities and hadn't ruled anyone out until today."

"You don't think I had the right to know?"

"Of course, but not until I got more proof and ruled out at least one of the other two possibilities. Besides I didn't want you racing around wildly and charging in and doing something dumb."

Silence.

"Fair enough, I guess. I have done a bunch of dumb things, which is why we're here. What else have you withheld from me?"

"Julie Ann, it's a murder investigation. You're the daughter of the victim, not a police officer or even a lawyer. You could be the killer, and no I don't believe you are a suspect, and we've ruled you out following proper procedure. But depending on how this ends up, a defense attorney could use your intervention against the prosecution and prevent them from getting a guilty verdict."

"I hadn't thought of that."

"That's not your job. It's mine, to investigate, follow the law and proper procedure and build a solid case against the criminal to hand over to a lawyer. Some of the information is confidential. And, I didn't want you in more danger than you already are."

"Maybe you should have given me the opportunity to make that decision. It's my life and my choices."

"Yeah, like the one you made to meet Monique at her house. And why we're trying to escape before they come back and kill us both. I just explained about proper procedure."

Julie Ann shut her mouth for several seconds. "I know. You're right. I deserve that. I tend to be emotional. It's what make me a good designer but a bad investigator. If I hadn't been so gung-ho to try and solve this myself, we might not be this position and Mom might not be dead. I need to think things through and trust other people. They keep killing all because of me. When will it stop, after they kill you and me?"

The knife sawed through the last strand.

"Who knows? I guess until everyone is out of their way. I'm hoping we stop them before they kill us. You're free. Here take the knife and cut the rope around your ankles, then get to work on me."

Julie Ann grasped the knife and bent forward to saw at the rope between her ankles. The rope fell off quickly. She moved her hands across his back searching for his hands. "Got it. Hold still."

She began cutting through the rope.

"Hurry, I hear someone coming." Connor whispered. "Faster."

"I'm trying." Julie Ann sawed faster. "Almost through."

The doorknob turned.

"Give me the knife."

Julie Ann slipped it into his hand, stood up and raced across the room. She hid behind the door.

The light from the hall crept across the room when the door opened.

"Okay you two, show time." Freddy flipped the light switch. "Wha…"

Julie Ann moved quickly, kicking him in his balls, then bringing her hands down hard on the back of his neck.

"Bitch," he groaned.

Julie Ann pivoted and made large circles with both arms, trapped Freddy's arm and locked his elbow. She dropped her weight down and pulled his face close to her. She reversed her pivot and struck him upwards with a palm-heel to the mask area of his face.

Freddy's eyes teared up.

Connor finished cutting through his wrist restraint and switched to his ankles.

From the look and movements Freddie was making, Connor figured Freddy's vision had blurred from that last hit.

Where had Julie Ann learned to fight like that?

She pulled on Freddy's arm that she had the locked at the elbow. His balance swayed. Then with the other hand she gave a reverse punch to his head.

She released and re-centered her balance so she was opposite him. She threw a tight elbow to his temple and another kick to the groin.

Freddy screamed in pain and floundered trying to keep his balance. He jabbed with his fists but hit nothing but air.

Julie Ann punched the base of his nose.

He screamed out in pain as blood spurted from his nostrils.

Connor sawed through the rest of the ropes. They dropped around his ankle and fell to the floor. He stood up, stepped over them and assumed a fighting stance, ready to step in and help Julie Ann but he waited, the knife clutched in his hand if needed.

She had a lot of anger and hostility to get out. This might help. And Freddy looked like he was about to give up and collapse.

Julie Ann gave Freddy a shove and he fell to the floor in a pool of blood. His eyes closed and his tongue lolled to one side. He was out cold.

"I knew I couldn't trust you." A woman stepped into the room and aimed her gun at Julie Ann.

Connor watched her finger squeezed the trigger. His knife flew through the air and hit her chest.

He swore he saw a small dog leap through the air at the same time, aiming for her gun. The gun shot upward toward the ceiling.

Naw, he was seeing things. He had no idea how to explain it, but he wasn't going there. If there were any paranormal forces involved, they were beyond his belief and comprehension.

The woman fell back. The bullet hit the ceiling.

The older woman lay on the floor, eyes stared blankly at the ceiling, the blood seeped out around the blade of the knife.

Julie Ann stared at the woman. "She's dead."

Connor nodded. "She would have killed you. She pulled the trigger. The bullet went off target."

"I know. Marie knocked the angle of the gun. Thank you. Who is she?" Julie Ann stared down as the blood seeped out the woman's body. Her hand rubbed her arm.

"I'm guessing it's Emily Dufour, Beau's mother."

"His mother? She's part of all the killing?"

"I'm guessing she's the one behind it, trying to protect her son, especially now he's running for governor."

Julie Ann ran her hand over the blood-soaked top that stuck to her injured arm. If the bullet had done more than scratch her arm, she wouldn't have been able to fight. But damn it hurt now.

"O'Reilly, you in there?"

"In here, Jerry."

"Shit, what the hell happened here? I heard the shot." The tall, beefy deputy stormed into the room.

"Well, this woman took down Freddy Martin. He's alive. She knocked him out cold. I killed the woman, who I believe is Mrs. Emily Dufour. She was about to shoot Julie Ann."

"I'll call for a bus. We picked up another guy outside. I think he was going to drive the get-away car. Just couldn't wait for back-up, could you? You two okay?"

"We are now. Julie Ann needs her arm checked. Thanks, Jerry."

"Can you call me a taxi?" Julie Ann asked the deputy. "You know where I live. You can find me there."

"You need to get that arm checked. I'll drive you." Connor offered.

"No, thanks. It's a surface scratch so it bled a lot. I can clean and bandage my arm at home. It will be fine. What I need now is some time to process. I'm confused and exhausted. Thank you for saving my life. That woman could be my grandmother. There still doesn't appear to be a motive for so many killings. I don't know who anyone is anymore. I don't want to make any more bad decisions. I need to think."

Connor reached out to touch her shoulder.

"No, don't touch me. You saved my life and I'm grateful. But I need to have people be honest with me, even if I make really bad decisions. And I do understand about proper procedure and that not following it could be used to get a killer off. I get it, but not deep down. I get that I could have got us both killed, but I need to process everything and get it resolved in my head. And there are still loose ends to tie up both for you and for me. Please try to understand. Give me a little space for a day or two. Deputy?"

"The taxi is on it's on the way, ma'am. It should be out front in about five minutes. You will need to give a statement and we will need to interview you" Jerry glanced at Connor.

"Thank you. Connor knows where to find me. I'd appreciate if I can do it tomorrow." Turning her back on Connor, she pulled held her arm and marched out the door.

"Tomorrow will be fine. Are you sure you don't need to go to the hospital and have that arm checked?" Jerry asked.

"I'm sure. Physically I'm fine except for my arm and a few scrapes and bruises."

Jerry nodded. "I'll have an officer escort you out to the taxi."

Jerry walked her out into the hallway.

"And you stay in the house until we find out if anyone else is involved in the killings." Connor shouted after her. "Shit."

"Looks like you screwed up big time there, buddy." Jerry commented.

"Shut up," Connor snapped. He took a good look around the room, but no sign of a dog. Did she leave with Julie Ann? Or what is it all his imagination? He needed time to sort a few things out, too.

"Oh man, you've got it bad. The great Con man has finally fallen."

"If you say one word to anyone…"

"Don't worry, bro, your secret's safe with me. Although I'm guessing you're going to have to work damn hard to get her back."

"Don't I know it? But she's right. I can see how she needs some space to process. It's been a rough week for her. And tonight she almost died. I can give you my statement. It will partially cover hers until she's up to talking to you."

"That'll work for now."

"Call forensics." Connor snapped.

"Already did. Forensics are on their way. They're going to be right ticked with you tonight. That's two bodies and two crime scenes in a couple of hours."

Freddy moaned.

Jerry bent to put handcuffs on the man.

Connor strode out the door.

"Where are you going, man?"

"I have to see a man about a baby."

Julie Ann stumbled through the front door. Marie L. raced across the floor, jumping up on Julie Ann as she headed toward the stairs. When she didn't stop, Marie barked sharply.

"I'm sorry, Marie." Julie Ann dropped to one knee and hugged the dog. "I'm just so confused. Tired, sore, confused and mad. I'm madder at me because I'm confused as to why I'm so mad. I don't even know who I'm mad at, myself, Connor, the Dufour family, the whole damn world."

The dog licked her face and Julie Ann smiled. "Yes, I love you too. And how did you get home? I left you in the car outside Monique's. Connor thinks he saw or felt you at the warehouse. I gather you helped him. I saw you jump at the gun. And now you're here. Is there something you want to tell me? Are you here to make sure you could keep me safe? Am I still at risk?"

Marie nuzzled Julie Ann's ankle and barked.

Julie Ann flopped down on the bottom stair and ruffled behind Marie's ears. A sigh slipped out and into the room.

"How the hell could he keep information about my father from me? How could Mom keep that information from me? What is it they don't want me to know?"

Julie Ann continued to hug Marie and buried her face in the dog's neck. A tear trickled down Julie Ann's cheek and disappeared in the fur.

"So the man who might be my father is running for governor, big deal. He wasn't thirty years ago. Why won't anyone tell me the truth? Is it too much to ask to want to know who your parents are? And yes, I guess I understand Connor, and him not telling me some things. Every time I find out something or try to find out something, I put someone at risk with my too stupid to live decisions. My head is spinning, and my arm is hurting."

The thought of confronting the gubernatorial candidate crossed her mind, but after the list of stupid things she'd done lately she decided against it. She'd stay in the damn house like Connor had shouted after her, and until Mr. Deputy Sheriff O'Reilly allowed her to leave.

Marie wriggled out of Julie Ann's arms and raced up the stairs.

Julie Ann followed her. "I need to fix this arm and take something for the pain."

She washed the sore and disinfected it. Covered it with a bandage and took a pain pill. "That's better. I need a shower."

Marie ran out of the bathroom.

"Marie L., where are you going? Marie, come."

She heard the dog scratch at a door. She followed the dog into her bedroom. Marie L. stood in front of the closed closet door. She scratched frantically.

"What? What's in there? We've checked it all over, top to bottom, twice." Julie Ann opened the door and the dog bounded to the back of the closet and began to scratch at the wall.

Shaking her head Julie Ann opened the secret door.

Marie L. charged forward and crawled under the cot, whining.

Julie Ann stood inside the door. "What are you doing? Come out from under there. I already checked under the bed."

The dog continued to whine. Julie Ann crouched down to try and drag the dog out, but Marie wiggled away.

Julie Ann pulled the cot away from the wall and crawled around it so she could reach the dog.

Marie L. scratched at the floor.

"What on earth are you doing?" Julie Ann bent down to pick up the dog and noticed a small knothole against the wooden baseboard where the dog was sitting.

"What is that?"

Marie moved to one side so Julie Ann could reach it. Julie Ann scratched at it hole and then it hit her. It was similar to the entrance to the closet. She pushed it and a floorboard slid back.

Julie Ann froze, stared at the open spot in the floor and then looked at the dog.

"You could have shown me this sooner."

Marie wriggled her butt, her tongue hung out.

"I've checked this room from top to bottom, twice. You sat and watched me. Why didn't you want me to find it sooner?"

She bent down and slipped her hand into the opening. Her fingers wrapped around a plastic bag. She pulled it out. There were several documents inside.

Plopping down on the edge of the bed, her hand trembling, she opened the bag. Marie L. jumped up on the bed beside her and dropped her head onto Julie Ann's lap.

The first document she pulled out was her birth certificate. It gave her mother's name and all information relative to her birth, except for her father's name. She recognized the signatures of the nurse and doctor who had signed it. They had both died, accidentally.

Placing the certificate carefully on the bed beside her she took out the next paper. It was a letter written in faded, spidery handwriting, when Julie Ann was eight months old. She read the signature first. It was signed by Elizabeth Watson.

Julie Ann took a deep breath and attempted to control her shaking hands. She began to read.

I don't know who might be reading this. I give it to my closest friend Perrine Dupré, along with my daughter's birth certificate. I trust her to do the right thing with it.

I fell in love with Beau Dufour. I believe he loved me too, although his family would never approve of our relationship. They are politically motivated and have high ambitions for their son. I wouldn't fit into those ambitions. I come from the wrong socio-economic group. Sometimes I think they might even have a criminal connection. It's just a feeling I get. Every once in a while, I hear someone say something about a shipment coming in. Beau doesn't seem aware of it and I am probably supersensitive because I know how his mother hates me. She is a strong woman. Beau said she is the Dufour Matriarch and runs the family and the family business.

When I found out I was pregnant I decided, against my parents' wishes, to keep my baby. I planned to tell Beau. He took me home to meet his parents for the first time. I hadn't told him I was pregnant yet. I wanted to meet his family first. The timing was coincidental. His mother was furious and ordered Beau to never see me again. She didn't want him to ever talk to me. I decided I didn't want anything to do with his family and that I didn't want them to find out about my baby. I didn't know what they might do, and his mother scared me. She's a very intimidating woman. I broke off our relationship and never told Beau about our baby.

After the birth of my beautiful daughter, Julie Ann, I got a small apartment close to downtown New Orleans. I worked a part-time job as a waitress in the evening and Perrine looked after Julie Ann for me when she finished work. After a few months I felt we were being watched. I still get the feeling of being followed but I have no proof.

I'm very concerned that if Mrs. Dufour finds out about me and the baby, something could happen to me. That's why I asked Perrine to raise my daughter, should anything occur. I gave her information about Julie Ann's father and the family. I have concerns that if Beau rises up the political ladder, which is his mother's goal, the closer he becomes to the top position the more his family, basically his mother, might want to eliminate anything that could affect their ambitions. That could include myself and his daughter.

I am hoping this letter can be used to assure the safety of my friend and my daughter. If anyone contacts me, I will tell them about this letter and that the information can be shared if there are threats against any of us.

Julie Ann, honey, if you ever read this, because I'm not there with you, please know you were the jewel of my life. I loved you so much and I know you are a very special person. Please live your life to the fullest and may you find a true love who will never abandon you.

Elizabeth Watson

Tears streamed down Julie Ann's cheeks and she buried her face in her hands and sobbed loudly. Marie raised her head and licked Julie Ann's cheek. Julie Ann dropped her head into Marie's fur and kept crying.

Finally the sobs became quieter. She wiped her face with her arm and pulled out the next document. It was the deed to the house, in Perrine's name.

The next document was a letter from Perrine, dated over twenty years ago.

To Julie Ann or To Whom It May Concern,

Hopefully you're the one reading this Julie Ann. However, if you are, it probably means I'm dead, hopefully by natural causes but it could also be from the hands of the same people who killed your mother.

It was not an accident. Beau's family found out about you. I think his mother had Elizabeth followed to make sure she stayed away from her son. Because of that, she found out about you. It wouldn't be hard, to figure out from the timeline Beau was the father. She would want to make sure no one ever knew Beau was your father or he'd had an illegitimate child from an affair. Elizabeth never identified Beau as your father or made any demands on their family. But there was always the unknown threat. So Elizabeth had to die.

Be aware that your life could be in danger. There are people who would prefer that you also were dead, because of who your father is—Beauregard Dufour.

It is my belief they are responsible for the death of your mother. After her death they came to me. They paid me a small sum in exchange for raising you and maintaining my silence about your parentage. They sent me a letter detailing the agreement. I kept it for protection in case they decided to kill you or me, along with the letter from your mother. I told them the letters wouldn't be released unless there were threats against you. The money I invested and used for your secondary education.

I've kept silent all these years, even though you begged me to tell the truth. I thought that as long as I had the letters, we'd both be safe.

Love
Mom
Perrine Dupré

At the bottom, a new paragraph had been added. It was dated a few weeks before she came home.

My darling, Julie Ann,

I'm no longer sure that the letters are going to be enough protection for myself or you. There have a been attempts on my life and threats. The only thing new and different is I've heard Beau Dufour is going to run for governor. They may be trying to tie up loose ends so there won't be any scandal about an illegitimate child. Believe me, I wanted to tell you everything I knew, but once you find out the truth they will try and kill you.

Forgive me, but I tried to do the best for you.
I'm not sure how much longer I'll survive.
I'm hoping you find this letter and can figure out how to protect yourself.

I love you
Mom

Julie Ann opened the last document. It was the contract signed by Mrs. Dupre and witnessed by her lawyer.

"Julie Ann, baby, are you all right? You left your door unlocked." Savannah's voice drifted up the stairs.

Julie Ann wiped her eyes and shoved the papers into the plastic bag. "I'll be right down. Come on, Marie."

Julie Ann closed the closet door, clutched the bag against her chest and headed downstairs.

Savannah stood arms akimbo at the foot of the stairs She glared up at Julie Ann as she descended the stairs. "You left the door unlocked. You outta your mind?"

"Savannah…"

"You bin crying, child. What's happened? What's the blood on your arm?"

"It's nothing. I was grazed by a bullet when I tried to escape."

"What?"

"I found out who my father is, and we caught the killer and Monique's dead and so is Beau's mother and he lied to me."

"Who lied? Beau? Who's Beau?"

"No, no, Connor. And I almost got him killed, too. I've hurt so many people."

"You mean that cop? Oh baby, I warned you about gettin' involved with that man." Savannah pulled Julie Ann into her arms and squeezed her.

"I know, but I can't help it. Damn him anyhow." Julie Ann sobbed onto Savannah's shoulder.

"And who's dead? Monique? What have you been up to? Tell Savannah."

"It's a long story. I think we solved Mom's murder. I'm so confused about everything."

"Okay, you comin' home with me tonight. We'll figure it all out in the mornin'. Charlie has the funeral set up for the day after tomorrow. He's takin' care of all the details, the band and invitations in the papers. The Angelique Hotel is doing the celebration of life, but we still got some cookin' to do. We can talk over cookin'."

Her arms around Julie Ann's shoulder, Savannah lead the her toward the door. "You got your key?"

Julie Ann nodded. Sniffing loudly, "Marie L.…."

"That damn dog, yes, she can come too. Get out here, you mutt."

Julie Ann locked the door and they headed across to Savannah's house. Marie followed at Julie Ann's heels. Julie Ann still clutched the bag of papers. She needed to make copies and put them all in a safe place.

"We're going to start cookin'. First for dinner tonight, in case anyone comes by and then for the celebration and you're going to tell me all the details of what you found out and who died."

"Connor said not to leave the house."

"He won't mind if you're with me. It's probably safer. Send him a message that you're at my house. What you got in that bag?"

"My life story."

Savannah paused and looked at Julie Ann. "Then we better get it and you inside and lock the door."

Minutes later a car drove slowly down the street. It pulled up in front of the Dupré house and turned the engine off. A dark figure opened the door and shuffled up to the front door. A few minutes later the door opened. The figure went inside. A faint light moved around the rooms. After several minutes, the person left, got in the car and drove away.

Connor strode across the marble floor to the copper and glass hotel registration desk.

The desk clerk flashed a smile as Connor approached. "May I help you, sir?"

"I need the room number for the Dufour's." Connor flashed his badge.

The desk clerk hesitated. "I'll check and see if he's registered."

"Police business, he's here. I need the number now or you'll be charged with obstruction of justice and I'll arrest you."

The man glanced over his shoulder.

"The room number and the key, now."

"They're in the penthouse." The clerk slid the key card across the glass counter. His hand inched toward the house phone.

Connor turned toward the elevators. "Don't touch that phone. That's a police order."

As the doors closed, he saw the clerk standing at attention, terrified to move.

Minutes later he knocked on the penthouse door. An attractive woman, in her late forties, looking elegant in some designer style suit, not a hair out of place, opened the door.

Connor assumed she was Lois Dufour. He pushed passed her into the room.

"Excuse me," she tried to protest.

Connor flashed his badge. "Police! Where's Beau Dufour?"

"I'm right here, officer. What can I do for you?" A tall, well-built man, graying at the temples stood in the door to the bedroom. He wore a hotel bathrobe and dabbed at his face with a hotel towel.

"Beau Dufour, I'm here to inform you your mother is dead and to ask you about your daughter."

The towel fell to the floor. The man's mouth fell open. He put his hand against the door jamb. "My mother… dead…what, what happened? Did she have a heart attack Where is she?"

"She died during the commission of a crime. Did you know anything about it?"

The color drained from his face. Dufour shook his head. He gripped the corner of the wall to steady himself. "What crime? My mother wouldn't be involved in any crime."

"How about murder?"

Dufour staggered to the closest chair and dropped into it. His wife hurried across to put a hand on his shoulder. "Beau, what are they talking about?"

"I have no idea, Lois. Dead? Are you sure it was my mother? How could that happen?"

Connor took a deep breath. It looked like Dufour hadn't been party to his mother's devious past. Either that or he was some kind of actor, because he appeared to be truly shaken.

"Mr. Dufour, I am sorry to be sharing this information at this time. There have been a long list of killings that can be traced back to your mother and her clean up guy, Freddy Martin over the last twenty-five years, or longer. They have increased since you decided to run for governor."

"Freddy? I mean I can believe Freddy might be involved, but my god, not my mother. She's dead! What crime was she supposed to be committing? I'll be having this officially investigated." Beaus slammed his fist on the arm of the chair.

"She had kidnapped me and your daughter. She was about to shoot your daughter."

"Mother was going to shoot someone. No, this whole thing is absurd. My lawyers will be looking into this. Oh my God, Mother's dead."

"Your mother has been the mastermind behind these

killings, your career, the Dufour fortune and possibly some drug connections for years. She also developed, or worked with, a corrupt police force. Hundreds of cases over the last twenty-five years or more have been covered up by corrupt police under her direction."

"No, no you're wrong. I don't know where you're getting your information, but my mother isn't part of anything like that. She's a seventy-year old woman. She's prominent in New Orleans society. She's the head of many local charity organizations. Where is she now?"

"She may have been a seventy-year-old woman, but she was corrupt and evil. I realize this is a shock to you. Your mother's body is at the coroner's office. You will be able to see her there, but make an appointment. We'll need you or your father to identify her."

Beau nodded. He kept shaking his head. He appeared to be in total shock and denial. His color was ashen.

Connor strode toward the door.

"Wait, you said daughter. What daughter? What are you talking about? Lois and I have two sons."

His wife squeezed his shoulder. Beau reached up and grasped it.

"You had a daughter with Elizabeth Watson."

"Elizabeth? That was over twenty-five years ago. We had a daughter. She never told me she was pregnant. I didn't know…"

"I understand she didn't want your family to know about the baby. I believe your mother found out somehow, and as a result Elizabeth died in a hit and run accident when your daughter was a year old."

"Oh Lord, I knew mother never approved of Elizabeth, but to kill her, no, she wouldn't."

"No, she probably didn't do it herself, but I'm pretty sure Freddy will confirm when we interview him, that she paid him to kill her."

Dufour shook his head. "I have a daughter?"

"Yes. No, thanks to your mother and Freddy. She's still alive. They have been trying to kill her."

"Oh my god. Lois, I'm sorry, I didn't know."

"It's okay, I understand." Lois dropped her head to rest on the top of her husband's head.

"My daughter is still alive? Where is she now?"

"She lives in the French Quarter, where she was raised by a foster mother, Perrine Dupré, who knew Elizabeth."

"I… I…don't know what to say. I think I recognize the name." He ran his fingers through his hair. "I…"

Lois gave her husband a hug. "We'll get through this. We'll talk about it after the shock wears off."

"If you weren't aware of any of this, it's going to take a while get your head around it. Where is your father?"

"He's down in the ballroom, getting everything ready for tonight's fund raising."

"I'll need you both to come down to the station. We will need a statement from both of you."

Beau nodded. "I'll get dressed."

As Beau left the room he turned. "Can I see my daughter?"

"I don't know. I'll talk to her. She's also going through shock. Your mother tried to have her killed today. If she wants to see you, she'll contact you." Connor replied.

"I can't believe it. My mother masterminded a series of killings. What proof do you have?"

"Her confession, as she tried to shoot your daughter."

"Oh my god, Mother, what have you done?"

"Is your father part of it?"

"No, I'm sure he isn't. He'll be as shocked as I am. He runs the car business and does whatever Mother tells him to do regarding my election. In his spare time he paints with watercolors."

"But you didn't think your mother was involved in any of this either?"

"No. I still don't believe it. I'll want to see all the

evidence you have. I'll also want details of her death. Lois, will you call our lawyers and have them meet us in the ballroom? I'll get dressed."

Twenty minutes later Connor followed Beau into the ballroom. About a dozen people were busy working on set up, sound system and lighting.

A man in his seventies, about six feet, in good physical shape with receding gray hair, saw Beau and hurried across to him.

"What are you doing here? You were supposed to be resting and reviewing your speech." Douglas Dufour put his hand on his son's arm.

"Mother's dead. She was killed by the police."

"What? What are you talking about? She's out working on getting campaign donations?" The older Dufour asked.

"Apparently those donations were in the way of eliminating any threats to the campaign." Connor said.

"What? What are you talking about? Who are you?" Douglas turned to Connor.

"Deputy Sheriff O'Reilly. Your wife told Freddy Martin to kill a Julie Ann Dupré. When he failed, she attempted to kill Julie Ann herself. She died in that attempt."

The senior DuFour stared at Connor, then turned to Beau. "I told her it would eventually catch up to her."

"Dad! You knew what she was doing?"

"No, not really. Certainly nothing about killing anyone."

"But you knew the business she was in?"

"She always said it was best if I didn't know. All I knew was she was involved in activities that may have been illegal and Freddy was her henchman. I didn't know she would actually hurt anyone."

"You'll have to come down to the station and give a statement." Connor said.

"Of course. We'll need to cancel the fund raising. I need to notify a few people." Douglas Dufour said.

Connor nodded. "Go ahead."

"And our lawyers are supposed to here shortly." Beau informed his father.

"Probably a good idea, but I don't think we'll need them. Your mother made sure she kept us out of it." Douglas Dufour closed his eyes briefly, then moved across the room to give instructions to several people.

Beau wiped a tear that drifted down his cheek.

Conner regard the man who was probably Julie Ann's father.

Would she see him? What would Beau do if he met his daughter?

Chapter Fourteen

Connor stood in the observation room, on one side of the two-way glass.

The balding man in his late fifties shifted in his chair. At one time he had been a tall, muscular man but age and alcohol or drugs had taken a toll. He slumped forward and winced with pain. His nose still had dried blood on it.

Jerry strode into the room, pulled out a chair and sat down. "You're in trouble now, Freddy. Your boss is dead. It's all going to come down on you."

"I want a deal."

Jerry shrugged. "We'll have to see what you've got to offer.

Connor left the observation room and entered the interrogation room, the file in his hand. He tossed it on the table and sat beside Jerry.

"He wants a deal."

"Really?" Connor opened the file. He moved his finger down a long list on the page. "I'm looking at more than a dozen murders here, Freddy. I don't see much of a deal available for all those. Maybe life instead of the death penalty. But I'm not even sure that's an option."

"I've got info on Mrs. Dufour and everything she did."

"She's dead, Freddy. I don't think anyone's going to deal on that. Let's start with this list of people you've killed." Connor slid a pad of paper and a pen in front of Freddy. "Start writing. I want a confession on each of the people you've killed and how you managed to avoid being caught or being charged with any of their deaths."

A flash of panic crossed Freddy's face. "Can I get a deal if I write that down?"

"Start writing."

Freddy darted a look around the room then back to Connor. "Not without a deal."

"Write and don't leave out any details."

"I can give you more info on Mrs. Dufour. She is, was, into money laundering and drugs. I can give you information on her drug ring and the next shipment."

"Racketeering such as money laundering, along with murder, what do you think, Jerry? Anybody might be interested in dealing for that information?"

Jerry turned the file and ran his finger down the list of names. "I don't know. You killed a lot of people over the last twenty-five years. I'm not sure the racketeering info is going to go very far. I think it's going to be the death penalty for you."

"I agree with Jerry. And the Dufours aren't going to come to bat for you. It's going to be a quick trial with a public attorney and the death penalty. Write and maybe we'll see." Connor closed the file.

Perspiration beaded on Freddy's forehead.

He started to write. Then he stopped. "Wait. What about the crooked cops?"

"Crooked cops? What about crooked cops, Freddy?"

"The ones on the Dufour payroll. They get paid every month to follow Mrs. Dufour's orders and directions."

"Who are they?" Connor asked.

Freddy hesitated.

"Come on Freddy, you're doing good. We'll let the

District Attorney know how you've cooperated. He might take the death penalty off the table. What cops are on your payroll?"

"There are a lot of them, but I only know the names of three."

"Okay, who are they?" Connor asked.

Freddy sighed. "Westlake in the 9th District, Smithwaite in Garden City and…"

"And…" Connor prodded him.

"Tozer, here."

Connor nodded. He wasn't surprised. "How long has Tozer been on the payroll?"

Freddy shrugged "Twelve, fifteen years, maybe longer."

Connor nodded. "He was involved with the cop that was killed ten years ago. Did he kill him or did you?"

"Hey, I didn't kill no cop. I've never killed a cop. That was him. His partner was getting close to finding out Tozer was on the take. Tozer had to take him out. It had nothing to do with us."

"Mrs. Dufour did help cover it up."

Jerry looked across at Connor. "Sorry, man."

Connor nodded. "Thanks. Now at least I know. I've suspected for a while. Can you finish off here while I go make an arrest?"

"Yeah, sure."

"Okay, Freddy, finish writing it all down, your confession to all your crimes and the crooked cops. The DA might deal on that." Connor said.

Freddy went back to writing, confessing to following orders and shooting Elizabeth driving a stolen car which he dumped in the lake immediately after. He wrote how Mrs. Dufour had paid the police chief at that time to rule it an accident.

He continued to write about the deaths of the doctor and two nurses and how they, too, were covered up.

"Make sure he confesses to Perrine Dupré's death and the

details of the money laundering and drugs. Also, how does Sammy fit in. We'll interview him, too. I'll catch up with you later." Connor left the interview and strode down the hall.

He slammed the door open into Tozer's office and stormed inside.

"What the hell do you think you're doing, O'Reilly?" Tozer scrambled to his feet.

"Arresting the scum bag that killed my father." Connor crossed the room. He grabbed Tozer and slammed him across the desk.

"Take you hands off me. I'm your superior officer."

"Not anymore. You're a corrupt, murdering son of a bitch." Connor pulled Tozer's hands behind his back and snapped on the cuffs.

"You don't know how hard it is for me not to beat the hell out of you right now. You're a disgrace to the uniform."

"I don't know how you found out, but I didn't hurt your girly friend. I just went inside to make sure she was okay."

"You what?"

"I heard she might have been hurt. She wasn't there when I checked. I never saw her."

"You were in the Dupré house tonight? And what did you plan to do if Julie Ann was there?"

"Nothing. Make sure she was okay. You didn't know? I don't know what you've got you shirt in such a knot for then. You won't get away with this. I'll be out in no time and you'll be out of a job."

"If you think Mrs. Dufour is going to come riding in on a white horse and save you, you're out of luck. She's dead."

"What?" Tozer started to shake. "What do you mean?"

"I killed her earlier today. And Freddy, her right- hand man is in custody. He gave you up as the person who shot my father."

"No. I don't believe you." Tozer shook his head.

"You will when you make your one phone call, and no one answers."

Connor dragged Tozer through the office.

"You're going to pay for this. Believe me, you'll be lucky to escape with your worthless life." Tozer shouted.

"And that's coming from a cop killer."

People in the office stared in silence as Connor marched Tozer past the desks to the jail cell area.

Julie Ann waved to Savannah when she and Marie reached their front door. Savannah had wanted her to sleep over, but Julie Ann figured it was safe to go home. Everyone was dead or arrested. No one would be breaking in tonight.

Marie barked.

Julie Ann turned the front doorknob, the envelope with the documents under her good arm. It was unlocked.

A shiver raced down her spine. This was supposed to be over. Was someone inside?

She pushed the door open cautiously. Marie barked and raced inside. She ran in a circle and came back to Julie Ann. That made her feel better. There probably wasn't anyone in the house.

She locked the door and checked the house. It was clear. No one was there. She decided she needed a drink and put the documents in a kitchen drawer. She opened a bottle of Merlot.

"Hey, Marie, I'm glad you're here. It's been a rough day. You know, you were with us. I'd offer you some wine, but it's not good for dogs."

Marie barked and sat down at Julie Ann's feet.

She poured a glass of wine and curled up in a chair. It was going to take a while to sort things out. Now she knew who her father was. And he knew about her by now. She took a sip of wine.

Connor would have informed him about her. *How did he*

take it? Would he want to meet her, or maybe not? Did she want to meet him?

She took another sip of wine. There was so much to take in and process, including the information her mother had shared in her letters. The woman who had tried to kill her had been her grandmother. That was a shock. How did anyone process that?

There was a knock on the door.

Julie Ann put her wine down and checked to see who it was before she opened the door for Connor.

He stepped inside and wrapped his arms around her, gently. "Are you okay? I know I was supposed to come by but I had to see you."

"Depends. Physically I'm fine but emotionally I'm a confused wreck." She leaned into him. He always made her feel safe and secure.

Marie sniffed his shoes and barked.

"Sorry for my temper tantrum at the warehouse. Everything was overwhelming. It got to me."

Connor kissed her forehead and squeezed her tight. "I got it. I'd say it was normal under the circumstances. It's going to take a while to process it all and debrief. Make sure you take time to do it."

Connor released her. "As for you, Marie, I don't know where you were all day, but I swear you helped us in that room. I don't understand it but thank you."

Julie Ann chuckled. "She was there, helping us out. Can I offer you a glass of wine?"

"I'll pass right now. Thank you. I have something I want to do when I leave here."

"Anything to do with the case?"

"Not this case. We arrested Sheriff Tozer. I want to do some follow up."

"The sheriff?"

"He was on Mrs. Dufour's payroll. She had a whole bunch of crooked cops so we're working on that. Hopefully we'll be able to find there are honest cops and others in government."

"Wow, one thing leads to another and it keeps growing. Speaking of the Dufours?" Julie Ann looked at him.

"Yes, I talked to Beau Dufour and yes, I told him about you."

"How did he take it?"

"I'm not sure. I told him right after I told him his mother was dead and she was a crook."

"Not the best time. We're probably both in the same boat, confused and overwhelmed."

"Do you want to meet him?"

"I think so, but not right now. Like you said, I need to process a lot and get a handle on everything. And I have Perrine's funeral, parade, and the celebration of her life coming up."

"Right. How's that coming?"

"I think Charlie has it all under control. It's planned for Saturday."

"I'll be there, but I'll see you before that. Now I'm going to take off. Are you okay?"

Julie Ann nodded. She debated mentioning the unlocked door but decided Connor had enough problems right now. Everyone involved appeared to be arrested. "I'm good."

After Connor left, she locked the door and leaned against it. Connor made her feel better just being close. She wanted to be with him, not just for the sex.

Did she want a relationship?

It felt like it. But what about her job and her business? That was one of the things she need to process and work through.

After the funeral she'd have to do some soul searching about the direction she wanted her life to take.

She picked up the information Charlie had left for her. "He's done a great job. Perrine's funeral is going to truly be a celebration of her life. I think she'll approve."

Marie barked and wagged her tail.

"You agree, huh?" Julie Ann bent down and scratched behind the dog's ears.

"Okay, so what do I do, go back to New York or stay here?"

Marie jumped up and licked Julie Ann's face.

Connor slowly drove the car along Basin Street and turned into the alley where his father had died. He pulled over to one side and parked. He climbed out of the car, paused and stared at the end of the alley.

Once again, he tried to figure out what had really gone down. The file said nothing. Tozer had barely written a paragraph on the death of a police officer, his partner. He refused to answer any questions after he was arrested. This time Connor was going to find out what really happened. He was going to nail Tozer for the murder.

He ripped a five-dollar bill in half and waved it at a boy leaning against the brick façade watching him.

"Here, keep an eye on my car. If it's still here and in good condition when I get back, you get the other half of the five-dollar bill."

The boy grabbed it. "You got it, mista. I watch it for you."

Connor left the alley and strode down the street. At each store that was still open he stopped and stepped inside to talk to the owner or the manager. If they'd been operating ten years ago, he asked about the night when a police officer was shot in the alley. A few of them remembered that night, but either they were already closed up or they had gone home.

At the corner an old man leaned on the counter of his news stand. He flipped through a sports magazine, watching Connor.

Connor reached for The Times-Picayune.

"You gotta name?" he asked the man as he paid for the paper.

"People call me Joe."

Connor nodded. He folded the paper and put it under his arm. "So what time do you close up, Joe?"

"Depends," the old man answered. He scratched the grey fuzz around the back of his head, below his wool toque. "Why you want to know?"

Connor pulled his suit jacket back and exposed his badge. "Deputy Sheriff Connor O'Reilly."

"Shoulda figured."

"So, what time do you close up, Joe?"

"Like I said, it depends. Depends on business; depends on the time of year. You have any specific time you interested in?"

"Thursday night, June 17th, ten years ago."

The old man closed the magazine and adjusted his bifocals.

"Nobody ever asked me about that night before. I was surprised, especially considering the victim was a cop. How come you comin' around now?"

"My father was killed that night."

"Your old man the cop that got shot?"

Connor nodded.

"Sorry about that. Yeah, I had just closed up my stand. I was bent down behind the counter putting the money away. No one could see me."

"So you saw what happened?" Connor pulled out his notebook.

The man nodded. "I saw some of it, heard the rest."

"What happened?" Connor asked.

Joe shook his head. "Two cops showed up that night and went into the alley. Funny thing, I think the alley was empty that night, like maybe the dealers had been told to stay away. Cause usually there's a few deals going down there, but I never saw or heard anybody that night."

"So there were no dealers there that night? Are you sure?"

Joe nodded. "Oh yeah, I remember that night real clear. The whole thing didn't smell right."

"What happened after the two cops showed up.?"

"They went into the alley. I thought it was odd since I didn't see no one else go down there before they did, and it was quiet in there. A few minutes later I heard two shots. Then silence for maybe five minutes. I stayed where I was, didn't want to get involved with any cops."

Connor scribbled furiously. "Then what happened?"

"Like I said, it went quiet for about five minutes, then I heard the one cop phone for help, yelling that a cop had been shot. He came out of the alley, checked up and down the street, maybe looking for witnesses. I hunkered down a little more and hoped he didn't see me. Cause I figured I might be the next one shot."

"So it took him maybe five minutes to call for help after you heard the shot?" Connor frowned.

"At least. I thought it was funny, but I didn't want to get involved. Then all the cops showed up and then the ambulance. I slipped away and went home."

"No one ever asked you any questions?"

"Nope, the cops didn't talk to anyone down here. I asked some of the other workers the next day. They said no one ever talked to them. I guess they wrote it off as an accident. I did read the cop died."

"Thanks, Joe. I appreciate that. I may need to bring you in to be formally interviewed. Are you willing to testify to what you told me?"

"Sure. No one should get away with shooting a cop. And not another dirty cop. I thought I might be called in back then."

"Can you identify the cops?"

"Not by name but I'd recognize the one that came out of the alley."

"Good. I'll be bringing you in for a line up." Connor shook the man's hand and headed back to the alley.

Five minutes would give Tozer time to get rid of his throwaway piece, if that's what he used to shoot Devon O'Reilly. And it certainly sounded like Tozer had shot his dad, if there was no one else in the alley.

This had set-up written all over it. What had his father found out? Who had put the hit on him? Tozer? Or was it someone else? Tozer had shot him, but who ordered it?

He knew his dad had kept a notebook, same as Connor did. If the notebook was still around and Connor could find it, maybe he'd be able to figure out why his father had been shot. He looked right after the shooting but never found the notebook. Maybe he could find it if he looked again.

Connor left the alley and headed back to his car. The boy sat on the hood of the car. Connor waved the boy off. He handed him the other half of the five before driving off.

Maybe his mother might remember where the notebook might be.

Connor sat on a box of Christmas decorations stored in his mother's basement. His mother said she never found a notebook. His father's clothes, shoes and most of his stuff had been given to Goodwill.

She said anything else he had she'd boxed and stored in the basement. She didn't want to come down with him. She said she never came down here.

He had told her about Julie Ann. She was pleased and excited to meet her. It was the happiest she'd been in years. He'd bring Julie Ann over after the funeral. She had enough to cope with now with the funeral and her new father.

His eyes scanned the boxes pile up against one wall, a

bassinette, an old wringer washer; garden tools all piled in one corner and his father's old tool bench. A few tools were still where his father had left them.

Where did a person start? Did his father have the book with him that night? Did Tozer take it?

Connor scratched his head. He had Tozer on the murder. He had an eyewitness, and a witness who said Tozer had shot the cop. That should be enough to make sure he was found guilty, maybe even get the death penalty, although no one had been executed for ten years. Maybe he should give it up and accept that. But the shooting had left questions about Devlin O'Reilly's death. Connor wanted to clear his father's name.

Tozer had written his report. He'd said Connor's father had entered the alley first. He'd had a conversation with a drug dealer. Tozer hadn't heard what he said but it looked like maybe something had exchanged hands. Then the dealer fired two shots at close range. Devlin O'Reilly fell to the ground.

Tozer rushed over.

The dealer escaped out the other end of the alley. Tozer called for help. That was the whole report. There had been no investigations, no corroboration of the story Tozer told. The Department had written if off as an accidental shooting by a drug dealer. The dealer was never found, neither was the gun that had killed his father.

According to Joe, there hadn't been any drug dealer that night. No money or anything else had been found on Devlin's body. Tozer said the drug dealer must have taken it back.

Connor stood up and edged his way through the clutter to the tool bench. He picked up a rusted chisel. Memories of sitting watching his father work, fixing an old clock or putting a leg back on an old end table, rushed over him.

Sometimes his father would get Connor to help him. Damn he missed him.

He put the chisel down and reached for a screwdriver. He caught a glimpse of the bench against the wall. His father had put hooks and shelves on the wall to hold his tools. Devlin had been a very organized man.

Staring at the wall Connor couldn't put his finger on it, but something felt out of place. He moved his fingers slowly across the wall over the hooks and shelves. One shelf stood farther out from the rest.

When Connor touched it, it wobbled slightly. He returned to the shelf, moving his fingers around the piece of wood. Wriggling the wood, it slipped forward. Connor pulled on it and it came away from the wall.

Squinting at the spot where it should be anchored Connor could see something jammed in behind.

He slipped his fingers in the small gap. It took a lot of wriggling. Eventually he managed to pull a small notebook from the slot.

His hand trembled. His breathing ramped up. Connor slowly opened the first page. It was his father's notebook.

Connor dropped down on the bench. He flipped through the pages. In the dim basement light some of the faded writing was difficult to read, but he could read enough to get a good idea what had been going down when his father had been killed.

Drug deals, racketeering and crooked cops were some of the things his father had documented. He listed names and dates. One that showed up frequently was his partner, Harvey Tozer.

Connor slipped the notebook in his pocket and headed up the stairs.

With Emily Dufour dead and Freddy under arrest, was there anyone else prepared to step up and take over that organization? What about the corrupt cops? What were they willing to do to protect themselves? Would the corruption continue?

Who could he trust? Who could he share the information

with and not have it get lost or covered up? Who would make sure there would be an honest investigation?

Paul Arnett was the new District Attorney. The man said he would clean up the corruption in New Orleans. So far, he'd laid two hundred charges and had managed a ninety five percent conviction rating. The police commissioner had been replaced by someone from out of state.

Connor decided to skip his superiors in the police department and go straight to the new District Attorney.

The receptionist opened the door and announced Connor.

Connor stepped into the room.

"Deputy Sheriff O'Reilly. Please have a seat. What can I do for you?"

Connor perched on the edge of a chair. "I'm not sure. How do I know I can trust you?"

"You don't, but you've seen my record. I've arrested cops, school board members and government officials. You came to me. If you've got information or concerns about anything illegal, I'm your best bet."

Connor nodded. "It's information my father collected ten years ago. It got him killed. It's a list of corrupt police and supervisors with dates and documented cases they covered up. Many of the same people are still around and still covering up whatever they don't want people to know about. The latest cover up was the murder of Perrine Dupré."

"I heard she was a robbery victim."

"That's what they said but she was murdered. I don't know what you've heard but Emily Dufour was running a racketeering organization. She'd been doing it for years. It included money laundering and having people killed. One of those was Perrine Dupré. Mrs. Dufour also had numerous cops on her payroll."

"I've heard some information. I don't have any facts."

"We have a witness who is giving us a lot of information on Mrs. Dufour and her organization if we take the death penalty off the table. He's also giving up the names of the police on the take that he knows. He says he doesn't know all of them. We're going through Mrs. Dufour's records to find other names of people who were on her payroll."

"That sounds like you've been gathering relative information following the correct procedure. I think we can take the death penalty off the table for his information if it's proved accurate. Anything else?"

"Most of the officers that are working on the investigation are men I know, and hopefully are honest. One of the corrupt police officer is Sheriff Tozer. We are gathering information on his involvement with Mrs. Dufour. It looks like it goes back over twenty years."

"That's not going to be good for the department."

"No, sir it's not. The reason I'm here is because Sheriff Tozer shot and killed his partner, my father, ten years ago. The reason was Devlin O'Reilly was gathering information on Sheriff Tozer's criminal activity. He was getting ready to expose him."

"You have proof?"

"I have my father's notebook with names and dates. And I have a witness for the night Sheriff Tozer shot his partner, my father."

The DA nodded. "Go on."

"Sheriff Tozer has been arrested and charged with murder and the cover-ups he was part of over the years. Tozer has a lawyer and they're trying to get him out on bail. I don't know how honest the judicial system is."

"I'm hoping most judges are honest."

"Good. I would like to see Sheriff Tozer held on those charges without bail. I realize that's up to a judge. If he's an honest judge, I'll accept his decision. I also want to make sure the sheriff has a fair trial, not covered up."

"What do you expect from me?"

"I'm hoping you're honest and fair. If people, particularly the corrupt police, know that you have all the information and will be watching the case they may not try to destroy or muddy the evidence. If enough people are aware of the evidence, there won't be a cover up and Tozer won't get off because of his ties to racketeering."

"That sounds fair. I run an honest office. I'll keep an eye on the case and let people know that I'm keeping tabs on the process."

Connor stood up. "Thank you, sir. Here's a copy of my father's notebook and a transcript of the interviews of both witnesses. You don't need to read them at this time. I just want someone to have a copy of them in case the originals ever go missing."

"Understood." Paul took the package.

Connor extended his hand.

Paul shook it. "Nice meeting you, Deputy Sheriff O'Reilly."

Connor left the office. He nodded to the receptionist.

That had gone well, he thought. Now to drop by the jail cells and let Tozer know the DA was aware of the case and Tozer might be spending a long time in that cell.

Connor grinned to himself. It might not bring his father back, but it restored Devlin's credibility and hopefully destroyed Tozer's at the same time.

CHAPTER FIFTEEN

The small chapel of the funeral parlor held a few close friends of Perrine's. Savannah kept her arm around Julie Ann. Julie Ann tried to hold it together and sobbed quietly during the brief dismissal service. Connor patted her thigh on the other side.

Outside, Charlie and twenty or thirty of the old jazz musicians from around the area started to play 'Just a Closer Walk with Thee'. Six younger men carried Perrine's coffin and headed out the door and down the street. Another seventy or eighty people, who had waited outside, fell in behind the band.

Julie Ann walked behind the coffin, Connor on one side of her, holding her hand. Savannah on the other side, holding her other hand. They didn't talk. Julie Ann was grateful. It allowed her to stay focused on her mother.

The band led the procession slowly through the neighborhood and past Perrine's house. A black wreath hung on the front door.

Julie Ann glanced around for any sign of Marie, but there was no sign of the dog. She disappeared the day before. Martha Wright sat in a chair out front, watching the procession. She put her hand over her heart.

Julie Ann noticed Laura walking a few steps behind her, beside Princess Ava. George and Monet Smith were behind Laura.

The band switched to an old protestant hymn. People hummed or sang along. The music echoed through the neighborhood. Some people came outside and stood somberly while the procession passed or placed their hand over their heart.

The cemetery was only a few blocks away. At the cemetery, Priestess Ava conducted the internment ceremony. Julie Ann couldn't control her sorrow and sobbed uncontrollably. Both Savanah and Connor kept their arms around her shoulders.

"It's okay, baby. Let all that sadness out." Savannah said.

Connor gave her a squeeze.

After she finished her eulogy, Priestess Ava crossed over and hugged Julie Ann. "She's in a better place. She's at peace and loves you. Hold that thought."

"Thank you," Julie Ann whispered.

Priestess Ava stepped in behind Julie Ann.

The band led the procession from the gravesite without playing for about half a block. Then Charlie raised his sax and played a two-note preparatory riff to alert his fellow musicians. At this point, the drummers begin to play what has become known as the 'second line' beat. Lenny blew on the trumpet and marched behind Charlie. The band swung into "When the Saints Come Marching In". People started to sing and clap as they wound through the streets to the Angelique Hotel. Some people opened elaborately decorated umbrellas. Other people joined the procession as it passed.

A man in his early fifties and his wife stepped into the procession.

It was a joyous procession. Julie Ann smiled. Mom would approve.

The doors of the Angelique were open. The band and the people piled inside. Julie Ann noticed the couple that came in toward the end. She didn't recognize the woman, but the man was Beau Dufour.

Charlie came over and gave her a hug.

"Thanks, Charlie. You did a great job. She would have loved it."

"She deserved it. Everyone wanted to remember Perrine and celebrate her life."

"She did have a good life. It's too bad it was cut short, but I'll keep her memory alive." Julie Ann stood on tiptoes and kissed Charlie on the cheek.

She glanced around. Beau Dufour had disappeared.

Why had he come?

The next morning Julie Ann searched through the house one more time looking for Marie. She checked when she got home last night, but the dog was nowhere to be found.

She poured a coffee and went out into the garden. "Was that you, Mom? Were you Marie? Were you trying to keep me safe? And now you're gone? I'm going to miss you, both of you."

She sipped her coffee. No response. "Priestess Ava said you're in better place."

She shivered. There was a cool breeze. In the corner a faint shimmer appeared. She heard a soft 'I love you.' There was a wave goodbye and the shimmer was gone.

She was alone in the courtyard.

"Love you, Mom." Julie Ann took another sip of coffee.

The phone rang.

She hastened inside expecting it to be Connor, but the image that flashed across her mind when she picked up her phone, was someone else.

"Hello."

"Julie Ann Dupré?"

"Yes."

"This is Beau Dufour, your father."

Julie Ann tightened her grip on her phone.

"Are you there, Julie Ann?"

Julie Ann released the breath she'd been holding. "Yes."

"I'm sorry to surprise you like this. I realize it's awkward, for both of us. I had no idea I had a daughter, until recently. I was going to wait, but I'd like to meet you."

"You were at the funeral."

"Yes. I was told how the woman who raised you died and that there was a funeral and celebration of life for her. She raised my daughter. My wife, and I wanted to pay our respects to her. From what I saw there, she must have been a special woman."

"She was." Julie Ann swiped at a stray tear that escaped.

"I also wanted to see you, but I knew it wasn't a good time to introduce myself. I realize I can't make up for the last twenty some years, but I would like to get to know you. Maybe we can have a relationship starting now. My wife would like to get to know you, too. We have two sons and she always wanted a daughter."

Julie Ann flopped down in a chair. "I appreciate your call. I'm a little overwhelmed by it all. I'm not sure what to say."

"I can understand that, especially after everything you've been through lately and the death of your mother. It doesn't have to be right away, whenever you're ready."

"Are you still running for governor?"

"No. I've withdrawn from the race."

Julie Ann nodded. "I would like to meet you. I'd like to ask questions about my birth mother."

"I'll share what I remember. She was a special person to me back then. I had no idea what had happened to her or about you. Maybe we could start by meeting for lunch and have Lois, my wife, join us for dessert."

"That would work for me. Maybe next week?"

"That would be good. Would you like to call me when you're ready?"

"Yes, I'll do that. Thank you for calling." Julie Ann hung up.

She pulled her knees up onto the chair. Her father had reached out to her. And he'd come to Perrine's funeral. His mother had ordered the death of Perrine and then been killed. He must be going through as much confusion as Julie Ann. It would be interesting to hear what he had to say.

She had a week before she met with him and she had a lot of other things to decide before they met, like what was she going to do when she grew up? And what was she going to do with her immediate future? How did Connor fit in?

Julie Ann curled up in the corner of her couch. Connor slouched beside her. He draped his arm around her shoulder.

"Marie never came back after the funeral?" He glanced around the room.

"No. I think she realized I was no longer in danger. It was time for her to leave."

"Leave?"

"I know you won't believe it, but I'm sure it was Perrine. She came back in spirit to be here while I was in danger and try to protect me. She realized the people couldn't be bought off any longer and when they killed her, she knew I would be next."

Connor shook his head. "If you say so, I'll believe it. I admit there are things that cannot be explained. I believe Marie was in that warehouse with us. I don't know how."

Julie Ann grinned up at him. "That's a start. Between the two of us we may manage to keep some of Perrine's psychic abilities."

"Maybe. We'll see. Do you want to live here?"

"What do you mean? New Orleans? This house?"

"Both, I guess, but specifically, after we're married, do you want to live in this house?" Connor asked.

"Excuse me? After we're married? I don't believe we've discussed marriage."

"Of course we'll get married. We'll figure out the details. Have you considered moving to New Orleans permanently?"

She nodded. "Yes, I've thought about it and checked it out. I can move my business here and rebuild it. In fact, I've already found the perfect spot in the French Quarter and put a down payment on the location. And yes, I'd like to live here in my house. It has a lot of good memories."

Connor let out a breath. "That's perfect. And I'm happy to live in this house. It's a great location, good neighbors and we'll be close to Savannah, if she needs anything."

"Thanks for saying that." She pulled his head down and kissed him. "She and Charlie and Lenny and all of them are neighbors and family. I want to be close to them. I'll have to go back to New York. Allison said she'd buy my half of the New York business. I need to arrange all the legal details and give up my apartment."

"That's okay, as long as you're coming back to me."

"I'll be back. I love New Orleans. I should never have left. I'm not leaving again. Besides, I've also found my father."

"You went to lunch with him. How did that go?"

"Good. He's a nice person and never knew about me. He feels bad about that and that it was his mother who killed or caused the death of Perrine. He's still in shock. His wife is very sweet and wants to spend time with me. They both want to include me as part of their family."

"Good. Beau's going to have to accept his mother's death and everything she'd been doing. They had a very small funeral when the body was released. It was just the immediate family and she was buried in the family cemetery. Beau's in the clear but his father had some knowledge of Emily's activities, so he is either an accomplice or he obstructed justice by not providing information. I'm not sure what they are going to charge him with, but he will probably be found guilty and given a suspended sentence."

"That's one more thing my father's will have to work through." Julie Ann sat up and put her hands on both sides of Connor's face. "How are you doing? What's happening about your father's death? What's happening to the sheriff?"

"They've reopened the investigation into my father's death and Tozer's history of corruption. The District Attorney checks on the investigation occasionally. I think he's trustworthy and he's keeping the investigation honest. Tozer is still in jail. He didn't get bail. The department offered a formal apology to my mother and our family. The police now know the truth."

"I'm glad. That must be a weight off you. Do you know who's going to be the new sheriff?"

"No. I heard they're bringing in someone from up north. They want to prevent further corruption. He sounds competent. We'll see. Now let's get to the important stuff."

Julie Ann laughed. "And what would that be?"

Connor reached in his pocket and got down on one knee. "Julie Ann Dupré, will you marry me?"

He opened the small box. "It's my grandmother's ring. I got it sized with Savannah's help."

The ring was a small diamond set in a circle of rubies in an old gold setting.

"It's a beautiful ring. I love it. Yes, Deputy Sheriff Connor O'Reilly, I'd be honored to wear your grandmother's ring and marry you."

"Whew! I was a little nervous about your answer." Connor slipped the ring on her finger. It fit perfectly.

Connor reached up and kissed her. "I love you so much. You make my life complete."

"I love you, too. When I thought about my priorities, I knew I couldn't leave you. I want to spend my life with you."

"Can we get married quickly?"

"We'll have to see. I gather Savannah knows about this. She'll want to be part of the planning."

"Yes, and she said you'd say yes. She's already started to design the wedding with Charlie. And I told my mother about you and that I was going to ask you to marry me. She's very excited. It's the happiest she's been since Dad died. She'll want to be part of the planning, too."

Julie Ann laughed. "Of course. I'm glad she's happy. I can't wait to meet her. Mom would be happy, too, if she knew about it. With everyone who wants to be involved, I don't think we can be married too quickly."

The back door flew open. A breeze floated around Julie Ann and Connor and drifted back to the open door. In the distance a dog barked.

The door slammed shut.

"What the hell was that? It sounded like it might have been Marie."

"I'm guessing that was my mother, signaling her approval and leaving for her final destination."

"Am I going to have to get used to her dropping by?"

"No. I think she hung around to make sure there was a happy ending here. Now she knows all is good, she can leave. I don't think she'll be back."

"Is this part of the voodoo stuff?"

"Maybe."

Connor sighed. "Okay, I'm not a believer yet, but I'm open to it. Teach me."

Julie Ann wrapped her arms around him. "As long as you're open, we're good. Our life will always be special. I love you."

COMING SOON

LIABILITY WIFE

Book 2 in The Foundation Series

by Beverley Bateman

Excerpt

Lydia hesitated at the door of her Miami home. It had been almost five months since she'd been back. She'd had the locks changed so her wonderful, cheating husband couldn't get in. Still...

She knew he'd hired a hit man, but she hoped she had slipped back into town unnoticed. If she was quick, she could get in, do a quick check and remove some of her stuff before her husband or the hit man knew she was back in town. She had a flight back to New York tonight.

Her first stop had been to her lawyers to sign the changes to her will. With that done Charles wouldn't get a penny if anything happened to her.

A quick glance over her shoulder showed a street that looked empty. She turned the key. The locked clicked. Lydia slipped quickly inside and locked the door. The place had the musty scent of being closed up for a few months. It didn't look like anyone, including Charles, had been inside. He was still staying at the Men's Club. She'd checked out his location and itinerary before she'd come back to Florida.

The house gave off unwelcoming, almost threatening vibes. She felt a little vulnerable without her team. A smile touched her lips briefly. She'd never expected to become a special operative with a strong supportive team. If they were here, they'd cover her back. She wouldn't feel so vulnerable. They were back in New York, but she knew they would always be there for her if Charles continued to try and have her killed.

She hurried to her home office, opened a couple of drawers, grabbed a diary and some computer flash drives. Lydia dropped them into the backpack she'd brought with her and hastened up the stairs to her bedroom. In the closet she removed a few favorite outfits. At the back of the closet she opened the secret compartment where she kept her good jewelry, dumped everything into the backpack, and ran down the stairs. A shiver raced through her body Something felt off. Someone was coming.

She wanted out of the house. She darted down the hall to the back door. A click from the front door made her stop. Lydia's stomach clenched. Someone knew she was here. They were trying to break into the house.

Lydia turned and focused her mind on the front door. She visualized the lock. Using her power of telekinesis she visualized a pick being pushed into the lock. She focused all her energy to slide it out of the lock and fall in the plant beside the door.

She heard someone swear.

Racing to the back door she let herself out, locking the door behind her and running down the steps to her car in the driveway.

Seconds later the rental car was flying down the road. Lydia checked in her rear-view mirror. She couldn't see anyone following her.

She'd sell the house. She couldn't go back there. She knew Charles hired someone to kill her. The Foundation had found out during the background check on her when she was screened for special op training. They'd told her, but the reality hadn't actually hit her until today. He had been very close to finding her.

It was hard to believe Charles hated her that much, or maybe it was just he wanted her money. Well, he wasn't getting any of that. He'd be shocked when he found out she'd cut him completely out of her will.

She pulled over and punched in the phone number for the local police and reported someone breaking into her house. They said someone was on their way to check it out.

She drop the car off and head to the airport. She needed to keep a low profile until she got back to New York. Then they needed to come up with a plan to catch whoever Charles had hired. And get Charles arrested as an accomplice.

He couldn't believe his luck. He'd been in the process of picking the lock on the back door when he heard her. She was inside. He'd shoot her. They'd think it was a break and enter. He'd get his money and get out of town.

The pick he'd been using fell into a plant by the door. He swore and started to dig around until he found it in the damn planter. His hands were filthy. By the time he got inside she'd gone. There was no sense trying to follow her. She had too much of a head start. He began searching for anything that might tell him where the bitch had been hiding and where she might be going now.

Apparently, she hadn't been back in the house for over five months, but she'd made sure the husband hadn't been able to get back in either.

He chuckled. Hate was an interesting psychological emotion. One he appreciated.

He carefully searched through the drawer's downstairs, removing anything he felt might be of help. Moving upstairs he began to go through her drawers.

A car stopped outside.

He slipped across to the window and pulled the curtain slightly apart.

Shit, the cops were checking the house. The bitch had called in a complaint. Moving quietly downstairs he headed to the back door and grabbed a memo pad from beside the phone as he left. In the small yard he moved around the house, hoping he'd chosen the opposite direction from the police who would be checking the yard.

Once he found her, he would enjoy killing this woman.

About the Author

Beverley Bateman is a Canadian author of several books who loves traveling, good wine and a mystery. She lives with her husband and their rescue Bichon-poodle on the Canadian prairies during the summer and snowbirds to Arizona in the winter months.

She loves to hear from her readers. You can contact her at babateman@shaw.ca.